RIDING A CRESTED WAVE

A Mystery

Peter Bernard

The characters and events portrayed in this book are fictitious.
Any similarity to real persons, living or dead, is coincidental
and not intended by the author.

RIDING A CRESTED WAVE.

ISBN 9798679633247

Chapter One

If Harry could have told it, he'd be standing right here next to the high-arched, dark brown, double oak doors of this magnificent church, savoring the long line of mourners coming to pay their final respects to him. And knowing him as I did, he'd bestow that arrogant smile of his while shaking hands with each one, expecting in return their heartfelt gratitude for providing the cherished gift of financial security for the rest of their lives.

But as I stood by these doors, reality proved to be surprisingly different, for no one who walked by appeared to be grieving Harry Miller's shocking death last Saturday night. Rather, most of them wore a look of smoldering, tight-lipped anger, as if ready to explode at any second. The kind of anger that comes from being fleeced in the most despicable, unforgiving way, and severely hurt financially in the process. From their expressions, I could only assume they had come today for the same reason as I had: to curse Harry Miller out one last time for the vile things he had done to us. As I watched the final person enter, I couldn't help but silently applaud whichever one of them had murdered Harry for destroying their lives, the ultimate revenge that Harry so richly deserved.

I lingered by the doors until most everyone had found their seats, and then walked slowly down the long center aisle that sloped gradually toward the foot of the dais in search of an empty chair. I finally spotted one on the right side near the center. As I made my way there, I graciously thanked those who stood up to let me pass and frowned at those forcing me to squeeze by. Only a handful acknowledged either my *thank you* or *excuse me* as the rest were too deeply engrossed in grumbling to one another, the essence of which was, *I'm glad the bastard is dead*!

When I finally reached my seat, the white-haired gentleman seated next to me looked at me angrily, and in a loud whisper you could hear three rows in any direction, hissed, "Did he steal your money too?"

"Not recently," I whispered back, loud enough to make sure everyone around us heard me as I sat down.

He appeared confused; my answer wasn't what he had expected. He shook his head, clearly unappreciative of my being evasive. Yet, given the look on his face, it was obvious he was dying to know whether I thought Harry Miller was a godsend or thief.

Just at that moment, the double doors banged shut, abruptly stopping the din of conversation throughout the church. Almost in unison, the entire congregation turned towards the center aisle to watch eight pallbearers slowly carry Harry's heavy mahogany casket down to the waiting gurney covered with a white sheet stationed in front of the dais. When the leader commanded *now*, they lifted the casket off their shoulders and carefully set it down. Each one stared silently at the coffin for a brief moment, then turned and disappeared to their respective seats.

The silence continued throughout the church for another minute or two as all eyes were still riveted on the casket. Then slowly, the church began to buzz again. Around me, the talk consisted of angry words about being denied one last chance to tell Harry just how much they despised him for stealing their money. Listening to all this bitterness, I began to realize the magnitude of just how much money he had screwed them out of, which was a hell of a lot more than I had imagined!

"My name's Frank Ellis," the well-dressed, tanned, elderly gentleman said to me.

"I'm Davis Lowe," I responded with a pleasant smile, my voice slightly above a whisper.

"So he screwed you out of money too?" His voice was getting louder.

"Yes, but that was a long time ago," I whispered back, hoping to end our conversation.

"Was the bastard running another Ponzi scheme before he started his scam here in town?"

"No. It was a private investment company, just buying and selling stocks," I replied sharply, my voice still reflecting anger at what had happened to me.

Before he could ask me another question, an attractive, blue-eyed, silver-haired lady on my right gently pushed me back so she could lean in front of me to admonish him. "Frank Ellis, how could you call Harry Miller that?"

"How? I lost a hell of a lot of money through Harry Miller, Millie. That's how!"

"I lost some money, too," she admitted softly. But with her next breath, her outrage returned. "Still Frank, how can you forget all the good things Harry did for our town? Why, without his generosity, Lymouth would never have been half the town we are now. You know very well that Harry paid the building costs for most of this magnificent church. He was the biggest donor towards renovating the town hall. And don't you forget it was his generosity that rebuilt the town library and put on that expensive addition. He even donated all those school uniforms and Little League uniforms. You know very well, Frank Ellis, that Harry Miller had a good heart no matter what he did to us. So appreciate that, and pray for his soul!"

"Damn his soul, Millie! You know the man was a con artist, a swindler, and a thief!" Frank's face had turned red to the point where I thought he was going to explode. Millie must have thought so too, as she quickly sat back. Hoping to calm things down a little, I turned around to introduce myself and found her looking just as mad. Lips pressed tightly together, eyes hardened into an angry stare, she was obviously preparing to do battle with Frank again. She was ready…and how! Shoving me back, hard this time, she began loudly scolding him. "Well then, Frank Ellis, you shouldn't have invested your money with him!"

Frank's face was now beet-red face as he glared at Millie. I thought he was going to have a heart attack or stroke or try to push me out of the way so he could jump up and unleash a verbal tirade at her right here in the church. I started to say something to calm him down when I caught sight of the door off to the right of the dais opening. Out stepped the Bishop, followed by the Monsignor, and six priests who, in turn, walked slowly and reverently towards their respective chairs behind the pulpit.

"Shhh!" I put my finger to my lips, then quickly whispered to Frank, "The service is starting."

Instantly distracted, he whispered eagerly to me, "That's Bishop Henry Frey. Such a wonderful man. I don't know how many times he tried to get Harry to stop selling his scheme here in town, but it was too late. Harry had locked up most of everyone's money by then. Rumor has it the Bishop invested some of his own money too, but no one really knows for sure."

"Please, Frank," Millie hissed, peeking around me. "Can't you see the service is starting?"

The Bishop moved slowly to the pulpit, then peered down at Harry's casket for a long moment. He was a handsome, dignified man with a prominent square jaw and large blue eyes, standing tall with a commanding presence in his gray and scarlet robe and scarlet skullcap. He looked up and out at the parishioners, waiting patiently for everyone's attention. Once they quieted down, he stared at Harry's casket again, his face now saddened with evident compassion over Harry's demise. Raising his hands for complete silence, he bowed his head to lead a silent prayer for Harry. I looked around and saw only a handful of parishioners bowing their heads in prayer. Upon finishing, the Bishop stood patiently waiting for them to finish. He appeared quite sad not to have had the chance to save Harry's life…and soul.

The Bishop looked out again at the sea of faces, nodded slightly, then walked over to a white folding chair near the pulpit. Turning it around, he sat down with his back to the congregation. A moment later, he tilted his head down, I assumed to say another silent prayer for Harry. But praying to save Harry's soul, I was convinced, was a lost cause, as he clearly had been devoid of a conscience.

Standing a short distance behind the pulpit was Monsignor Albert Gerrity, a short man with sparkling blue eyes and a large but very straight nose. Dressed in a white robe and a skullcap that could barely contain a shock of white hair, he respectfully waited for the Bishop to finish. He then stepped up to the pulpit, gripped both sides tightly, and waited patiently for the congregation's undivided attention. It was not hard to see by his kind face and caring demeanor that he was a man who chose to serve God early in life.

The priests in their white robes and skull caps, each carrying a prayer book, had moved silently to their respective white chairs, which formed an arch behind the pulpit. As they sat down, Frank leaned over to whisper loudly in my ear, "Let me tell you something, Lowe. I'm not the only one pissed off at Harry Miller. Just look around. You'll see the whole town feels the same way. Yes, sir, most of us lost our shirts investing in Harry's siren song of high-yielding, risk-free investments. And by God, we're all a damn sight poorer because of him!"

I was just about to commiserate when he shoved me back against my chair. Staring coldly at Mille, he hissed, "Renovations and additions and uniforms certainly didn't satisfy someone in this town, now did it, Millie? Someone was angry enough to put a bullet right through Harry's heart before trying to dump his body out to sea. And if you ask me, he deserved it!"

Looking surprised, Millie then shook her head in disgust, never taking her eyes off of the Monsignor.

"I heard that's what happened," I said softly.

I was about to ask for details when Millie peered around me again. "If you keep talking that way, Frank Ellis, the police are going to think you murdered him!"

Ignoring her warning, Frank solemnly declared, "Millie, if I had done it, I would have strangled him. Shooting was too good for the bastard!"

"Nobody deserves to be murdered, Frank."

Frank matched her angry stare for a second or two before looking up at the Monsignor, who had begun the service with an opening prayer: *Lord, for your faithful people life is changed, not ended. When the body of our earthly dwelling lies in death we gain an everlasting dwelling place in heaven.*

Chapter Two

As the congregation sounded a quiet amen, the Monsignor gazed out at the sea of faces. Nodding to himself that he had everyone's undivided attention, he began to read from the Old Testament in a strong, but somber voice. *There is an appointed time for everything, and a time for every affair under the heavens. A time to be born, and a time to die; a time to plant, and a time to uproot the plant. A time to kill, and a time to heal; a time to tear down, and a time to build; a time to weep, and a time to laugh; a time to mourn, and a time to dance...*

Listening to the litany, I started to reflect on Harry's journey through life as I knew it, and how his journey had changed mine so dramatically...and not at all for the better. I still can't believe how willing I was to work for him when he started out fifteen years ago. What a costly mistake that proved to be. But I was young and naive then, and under the illusion that I was smart enough to deal with him. Another major mistake of mine!

As the Monsignor read on, I couldn't help analyzing for the hundredth time why I made the choice I did. And for the hundredth time, it came down to one answer: money! Lots of money! More money than a 22-year-old like me had ever dreamed of making. What a fool I'd been. Even though I had known it would be high risk and a wild ride with Harry, I had told myself it would definitely be worth it in the end. Well, it wasn't! And it changed my life forever. And from what I was hearing around me today, Harry went on to change a hell of a lot more lives. Too many, it turns out, which finally did him in.

****

I tried listening to the Monsignor again but soon found myself drifting back to Harry and my first meeting with him. It was unconventional, to say the least...but so was Harry. I guess that's what impressed me. He was about my age, seemed very smart, and was blessed with an uncanny ability to think fast on his feet. Faster than anyone I had ever known. He could make a strong case using glib answers that made you just nod in agreement. In fact, he was an absolute master at it. It wasn't long before I learned about his other notable gift: an ability to quickly size up human desires and frailties and then take full advantage of them. Which he did at every turn, using his superior attitude to convince you that he was always right.

But Harry had his weaknesses, too. Starting with an arrogance fueled by his belief that he was smarter, more knowledgeable, and simply better than everyone else at everything. And he damn well made sure you knew it! It was that arrogance of his that launched his career. And he coupled it with a bulldozer-like, over-the-top drive to become a mover and shaker in the financial industry. It didn't take me long to learn just how willing he was to do or say anything, truthful or not, to gain any advantage as long as it opened a door of opportunity. He truly had the killer instinct.

Despite my sizing Harry up at the outset, he still drew me to him like a magnet. Early on working with him, I remember thinking how smart I was to grab onto him with both hands to share his wild ride. It was as though I had met the Pied Piper, and he was going to lead me into the promised land of money. Lots and lots of money!

I became Harry's first follower...and why not? The 1980-82 Recession was coming to an end. The financial community was struggling to escape from the stagflation of the late 1970s when the Dow Jones Industrial Average had sunk to its lowest level since the early 1960s. Jobs at brokerage firms remained a scarce commodity, and making money was even tougher. So when Harry came along and held out this large, enticing carrot of how he was going to turn Wall

Street on its head and make tons of money, how could I say no? How could anyone say no? Success on Wall Street had been a dream of mine since I bought my first AT&T shares back in my freshman year at college. Now here was Harry offering me a chance of a lifetime to get in on the ground floor to make it big! It was that simple. All I had to do was to latch onto his shooting star.

I couldn't help but smile, remembering what I liked most about Harry in those early years...that I could trust him! If I told that to the people sitting around me today, they'd probably look at me in shock and disbelief. But Harry back then was a man of his word. If he said he'd do something, he did it and didn't care how it got done, whether through quiet persuasion or extraordinary ruthlessness. It just turned out that in Harry's run to the top, ruthlessness seemed to win over quiet persuasion every time.

****

I still shake my head in amazement at my first meeting with the Pied Piper. It was at the most unlikely of places...a Sabrett pushcart at the corner of Broad and Wall Street near the New York Stock Exchange. I was standing in line to buy a hot dog for lunch. My introduction to him was odd, too. This tall, lanky guy with an unusually handsome face, a turned-up nose, short, dark brown hair, and large, penetrating blue eyes, suddenly turned around and snarled at me, "This is the last time I stand on this line, I swear to God!"

Caught off guard, I stepped back to wait and see what he'd say or do next. He quickly broke out in a broad grin, realizing how stunned I was by his remark. Seeing his smile, I immediately understood and smiled back, nodding in agreement and appreciation. He was absolutely right! Standing here at the crossroads of the financial capital of the world buying a hot dog from a street vendor was definitely not a sign of success. *Now, there's a smart guy,* I thought. He extended his hand to shake mine and introduce himself. "I'm Harry Miller. Say, don't I know you from somewhere? College, maybe? I'm out of Cornell, Class of '79."

"Davis Lowe," I answered, impressed by his firm grip. "Cornell '80."

"I knew I had seen you before, Davey. Say, now you're my witness to this solemn vow I'm taking: *From this day forth, I shall never eat another hot dog on the street again!*"

"I'll hold you to it, but how do you plan on doing that?"

"Well, tomorrow I start my climb to the top of Reynolds & Coleman as the new junior broker. It's a real shame my predecessor bit the dust with, let's just say a little push from...oh, me," he answered with a sly smile.

"You got him fired?"

"Damn right!" he replied. "Either he had to go, or I'd be eating these lousy hotdogs for the rest of my life. And frankly, sitting around every afternoon with acid indigestion waiting for him to screw up was not part of my plan to quickly make it to the top of the financial ladder. So, I gave him a little shove...that's all."

"Remind me never to get in your way!"

With the broadest of grins, he raised his right hand and said, "Davey, you have my solemn promise to never step on you, or over you, on my ride to the top."

I distinctly remember not smiling back, as my gut was warning me to be wary of a guy with such a killer instinct.

"Who you with, Davey?"

"It's Davis, and I just started with Brown, Johnson, and Partners as a broker's assistant while working on my MBA at the Baruch Graduate Business School at night. I'm looking to climb the same ladder as you as fast as I can."

"I got to tell you, Davey, I love your name," he said with a broad smirk. "It fits in perfectly at a big, white-shoe investment house like Brown, Johnson. Hell, with a name like Harry Miller, they'd lock and bolt the door to keep me out!"

"Thanks," I answered sarcastically. "But you just watch me climb the ladder. Someday I'll be one of those successful big shots who steps into his limo at 5:00 pm to ride uptown for drinks and dinner at the Four Seasons or Tavern on the Green, recounting all the successful trades I made that day."

"That's the way to think, Davey!" He patted me on the shoulder. "I say the exact same thing to myself every morning."

I looked at him, wondering if my initial wariness was still valid. I thought he seemed okay, but his mean-spiritedness bothered me enough to end our conversation. He must have sensed my backing away as he quickly gave me a warm, friendly smile and asked, "Hey, Davey, how about celebrating my hard-won promotion with me tonight? Have dinner with me at Harry's at Hanover Square. I'm buying. It's on Pearl Street."

"It's Davis. What time?" was my quick response.

To this day, I still don't know why I jumped to accept his invitation.

****

Harry's at Hanover Square was where the movers and shakers of Wall Street dined on steak and expensive wine. It was definitely out of my league on a lowly assistant's salary, but if Harry was buying dinner, how could I say no? When I got there, Harry had already bought a round of drinks for the table next to ours and was bragging to these two Wall Street types about how he had just outmaneuvered his boss, not only for his job but his client list as well.

"This is my pal, Davey Lowe, and the two of us are going to set Wall Street on fire!"

The two of them seemed amused at Harry's bragging. They turned to size me up, then looked back at Harry. Shaking their heads in disbelief, they started to laugh.

"Wall Street buries guys like you if you're not as smart as you talk," one said seriously. "Too many guys on the Street thought they'd set the world on fire, only to end up as very tiny flickers."

"Not me!" Harry declared. "My name will be known up and down

Wall Street. Mark my words!"

I watched as they continued to stare at Harry for the longest time. Finally, shaking their heads at anyone who could be so naive yet so full of themselves, they thanked him for the drinks, paid their bill, and left.

Harry appeared perplexed. "They didn't believe me...did they?"

"Why would they believe you, Harry?" I asked, signaling to the waiter to take our order.

"For starters, I know I can do it! Don't ever doubt me on that, Davey. Those guys are like a lot I've met on the Street...damn negative! Their kind always talks about the one big killing that got away or the one big trade they made years ago that was their claim to fame but never followed by another."

I guess my doubting expression really riled Harry as he launched into a fist-pounding tirade. "I'm different, Davey. I know I'm going to be a big winner...it's in my blood! It's something I've always known. When I'm told something can't be done, it sparks something deep inside me to go out and prove everyone wrong. And I always get it done...and damn well! And I'll do it again this time, too!"

I waited for an accompanying laugh to follow the line of crap he was feeding me. But Harry's eyes were blazing with a passionate determination. He wasn't kidding! He actually believed everything he'd just said!

I remember being surprised by this and quickly changing the subject before he could fire off any more zealous proclamations that could destroy what promised to be a great meal. I began to reminisce about the good old days at Cornell, with Harry nodding in agreement as he slowly cooled down. Suddenly, I felt the presence of someone leaning against the back of my chair. I looked across at Harry, who was staring up at the person. I saw his face tighten, and his blue eyes harden. He slowly stood up and walked around the table to go face-to-face with him.

"Davey, I'd like you to meet my ex-boss, Fred Simmons, who I'm sure didn't come here tonight to congratulate me on my promotion."

As I started to get up to shake his hand, I felt two strong hands press down on my shoulders. I began to say something, but Harry and Simmons weren't listening.

"What do you want, Simmons?" Harry asked calmly, knowing full well why his ex-boss was here.

"Why'd you do it to me, Miller? Why would you want to get me fired? Explain it to me!" Simmons' voice was quivering with anger. "How could you sneak those two lousy stock buys into my biggest client's account? You knew they were dogs! Nobody in their right mind would've ever bought Penn Square Bank or Braniff for the long term. They were one step away from bankruptcy, and yet you went out and bought them. Why Miller? Tell me why, you bastard!"

I quickly stood up to get out of the way of what was about to happen. And that's when I saw Simmons, a tall, redhead with light blue eyes and a freckled face burning with anger. It was clear he was out for revenge.

"I did it to help you out."

"Help me out? You're full of crap!"

"Simmons, look at it this way. I was trying to save you from the humiliation of your client dumping you after all the losses you've rung up for him over the last three months. You know as well as I do that you're a lousy stock picker. Everyone at Reynolds & Coleman knows it, including Charlie Reynolds! And you know it was only a matter of time before he'd tell you to pack it up and find another line of work."

"How could you, Miller? How could you do this to me? I'd never make either of those buys, never in a thousand years! You made me look like a complete idiot! And after all I've done for you. How could you forget that I was the one who stuck his neck out to give you a chance at Reynolds & Coleman? And this is how you repay me?"

"Simmons, Wall Street is never going to be the right street for you. Picking stocks means making quick, hard-nosed decisions every day. And frankly, you're neither quick nor hard-nosed. You haven't got the guts to risk someone's big bucks to buy or sell large positions.

You're too slow and too cautious. The minute I met you, I knew you'd never survive in this business...the market would eat you up and spit you out!"

"You son-of-a-bitch, you did it intentionally! You destroyed my career!"

"You never had a career, Simmons," was Harry's quick response. "A career in this business is for winners. You're nothing but a loser. Goodbye, Simmons! And good luck with your next venture."

Simmons' face was now beet red, almost a match to his hair as he stood there, clenching and unclenching his fists. I thought Harry was ready for anything Simmons might do, but what happened next was so quick, and without any hesitation on Simmons' part, that Harry didn't even have time to raise his arms to protect himself. The punch landed squarely on Harry's nose with a loud cracking sound, knocking him backward onto the floor. Blood began to spurt all over his face and clothes.

When Simmons saw Harry lying there defenseless, he moved to stand over him, his fists still clenched tightly as if ready to beat the hell out of him. But then for some unknown reason, he did nothing, just stood there watching a dazed Harry wiping the blood from his face with his sleeve. It appeared as though he was trying to make up his mind whether to punch Harry out, or walk away satisfied that he had his just revenge. This hesitation lasted several seconds, seemingly confirming Harry's insight about him. I was beginning to think he was just too nice a guy to finish Harry off when he leaned over, having finally decided that being screwed out of a good job and a budding career deserved a couple more punches to ease his pain.

He started to rear back to throw the one punch that would have put Harry, and his career, in the hospital for quite a while. To this day, I still don't know what inspired me, but I grabbed Simmons's arm, straightened him up, and spun him around to face me. It surprised him and frankly shocked the hell out of me that I could even do something like that. I then hit him with a solid right to his left cheek, driving him backward until his knees buckled, and he fell hard on the floor next to Harry.

As I stared down at these two pathetic Wall Street brokers, a loud, almost uniform cry of "Oh my God!" rose from nearby tables. Patrons were aghast at seeing Harry try to control his bleeding nose with his sleeve, and Simmons attempt to shake the cobwebs from his head while trying to sit up. And then there was me, jumping up and down, furiously trying to rub the pain out of my knuckles. Before the three of us knew it, two tall, heavyset waiters, a dictatorial-looking maître de, and a smiling busboy came running over. One waiter threw a small towel to Harry to cover his nose, before practically picking him up. The other waiter and the busboy grabbed Simmons under each arm and stood him up, though quite unsteadily. They then unceremoniously dragged the two of them out of the restaurant, with the maître de pushing me out the door right behind them as he yelled, "Don't any of you ever, ever set foot in here again. If you do, we'll deal with you in our own way. Do you understand?"

Harry and I nodded and mumbled a collective *yes* as we stood at the curb next to the entrance awning. Harry was still trying to stop his bleeding nose when a cab pulled up, forcing us to step back quickly. We watched as a still-dazed Simmons was slowly assisted into the back. One of the waiters gave a few quick bangs on the roof, and the cab took off. Harry peered at me through swollen eyes, face and clothes spattered with blood, and said, "I owe you a big one, Davey. A huge one! And you can count on me paying you back in full."

I've never forgotten how absolutely sure I was in not wanting Harry to owe me *anything* after seeing how badly he had screwed Simmons. His words *in full* had me conjuring up all sorts of devious plots to get me fired from Brown, Johnson so he could replace me. Then and there, I made it a point to never press Harry, under any circumstances, to pay up on his pledge.

Chapter Three

The twelve-person chorus had just finished a beautiful hymn when Frank nudged me. "They can really sing, can't they?" I started to whisper back how beautiful they sounded when the Monsignor began to intone a short prayer: *Lord, for your faithful people, life is changed. When the body of our earthly dwelling lies in death, we gain an everlasting dwelling place in heaven.*

Listening to the blessing's promise, I couldn't help but wonder: who's going to pray for Harry Miller to enter the gates of heaven? I started to speculate on the reaction the Monsignor would get from those sitting here today as to Harry's worthiness to dwell in heaven. Without a doubt, there would be a loud, boisterous, and uniform cry of *hell no!* Then, I thought of how Frank might express his feelings: never would a scoundrel, a cheat, and a conniver like Harry Miller ever pass through heaven's gates. Heaven is reserved for those who had goodness in their hearts and souls. And there was no doubt in my mind that Harry didn't have one scintilla of goodness in his heart. In fact, I'd swear he would have interpreted *goodness* to mean something entirely different...something along the lines of *good fortune,* with him being the primary beneficiary. No, for Harry, the gates of heaven would be locked tight!

****

The Monsignor's voice trailed off as I drifted back again to my life and times with Harry Miller. It was at a little Japanese restaurant downtown where Harry's definition of *good fortune* was made clear, and it had nothing to do with 'goodness towards your fellow man.' For Harry, it was about finding a client who would trust him with millions to invest. As he explained it, his *good fortune* would result from first making a hell of a lot of commission money by buying and selling stocks for a big-time account. And then by becoming Reynolds & Coleman's leading account executive. At the time, I scoffed at these outlandish goals. But Harry was absolutely positive it was going to happen.

It wasn't more than a few weeks later when Harry called me all excited. "Davey, my boy, I've had the good fortune to find that perfect client. She just happens to be Reynolds & Coleman's largest account. Her name is Maude Williamson, probably in her mid-30s. Her husband Albert died four years ago at the age of 63. He was the retired president and major stockholder of one of the largest savings and loan associations in Illinois. He left the Mrs. with, get this, seventy-five million in stocks and bonds. I also learned that Charlie Reynolds and Al Williamson had worked on a number of real estate deals and became close friends. So naturally, Al entrusted Charlie to manage Maude's money."

I vividly remember saying to him, "Come on, Harry, who in their right mind is going to let a twenty-four-year-old with only a couple of months of real stock trading experience under his belt make the leap from a wet-behind-the-ears junior stock broker to Reynolds & Coleman's lead broker? You've got a hell of a lot of nerve to even try it! Don't you understand that a seventy-five-million-dollar account is way out of your league?"

But Harry just smiled as he confidently replied, "Davey, I see only one obstacle in my way to making this work, and that's Charlie Reynolds. But I'll figure out a way to get rid of him. I'm going to manage Maude Williamson's account…you can count on it!"

I remember laughing as I said to him, "Sure you will, Harry!"

✱✱✱✱✱✱✱✱✱✱✱✱✱✱✱✱

About a week later, Harry called me. "Davey, let's have drinks tonight. I've learned a lot about Maude Williamson, and I want to tell you about her. Meet me at the Regency at 6:00 pm."

Harry was excitedly waiting for me with drinks on the table. Before I even sat down, he told me, "Davey, here's what I found out about the very rich Maude Williamson! She's coming to New York for three weeks in September and plans to meet with Charlie Reynolds to discuss her portfolio. It seems the illustrious Mr. Reynolds lost a little over two million dollars in failed trades in her account last year alone. Davey, she's definitely ready for a new account exec!"

I remember shaking my head at his arrogance. But Harry didn't seem to notice as he continued, "I also learned she's staying in a beautiful suite in the Plaza Hotel and shops at expensive Fifth Avenue department stores and Madison Avenue shops for the latest fashions to take back to Springfield. And if the right situation arises with the right man, might be open to a little romance while here."

I tried to say something, but Harry talked right over me. "But that's not all, Davey, my boy! My source told me that Charlie is very concerned about possibly losing Maude's account. These last five years were really tough ones for the firm. The Market's low trading volume and depressed prices have badly battered Reynolds & Coleman's finances. To keep the firm afloat, Charlie used her seventy-five million to churn enough commission money from buying and selling stocks in her account to cover the large hole in Reynolds & Coleman's cash flow."

"How'd you find all this out?" I asked, frankly in awe.

"Trade secret, Davey! But there's more! My friend told me that Charlie has come up with a two-part plan to keep her business. The first part is typical of him: wine and dine her at New York's best restaurants, and take her to a couple of Broadway shows. He's counting heavily on New York's bright lights, his charm, and, most of all, his past personal relationship with her. All designed to gloss over any lingering concerns she may have about last year's losses.

And get this...he also wants to worm his way back into a relationship with her." Harry shook his head in disbelief. "The second will be all business. Charlie's going to ask her to come down to his Wall Street office, where he's going to present a detailed plan of exactly how he'll recoup last year's losses. He knows it's his last chance, so he's got his best analysts preparing a buttoned-up presentation designed not only to restore her confidence in him, but also generate genuine enthusiasm for his financial acumen. So you can see, Davey, how desperately he needs the business!"

****

It wasn't until early that September when I heard from Harry again. He was quite excited, so I knew something was up. "Davey, I've got to see you! You won't believe what just happened. I can't believe it myself! When can we meet?"

"How about tonight? There's a little bar down the street from me."

"Nah! Let's meet at the Bull & Bear at the Waldorf. What I've to tell you is big-time stuff, Davey!"

When I got there, I found Harry sitting at the far end of the bar, staring into a vodka gimlet, a broad smile on his face. "Hi Harry," I said, sitting down.

"What will you have, Davey? The sky's the limit!"

"Whatever you're drinking," I replied, wondering what in the world had happened to him.

"Bring three more vodka gimlets, bartender!"

"Come on, Harry, why are we going to get smashed tonight?"

Smiling from ear to ear, Harry answered. "Well, let me start from the beginning, Davey. Do you remember me telling you about Charlie's two-part plan? Well, I decided to formulate my own plan to meet the rich Maude Williamson. It wasn't elaborate or clever, just straightforward, and built upon my single guiding principle: over-the-top, in-your-face, win at all costs!"

"I'm becoming acquainted with your guiding principle, Harry."

He looked at me in surprise, and then broke out in a broad grin, proudly stating, "This time, Davey, I hit one out of the park! I'm on a roll now, big time!"

The bartender set down three drinks. I took two and downed the first one quickly to fortify myself before Harry could start his story.

"So here's what I did, Davey. Knowing that the rich Maude Williamson was in the Reynolds & Coleman conference room, I simply walked in and acted completely surprised. 'Oh…forgive me!' I said. 'I'm so sorry to barge in like this, Mr. Reynolds. I didn't realize anyone was using this conference room.'

"Well, Davey, you should have seen how shocked and annoyed Reynolds was as he growled at me, 'We are, so leave!' But, you know me! In my most charming voice, I said, 'Please forgive me, Mr. Reynolds. I'm so sorry,' as I bowed humbly to a well-dressed, striking blonde with the most beautiful, doe-shaped blue eyes. I got to tell you, her good looks really surprised me. As I stood there admiring her, Charlie hissed at me 'Get out! Now!'

"But then Maude…ah…Mrs. Williamson stepped in and with a gracious smile and a wave of her hand and said, 'Oh, Charlie, it's no big deal!' She then turned to me, smiled sweetly, and said, 'We forgive him, don't we Charlie?' Before a shocked Charlie could utter a reply, I asked her in a voice full of awe, 'Aren't you Mrs. Williamson?'

'Why yes…yes, I am,' she replied, surprised and pleased at the recognition. I never even looked to see how furious Charlie was at me as I continued, 'Forgive me for asking, but wasn't your husband, Albert Williamson, very prominent in national real estate circles?'

'Yes, he was,' she answered proudly.

'And wasn't he the key backer in building a significant part of Chicago's lakeside skyline in the '50s, and the motivating force behind making Springfield worthy of being Illinois' state capital?'

'He was indeed!' she answered, beaming at my knowledge of her husband. With an endearing smile, she added, 'He was such an inspiration to so many people who relied on his financial ability to help make Illinois what it is today.'

"At that point, Davey, a very suspicious Charlie blurted out, 'How do you know so much about Al Williamson? That was over 25 years ago!' Before I could answer, Charlie quickly recovered, saying, 'Oh, I'm sorry, Maude...Mrs. Williamson. This is Harry Miller, one of our up and coming young brokers.' Looking at me with barely contained anger, he continued, 'You were telling us, Harry, just how do you know so much about Al Williamson?'

'Well,' I said admiringly, 'we studied about him, and his famous real estate deals in college.'

"Davey, she never took her eyes off of me. Reynolds was about to order me to leave again when Maude's voice suddenly turned hard and forceful. 'Now, Charlie, I like this young man. Al would have too! He always liked young men who could think on their feet in tough situations. And he always carried on about needing sharp, young minds with financial insight to get deep into the details, as they were the ones who usually found the key to making a deal profitable. Say, why don't you put Harry on my account? Maybe he could help you straighten out my portfolio.'

'I'll consider it, Maude,' he replied grudgingly. 'But right now, I've got the three best analysts in the business working on your account. I guarantee your portfolio will be back in the black this year.'

'Now, Charlie, you told me the same thing two years ago when my account lost over a million dollars. And then again after last year's two million loss!'

'Maude, believe me when I say that my team has assembled a terrific group of stocks that will generate some very profitable gains as the economy comes out of the recession. The next twelve months are going to be big winners for you. Absolutely big winners!'

Maude didn't seem convinced. 'Charlie, we're up to three million in losses. You're going to need some really big winners to make up those losses. I mean huge winners, which so far you don't have any record of producing. Don't get me wrong, Charlie. I'm hoping you can do it, as my portfolio can't keep taking a beating like this! And oh, by the way, before I came East, I finally got around to looking over the monthly statements for the last two years. I was shocked to find all those trades in my account. Tell me, what was that all about?' 'Nothing to concern yourself about, Maude, nothing at all!' Charlie replied quickly, trying to cover his growing anxiety. 'We had expected some very profitable opportunities when it appeared Reagan would win the election, but we happened to buy in a little too early...that's all. As Al used to say to me, you've got to be aggressive to make money in the stock market. That's what we did...and we made a hell of a lot of money together in those days.'

"Davey, I could sense that the conversation had taken a turn and figured it was the perfect time to break in. 'I'd be honored to work on your account, Mrs. Williamson. I believe there are a lot of very exciting stocks that could make some major capital gains when the economy turns around. I'm sure we could rebuild your portfolio in no time at all.' She gazed at me for a long moment before saying, 'I believe you can, Harry. Yes, I'm beginning to feel quite confident you can!'

As soon as Maude left the room, all hell broke loose. 'Miller, you're fired! Get out!' an infuriated Charlie shouted. As I walked towards the door, I couldn't help myself. 'May I suggest, Mr. Reynolds, that firing me would definitely upset Mrs. Williamson, especially after she insisted that I work on her account. But I assume you're ready and willing to take the chance Reynolds & Coleman could lose her business?'

'Why...why you're nothing but a snake in the grass, Miller, you son-of-a-bitch! Who the hell do you think you are breaking into an important meeting like that, then trying to sell yourself as the answer to her problem? Not Reynolds & Coleman, but you, Harry Miller, a smart-ass kid out of college who thinks he has all the answers. Well, I've dealt with punks like you before, Miller. You better be damn good, or I'll destroy you fast.'

'But Mr. Reynolds,' I replied ever so innocently, 'I was only trying to protect the interests of Reynolds & Coleman!'

'The hell you were!'

"As I'm sure you can guess, Davey, I didn't waste any time. I called her that afternoon and set up a meeting in her hotel suite for that evening."

Harry sat back, a smug smile on his face. He picked up his drink, saluted me, and then took a healthy swallow. I watched him, not really surprised by his story, knowing that he honestly believed he was smarter and cleverer than the rest of us. However, what was unexpected was his doubling down on his *nothing to lose and everything to gain* strategy. I guess over-the-top cockiness can work, but I still wasn't totally sold.

I picked up my glass to toast his success, knowing I'd need the help to get through his forthcoming bragging. "My hat's off to you, Harry, for getting this far with Maude Williamson."

Harry acknowledged my compliment with an arrogant smile and said, "Davey, that's only the beginning!" He leaned closer, glass in hand, and said, "Let me tell you what happened to me that night. You're not going to believe it, but it's absolutely true!

"As you can probably imagine, I was quite excited when I left the office that evening. I took the subway uptown and walked the few blocks to the Plaza Hotel. As I approached the side entrance, I saw a long line of black limos, and right in the middle of them, stood a horse-drawn carriage ready for the usual ride through Central Park. It was absurd to see the driver standing there in a top hat and tails, feeding his horse between all those limos. It reminded me of pictures I'd seen of Wall Street financiers from a century ago, showing off their wealth as they rode through the park in fancy carriages with beautiful women at their side. With that, Davey, I began to imagine myself riding through the park as the newest wizard of finance, a beautiful, expensively dressed woman clutching my arm. Strolling people would turn and point at us, declaring, *There goes Harry Miller, one of the youngest and wealthiest barons of Wall Street!*

"I've got to tell you, Davey, that moment, that vision was like a sign that all my plans to make it big on Wall Street were going to come true that night. As I walked quickly past one stretch limo after another, I noticed how each chauffeur stood intently watching the Plaza side entrance, anticipating the door opening any second and their VIP passenger rushing out. When the moment actually happened, I watched the chauffeur snap to attention, opening and closing the door behind his passenger and then quickly running around to the driver's side, where he got behind the wheel and drove off, I'm sure, to an important meeting. I can't tell you how envious that made me, as I swore out loud, 'That's going to be me…and damn soon!'

"When I reached the Plaza stairs, I looked up at those double doors and felt my determination surge as it always does when I want something bad enough. And I really wanted this! I was absolutely convinced I was going to be a big winner…that when I left my meeting with her, I'd be the newest superstar on Wall Street. Frankly, Davey, I never doubted it would happen. I felt certain she wanted me as her financial adviser...and maybe more. All I had to do was play my cards right, and it was in the bag!"

Harry paused to sip his drink before continuing, "Well, Davey, you should have seen me climb up those stairs to the Plaza door. My mind raced ahead as to how I'd close the deal, knowing all I had to do was mix a bit of Harry Miller charm with a buttoned-up plan to recoup her losses, and then show her how I'd make a ton of money for her. How could she say *no* to that? Taking a quick look back at that line of limos, I felt even more convinced this meeting was my stepping-stone to the big time. I gripped my briefcase tightly, stood tall, looked important, and strode towards the doors, causally nodding as the doorman opened them for me."

Before Harry could say another word, I reached for my second gimlet and gulped it down, grateful for a moment of silence. But Harry didn't seem to notice. He kept rolling on!

"At that point, Davey, I couldn't help but gloat at the thought of telling Charlie Reynolds and Reynolds & Coleman to go to hell! There would be no more piddling stock trades for me, only big ones!

A thousand share trades. Ten thousand share trades. What a feeling that would be!" As if to rub it in more, Harry gave me a look that said, *I'm a big-time winner now!* Which is when I signaled the bartender for another round.

"You know, Davey, when I pushed the elevator button for the tenth floor, I became almost giddy at the thought of how my life was going to change."

"So what happened next, Harry?" I asked hesitantly, knowing full well that a hell of a lot more was to come.

"Well, after I pushed the bell to Maude's suite, I stood there, briefcase in hand, a warm, slightly humble smile on my face, ready to make a grand entrance. I waited, then rang the doorbell again. Then I waited...and waited. Just as I was about to push the buzzer a third time, I heard the lock click. The door swung wide open, and there stood Maude, giving me a warm, sexy smile. She was wearing a tantalizing, tightly-wrapped, monogrammed blue silk robe, which, I have to tell you, shocked the hell out of me! Here I was all ready to conduct the most important business of my life, and she looked ready to climb into bed!"

I could hardly hold back a skeptical laugh as I asked, "Well...what happened then?"

"In the most matter-of-fact tone, she said, 'Why so surprised, Harry?'

"Davey, I couldn't even speak! 'Oh!' she said, 'it's the robe! Well...I was running late when you phoned, but I must say I'm impressed at your promptness, Harry!'

"I stood there frozen, staring at this pretty, older woman with beautiful doe-shaped blue eyes, and a terrific figure wrapped in a snug, blue robe, frantically thinking that my dream of becoming a Wall Street titan had just morphed into nothing more than a one-night stand with a very rich lady. It felt like all the air had been sucked out of me. And she just stood there, watching with amusement. Finally, she waved her arm, and with a knowing smile, commanded, 'Ah...come on in, Harry. It's only a robe!'

"I was totally disarmed at how causally she was treating this life-changing meeting for me. I just stood there, my mind running the gamut from defeat to panic. I guessed she sensed I wasn't following her because she turned around, put her hands on her hips, and practically laughing at me said, 'Come on, Harry, haven't you ever seen a woman in a robe before? Don't worry…I'm not going to bite you!'

"Davey, you can't imagine how I felt! I had no choice but to obey, and so I followed her into this low-lit living room designed to dramatize the magnificent view of Central Park at dusk. It was so overpowering that I became distracted. Sounding like a complete fool, I gushed, 'Wow! What a view! This is hard to believe! You can almost see the entire park from here. It's really beautiful!'"

"Wait a second, Harry," I paused, then asked, "How about another gimlet? I'm just about finished with this one."

Harry seemed surprised by the interruption but ordered another round. "As I was saying, while I stood gazing at the park's magnificence, desperately trying to regain my senses, I slowly realized how teasingly close Maude was standing to me. Close enough to overpower me with her perfume to where I almost forgot why I was there! I tried to fight my first impulse by telling myself I had to start making my pitch. But then I felt her arm around my waist as she pointed to the lake in the middle of the park. Between that and her perfume, I seriously started thinking maybe I should forget my pitch and just give in to her advances. Davey, I got to tell you, I was really torn between the two!"

"I can't believe she had you of all people, Harry, going around in circles like that!"

"I know! I suddenly thought about Charlie Reynolds and what my excuse would be for spending the night with Reynolds & Coleman's wealthiest client. I began to visualize myself standing in front of Charlie's desk as he interrogated me about the evening. I just knew he'd get the greatest pleasure not just firing me, but also destroying any future I had on Wall Street. At that point, I really was going around in circles!"

"I still don't believe it!"

"Well, it was a first for me, Davey," he replied, sounding annoyed. Harry paused to take a long swallow, trying, I guess, to decide whether to react any further to my sarcasm. Looking at me with a somewhat perturbed expression, he shook his head and then launched back into his story.

"Where was I? Yeah, so Maude took one look at my face, and then smiled as she took my hand and led me over to the large beige sofa facing the park, saying, 'The park is even more spectacular when the lights go on, Harry.' She then sat down in the middle of the sofa, curled her legs up under her, and patted a spot close to her, inviting me to sit down. Now…that made me damn sure of her intentions! Davey, here was this beautiful, older woman, looking so alluring in that revealing blue robe. I knew if I didn't sit down, I'd not only be an absolute fool, but would probably get thrown out, too! So, I slowly and cautiously sat down. Maude smiled, before mocking me with, 'There Harry, that wasn't too hard now, was it?'

"Davey, I swear, I've never been so confused!"

"I can believe that, Harry!"

"But you know me and how determined I get. I tried re-focusing on selling her my portfolio recommendations, but as I looked at her lovely face and oh…that blue robe…I felt my resolve slipping away. Taking a deep breath, I told myself to forget the sex and just concentrate on the business. *Don't be distracted*, I kept thinking. Otherwise, everything I ever dreamed of…the big money and all that fame…would disappear forever. Seventy-two million…gone! Why I'd be back eating hot dogs on the Street again. So, I picked up my briefcase, tried to look professional as I opened it, and pulled out a folder stuffed with my proposed stock picks guaranteed to recoup her lost money. She raised her hand to stop me. 'Now Harry,' she said most affectionately, 'before we talk business, I want to know more about you.'

"*Oh my God*, I thought, we weren't going to be discussing my stock picks at all tonight. I knew the sex would be great, but damn it, the business would be better. I gazed at her pretty face again, but this time I saw something different. It was the way she stared at me. Those beautiful doe-shaped blue eyes now had a hard, commanding look that clearly said, *Don't you dare challenge me.* That did it! I knew my business meeting was over!

"Davey, I've got to tell you, I've never been defeated like that! But before I could react, a new wave of anxiety swept over me. *Why does she want to know more about me? What should I tell her? What would she believe? And how close to the truth should it be?* God, I need time to think. Slowly, casually, I put my folder back into my briefcase, closed it up, and placed it on the floor beside me, all the while formulating my life story."

"I assume, Harry, you decided to tell her the truth?"

"Well, I did what I do best. I told her the truth...sort of."

"Okay, what exactly did you say?"

"That I was the son of a broken home. My father was a charming, handsome man with a decided weakness for women. And women couldn't seem to resist him. At least, that's what my mother thought when he went off on his many adventures. She was a beautiful woman, and I could never understand why my father treated her like that. I once asked her, and she told me it was in his DNA. My mother died when I was sixteen, and my father remarried a beautiful woman, twenty years younger. She and I didn't get along at all, so I was left on my own most of the time. At eighteen, I went off to Cornell to study economics and spent two more years in the business school getting my MBA.

"Anyway, that was the easy part...and mostly true. The harder part was convincing Maude of my financial credentials. I couldn't tell her I was a lowly runner until a couple of months ago. Why she'd kiss me off...real fast. But if I oversold myself, she could easily check with Charlie about my experience. So, I came up with a story with just enough truth scattered throughout that I thought she'd buy."

I just smiled and said, "Sounds like you, Harry."

"Thanks, Davey, thanks a lot," he replied with a smirk.

"I explained that I'd been with Reynolds & Coleman for close to two years. I started out as a runner but was shortly made a broker's assistant. My boss was a nice guy, but a lousy stock picker who'd made some grievous mistakes picking stocks for his biggest client. They were so bad they got him fired. After I took over for him, I not only got the client back on the right track, but picked some solid winners that made him a ton of money. I told her I have a unique ability when it comes to making money and could make a ton of it for her, too. Next thing I knew, her icy stare had melted away. She gave an approving nod, followed by a warm smile. I said a silent *thank you, God!*

"Then, Maude began to speak in a very soft voice. 'The difference between us was my father was a drunk. He left my mother when I was fourteen, and she raised me until she died when I was nineteen. After that, I was on my own until I met Al Williamson five years later. In between, I sang with a local band that traveled around Illinois doing supper club dates. That's how I met him in Springfield. He came into the club one night with his wife and some friends, and when I got up to sing, he told me he couldn't take his eyes off me. That he instantly fell madly in love with me. After that, he came into the club every night to see me, and then followed the band from club to club. I have to tell you: He was the most persistent man I'd ever known! Our relationship grew hot and heavy over the next several months. Before I knew it, he had divorced his wife of thirty years, told his two adult children he had found someone else and was madly in love with her, and told me he wouldn't take no for an answer until I agreed to marry him. I was twenty-four; he was fifty-three!'

"Davey, at first, I didn't understand why she was telling me all this. What's her history got to do with me? But then my intuition started flashing red that she had something else in mind. I guess I must have looked a little befuddled as she stopped and nodded at me before continuing. 'Al gave me anything and everything I ever wanted or even hinted at wanting. He was passionately in love with me, something I never had experienced before. I often wondered if the intensity of his love and devotion would cool at some point, or even stop because of our age difference. But surprisingly, it never did. He always tried to come down to my age, and do the things I liked to do. He treated me royally, Harry, just royally! I found myself loving him, really loving him!' Tears filled her eyes, and she pulled out a handkerchief from her robe pocket to dry them. 'We were together every single day for over five years. We traveled the world, stayed in posh hotels, and dined at expensive restaurants. I wore only clothes from famous designers, and jewels from Tiffany and Harry Winston.' She stopped again to wipe more tears away. 'I meant everything to *my* Al. Everything! There was nothing he wouldn't do for me...and I for him. Then, he got cancer, which ended our romantic travels. He died four years ago. And suddenly, my life was empty. I couldn't fill it without my beloved Al.' She started crying again.

"I must have still looked confused, Davey, because she took one look at me, and laughing through her tears said, 'You appear lost, Harry. Here I am, telling you my life story, and you don't have a clue as to what I'm saying.'

"Well, what are you saying?" I asked her nervously. But she just kept looking at me. Finally, sounding very sad, she answered, 'These last four years have been so hard for me with *my* Al gone. I've been lonely...very lonely. I can't tell you how much I miss him and everything he brought into my life; the excitement, the surprises, and the adventure. It was all so wonderful that I never wanted it to end. But now, all I have left are my memories. You may not understand what I'm saying, Harry, but when you're older, you'll learn that loneliness is something you'll never want to go through...trust me on that!'

"'I think I'm beginning to understand,' I replied.

"She must have seen the flash of anger in my eyes because she answered, 'I don't think you do, Harry. It's something that happens to people well beyond your years when they've lost someone they dearly loved, who they shared the good and the bad with every day.

Let me tell you something, Harry, it's hell being without the one you love! It changes your life and your perspective on life.' Shaking her head sadly, she added, 'Oh…I still don't think you understand what I'm talking about. I guess you're much too young.'

"Well, Davey, I understood her all right and told her so. 'I may not understand your loneliness, Maude,' I said, 'but I understand where you're going with this, and frankly, I don't want any part of it!'

"'That's too bad, Harry,' she responded, 'because I see in you all those wonderful traits *my* Al had. You're very good looking, like him. Smart and a real hustler just like he was. You probably will be a great dealmaker too, Harry. You're definitely full of yourself with a lot of determination to succeed, just like *my* Al. I saw it the moment you walked into the conference room. *My* Al would have done the same thing you did. Do his homework before barging into the room. Then use his charm to take command of the meeting to make his sales pitch. You did it perfectly, Harry, just like *my* Al would have done. It's amazing how much you're like him, especially knowing when the stakes are the highest. He took risks that never bothered him if it meant getting what he wanted. He never thought twice about failing. That's what made him unique, just like you're unique, Harry. It was one of the reasons I loved him so!'

"I thanked her for the compliment, but told her my answer was still *no thanks!* I'd make it on my own.

"Then she asked me, 'Don't you want to be rich, I mean really rich?'

'Yeah. But only on my terms!'

'On your terms, Harry? Well, I'm sure you'll be very rich one day as you have all the makings to become a success. But you need to ask yourself: how long will it take for that day to come? Five years? Ten? Maybe twenty years? Maybe never?'

'It will happen and soon, I guarantee it!'

"Maude just smiled. 'I can tell you're not the type to sit around and wait patiently for an opportunity to drop into your lap. And I'm sure you'll work and sacrifice, and do whatever it takes to make a deal as long as you get what you want. *My* Al did the same thing, and you're no different, Harry. But *my* Al had a rich father who staked him to his first real estate deal at a very young age. That success launched him into the big time. Harry, I know you have the same ambition as *my* Al. But think of it this way; a little help now can go a long way to making your dream a reality sooner than later.'

"At that point, Davey, I thought where she was heading might be interesting. And I've got to admit, I couldn't keep my eyes from wandering over her captivating body wrapped in that blue robe. 'I'll think about it,' I said, trying to sound noncommittal but still interested.

"She suddenly leaned closer to me, looked me straight in the eye without a trace of affection, and said in a cold, all-business tone, 'Well, let me help you make up your mind, Harry. Here's my deal for you. I'll back you with ten million dollars that you can trade as you wish. You can do it on your own or with Charlie Reynolds…it's your call. If you lose it, it's gone, and you're gone. If you make money, half of what you make is mine.'

"I sat back on the sofa, shocked. Her offer had taken my breath away. It was all I could do to hide the smile on my face. I got up and walked over to the big picture window, pretending to consider what she'd just proposed. It was the only way I could grin from ear to ear. This was the biggest win in my life, Davey! A dream come true! Now I was sure the world would know who Harry Miller was…a superstar! Once I had the ten million dollars under my belt and making money, the sixty-two million would quickly follow. I just knew it."

Wow! Ten million and keep half of the profits! That's one hell of a deal, I thought enviously.

Harry looked at me and said, "Davey, you ever thought about investing ten million any way you want?"

"No! I've never even dreamed of it, Harry."

Harry looked at me with a sly smile as if he already knew all the things he would do with ten million in the market and no Charlie

Reynolds looking over his shoulder.

"Davey, as I walked back to the sofa, it suddenly dawned on me, there's got to be some strings attached. Whatever it was, she was smart to save it for last, betting I wouldn't walk away from ten million dollars. Softly patting the same spot for me to sit back down, she folded her arms across her chest and, in a very tender voice, said, 'Harry, I want you to come live with me. Not in Springfield, but here in New York. You'll have the best money can buy…I'll see to it.' She paused to give me time to digest her proposal, before adding, 'But there's something I want from you in return and must have unconditionally!' I held my breath as she demanded, 'I want every bit of your attention outside of work. I want you to…no, I need you to do what *my* Al did for me. I want it very much, Harry. So very much! I like you, Harry. You've made me come alive again. And I promise you, Harry, you're going to like me as much in return!'

"I just stared at her in shock, Davey! What kind of life was she proposing for me? I was at a loss for words. All I knew was I had a hell of a decision to make and needed more time to think about it. I walked over to the window, where I stared out at the glittering lights in the park and struggled to decide if a ten-million-dollar stake was worth sacrificing my youth and freedom for this older woman. After a while, I turned back to look at Maude's pretty face and loving smile. Yes, I thought, she's still beautiful. And yes, the way she looks in that robe, I'm sure she knows how to make a man very happy. But she's at least ten years older than me. How could I make a woman her age happy? And what about me? Why should I give up everything in my life to satisfy her needs and wants? No! It just wouldn't work! I didn't even want to try to make it work.

"But then, Davey, I began to wonder…what happens to the ten million, and my breakout on Wall Street? How could I say no, when she was offering me everything I've ever wanted…to be rich and famous…and at twenty-four! The more I thought about it, the more I was convinced there was no way I could walk away from ten million dollars.

"As I stood there, wrestling with this life-changing decision, Maude walked over and looked up at me. That's when I saw the desperate look in her eyes. I knew then and there how badly she wanted this deal. Ignoring her, I kept staring out at the park. Finally, she took my hand in her shaking hand, and almost begging, said, 'Harry, I'll raise the ten million to fifteen million, and promise that you'll be very pleased with both ends of the deal.'

"Fifteen million, Davey! My God! Can you imagine how much money you could make with fifteen million bucks to invest? I couldn't believe it! I, Harry Miller, would definitely become the youngest financial wizard on Wall Street!"

Chapter Four

I was momentarily startled as my musings were interrupted by the sound of a chorus of parishioner voices joining in to recite the 23rd Psalm. *The Lord is my shepherd; I shall not want. He maketh me to lie down in green pastures: he leadeth me beside the still waters. He restoreth my soul: he leadeth me...*

Those simple words, *I shall not want,* brought Harry back into my thoughts. I had to smile at how those wondrous words became the mantra of his new life: not wanting for anything...anything at all. At twenty-four, he was a stock trader by day, and a young live-in lover at night. He was showered with every conceivable luxury from a woman who absolutely adored him. Looking back, there's no doubt in my mind that Harry pulled off one of the great coups of all time.

Even now, I can only shake my head in disbelief. Fifteen million to invest any way he wanted with the only stipulation that he give his benefactor half of his winnings...and his *full* attention. But it turned out that sharing the money was the easy part of the deal. The tough part for Harry was how to devote all of his non-working hours to pleasing his possessive patron.

****

It wasn't more than a couple of months after Harry had closed his deal that he called me. Typical Harry, he commanded me to meet him for lunch. "We're not going downtown. I'll meet you at the Top of the Sixes on Fifth Avenue at 1:00 pm."

When we met up at the restaurant, I immediately noticed a marked change in Harry's persona. It wasn't just how he was dressed, although I had to say he'd come up in the world of fashion. It was more that he exhibited an air of gentility instead of his usual aggressive arrogance. I could only assume his newfound wealth had lifted him into a position above life's everyday battles, and he no longer seemed the old hard-charging, take-no-prisoners braggart I had known. Frankly, it surprised the hell out of me!

As we shook hands, I couldn't resist saying somewhat sarcastically to the *new* Harry, "I must say you've come up in this world. Just a couple of months ago, downtown was the place to eat. Today, it's uptown at the Top of the Sixes. You've certainly enjoyed a meteoric rise to the top, Harry."

Ignoring my pun, he suddenly seemed to resurrect the Harry of old as he declared, "Davey, you can't imagine the great things I've accomplished since I saw you last. Now that I'm rich…really rich…I took the bull by the horns and opened my own investment firm: H. J. Miller Investments. Yes, me, Harry Miller, running my own show. And know this, Davey, I'm going to make one hell of a bundle of money…and do it all before my twenty-fifth birthday to boot! Didn't I tell you way back when that I was moving into the big time? And I plan to stay there for a hell of a long time."

"Congratulations, Harry!" I said as enthusiastically as possible, struggling not to show my envy. "You've climbed the investment ladder faster than anyone I've ever heard of. Wow! H. J. Miller Investments. Sounds damn impressive to me!" Harry nodded his thanks. "By the way, I heard on the Street that Reynolds & Coleman closed their doors last week. Do you know what happened?"

A grin slowly spread across Harry's face, but before he could answer, a waiter came over to take our drink order. Looking at me knowingly, Harry said to the waiter, "Two vodka gimlets, and two more in reserve." The waiter wrote the order and hurried off. Harry leaned back in his chair and closed his eyes for a moment before nodding a very definite…yes. Then, leaning forward, the old Harry came out in full force. "Yeah, I know what happened, Davey. I shot the bastard down in flames! And he didn't go willingly or quietly. Charlie Reynolds is now out on the Street looking for a job!"

With a smug look on his face, Harry leaned back again and started in. "Two days after I made the deal with Maude…you know, Maude Williamson, my backer, I walked into Charlie's office unannounced. When he saw me, he jumped up from behind his desk and began shaking his fist at me, bellowing, 'You're fired, you son-of-a-bitch! You've got ten minutes to clean out your desk and get your ass out of the building!

"I just smiled as he slumped back down in his high-backed, leather chair, and took a few slow, deep breaths. I guess it calmed him down because the next thing he did was start telling me how he planned to destroy me."

I was intrigued to hear how Harry handled this one. But Harry being Harry, I didn't have to wait long. "Well, Davey, I let Charlie ramble on for a while and then sat down in one of the plush chairs in front of his desk, crossed my legs, put my hands behind my head, and gave him my most winning smile. He went absolutely ballistic! He started ranting that I was a dirty double-crosser. That I was a blight on the financial community and ten minutes more of the same. When he finally stopped to take a breath, I casually said, 'Oh, by the way, Charlie, I'm here to tell you that I want my fifteen-million-dollar check from Maude Williamson's account in three days.'" Harry paused dramatically.

"Well, come on! Tell me what he said!" I practically shouted across the table.

"At first, he was practically speechless, choking on the words. His face turned bright red, and large blue veins popped out across his forehead…I thought he was going to have a heart attack right then and there. He started taking a lot of deep breaths to help get over his initial shock, and then he uttered every conceivable curse word at me. When he was done doing that, he screamed at the top of his lungs, 'You're fired, you son-of-a-bitch! Get out now! Fifteen million?

You'll never see it! Maude isn't about to give the likes of you fifteen million dollars just like that. I'll call her right now, so she can tell you that you're out of your goddamn mind, Miller! I swear you'll never work on Wall Street again. You're through! You're finished!'

"'Call her right now, Charlie,' I told him, not worried at all. He did, shaking his head from side to side, positive that Maude would never do anything like this to him. When she got on the phone, he demanded to know if she was giving this wet-behind-the-ears office boy fifteen million dollars. As he listened to her answer, his face turned from bright red to a ghostly white. After he hung up, he stared blankly at me in total disbelief, obviously too shocked to say anything, while I just sat there in sheer ecstasy watching him. After a while, I got up to leave, telling him to 'Cut the check, Charlie. You have three days.'

"At the door, I turned back and nonchalantly said, 'Oh…by the way, Charlie, I forgot to tell you that Maude is talking to a couple of investment firms about moving her remaining fifty-seven million from Reynolds & Coleman. Seems she is very upset about you churning her account at such a furious pace these last two years and losing a hell of a lot of money in the process. Frankly, Charlie, she doesn't trust you anymore.' I waited a moment, then added, 'God, I hope you haven't pissed away any more of her money!' With that, his jaw dropped. 'And Charlie, if I had to guess, I'd say you'll be out of business within the month.' I gave him a *that's too bad* headshake and closed the door behind me.

"I went back three days later to pick up my check. The office was dead quiet. A couple of brokers were cleaning out their desks. Charlie walked out of his office and spotted me. He just stood there and stared. Suddenly his eyes were filled with wild-eyed hatred, like he wanted to pull out a gun and shoot me dead. He didn't move or speak; just kept staring at me with a look of loathing I'd never seen before. Finally, I walked up to him and said, 'Think of it this way, Charlie, you're a hell of a lucky guy that Maude doesn't prosecute you for stealing her money with all the churning you've done.'

"I must say, Davey, the look he gave me was chilling. But then he suddenly seemed to give up. With head bowed and shoulders hunched in defeat, he slowly walked back into his office and slammed the door. I gave him a moment before following him in. 'I know you're going to be really short of money when Maude moves her account. So, I have a deal for you.' He looked at me with a vacant stare like he wasn't interested in any deal I'd propose. 'Charlie,' I said, 'I'm willing to buy your seat on the New York Stock Exchange for one hundred thousand dollars…and I'll pay you in cash.' His expression remained blank as he nodded faintly in agreement.

"You know, Davey, a seat on the exchange goes somewhere around three hundred thousand bucks. I told him I'd get my lawyer to draw up the papers and walked out."

Not sure how to respond to his story, I covered by asking, "So what investment firm is she going with, Harry?"

"I haven't decided yet."

"What do you mean *you* haven't decided yet? She's going to let you pick the firm to handle her fifty-seven million?"

"That's right! Maude's investing in a money market fund until I make a decision." He flashed a sly grin at me.

I remember just staring at Harry and trying to comprehend why she'd do that, but I couldn't come up with an answer that made any sense. It was then that I realized just how effective Harry was in taking a situation, whether personal or financial and turning it entirely in his favor. That's what he did with Simmons. And now, Charlie Reynolds. Still, I couldn't quite figure out what exactly provoked him to such heights of contempt and cruel humiliation. Was it to show the world just how tough Harry Miller could be? Maybe. But, it still didn't justify the lengths he'd gone to denigrate both of them…not at all!

Harry looked at me as though he understood what I was thinking. "Davey, let me tell you something. Reynolds was a nasty bastard and a lousy boss. The turnover in his shop was off the charts, what with firing people for the littlest things and giving brokers who didn't meet their monthly quotas no second chances. He deserved every bit of it. Trust me!"

I nodded a grudging acceptance, mainly to stay in his good graces…at least through lunch. "Harry, I get it; I've seen some of those things happen at Brown & Johnson too."

Harry smiled at my concurrence. Before he could say anything more, the waiter returned with our drinks. Raising his glass in a toast, he said, "Here's to Charlie Reynolds, may he never fire another living soul." We saluted each other, then drained our glasses.

Harry studied his empty glass for almost a minute before looking me straight in the eye and demanding, not asking, "Davey, you must come work for me. Be my partner. I know this sounds a little out of the blue, but I've been thinking about you ever since I got the fifteen million. It boils down to this: *I need your help to invest the money.* You're a smart guy who knows the market and can identify good money-making stocks. And what's most important to me is that you're honest and trustworthy. I'd feel damn comfortable working with you to build H. J. Miller Investments. And I've got to tell you, I've never been so sure about anything as the two of us making a fortune together. Bigger than either of us could ever imagine! When Wall Street people talk about being rich, we'll be at the top of their list. So what do you say, Davey, are you with me?"

What could I say? I was shocked beyond belief. I started to see all those dollar signs jumping out at me from every direction and knew I couldn't resist. Fifteen million was big money, and frankly, one hell of a way to start. Before I knew it, I was thinking about the stocks I'd buy, and the money I'd spend buying them. I looked over at Harry, sitting there, confidently waiting for my answer.

Then, it hit me. He knew I'd buy in all along. How in the world could I turn down an offer like that? He'd be dealing with big-time money, which any twenty-three-year-old like me would jump at. In the back of my mind, a yellow caution light started flashing wildly. Why pick me? There are guys with a hell of a lot more experience to choose from. Guys who know the ins and outs of the stock market far better than me, and who have dealt with major portfolios. And then come to think of it…how does he know how good I am at picking stocks? After all, we've only met a couple of times. And to be his partner, that seemed awfully strange.

My mind kept racing back and forth, trying to make the right decision, but it didn't take long to realize the cold, hard truth about myself…I simply couldn't walk away from the opportunity to invest fifteen million dollars, no matter what doubts I had about Harry. But there was that yellow light flashing wildly again. What about Reynolds and Simmons? Harry could do the same thing to me anytime he wanted, and I'd be out on my ass. Yet, all that money at my fingertips…what a great chance to make my fortune!

"Davey, you're hesitating. What's the problem?"

"Harry, let me be frank with you. You've got no idea if I'm the best stock picker in the world or the worst, or somewhere in-between. Why would you want me to invest your money?"

"Let's just say it's instinct, Davey. I saw how you backed me up with Simmons. You didn't have to do that, but you did. You showed me a lot in that moment of crisis. And I believe you'll always give me a straight answer. I need that! You know as well as I do that to run an investment business, there has to be someone you can trust, really trust, to tell it like it is without any sugar coating. In my mind, you're the guy who fits that bill for me. So, what do you say, Davey?"

"What about money, Harry? What are you thinking?"

"How's two hundred and fifty thousand to start, plus ten percent of my share of the earnings? Would that make you happy?"

My eyes practically popped out of my head at those numbers. How could I turn down an offer like that? It was a fortune. But that yellow light was flashing brighter than ever. I'd seen firsthand how Harry dealt with people. At the first sign of trouble, he'll boot me out, and damn fast too. But…all that money! If he's willing to pay that kind of money, who am I to argue? Hell, if he had offered me half, or even a quarter, of the two hundred and fifty thousand, and only five percent of his share, I'd still have jumped at the opportunity. Even if there's got to be another reason why he wants me so badly, there was no way I was going to say no.

"What do you say, Davey? You can buy a hell of a lot with a quarter of a million dollars and ten percent. You'll climb that elusive ladder faster than any other twenty-three-year-old on the Street!"

"Count me in, Harry. But no shenanigans or I'm gone."

"That's fair. Welcome aboard, Davey, and boy, am I glad to have you aboard. We're going to make a hell of a lot of money together." Harry then proposed another toast. "In no time at all, we're going to be the two wealthiest guys on Wall Street." We clicked our glasses and downed our gimlets.

"Say, Davey, I want you to meet my partner and benefactor, Maude Williamson, real soon. She's a terrific gal who I know you'll like instantly, just as I did."

Chapter Five

I remember it was almost three weeks later when Harry and I took a cab from the office up to the luxurious Fifth Avenue apartment he shared with Maude Williamson. "You live here, Harry?" I asked incredulously, awed at how a twenty-four-year-old, recent lowly runner on Wall Street, could be living such an opulent lifestyle. "I've got to tell you, Harry, this sure beats standing in line for a Sabrett hot dog," I said jokingly, as the doorman held the door open for us.

Harry ignored my friendly dig as he proceeded to tell me for the umpteenth time how much money I was going to make. "Davey, you're going to be rolling in money. An apartment like this will be yours for the asking!"

I gave Harry a hopeful glance, yet remained somewhat doubtful as I followed him into the lavishly appointed lobby to the elevator. We rode up to the penthouse in silence. When the elevator stopped, Harry unlocked the door to an elegant vestibule. He directed me to the large living room where a series of giant picture windows spanning the length of the room showcased a magnificent view of Central Park. I'd have to say breathtaking was an understatement.

"Well, Davey, what do you think of the view?" he asked boastfully while waving his arm at the panorama in a grand manner. "All this will be yours as soon as we lock into some high-flying growth stocks to get us off to the races."

The penthouse and its splendid view overwhelmed me. My innate greed took over, as I envisioned this kind of living within my reach. It drove me to buy into Harry's rationale for hiring me and choosing me as his partner. The hell with Reynolds and Simmons, I concluded, they were just one-time incidents. Every bit of this opulence was going to be my destiny. Every last dollar of it!

Harry left me standing there to look enviously around the penthouse and gaze out at the beautifully lit park. I practically started to drool over the thought of all the millions we were going to make in the market. *I'll be able to buy anything and everything I've ever imagined,* I thought, grinning to myself. My reverie was broken as Harry returned with Maude clinging to his arm, a friendly smile on her lovely, but clearly older face.

"Maude, I'd like you to meet Davey Lowe. His real name is Davis, but I like Davey better. He's my old college buddy, good friend, and now my associate; he's one of the smartest stock pickers on Wall Street. That's why he's H.J. Miller Investments' first employee. He's the man who's going to make a hell of a lot of money for us!"

"I'm so pleased to meet you," she said most graciously. Adding warmth to her already warm smile, she asked, "But please tell me, do I call you Davis or Davey?"

"Davis, if you don't mind. I'm too old to be Davey," I replied, slightly irritated at having to explain this to her with Harry grinning in the background.

****

I had never been to The Four Seasons before, but it was jam-packed that night. We followed the maître d' as he made his way to a quiet table. Along the way, I noticed quite a few heads turning to watch this stylishly dressed, attractive older woman leading two young guys who looked like they could still be in college.

"Harry, why don't you order some champagne to celebrate Davis becoming your first employee," she directed excitedly.

Harry smiled. "Great idea, Maude."

The champagne came, and we watched the usual fanfare of opening the bottle with sheer enjoyment. "Let me propose the first toast," Maude said with a youthful zest. "To Davis, may you pick a constant stream of winning stocks that make us all richer than we could ever imagine!"

Harry nodded his enthusiastic agreement and then raised his glass. "To Davey, my dear friend, and valued partner. Together we're going to make a fortune for all of us!"

They both looked at me, waiting for my toast. So, I raised my glass and said, "To Harry, for giving me this opportunity, and to you, Maude, for making this opportunity possible. I won't let either of you down."

Maude clapped softly and smiled warmly at me as if I was a dutiful son who had just promised his mother that she would be very proud of his accomplishments. Harry couldn't stop beaming at me, which for the moment, seemed to solidify our friendship; and, likewise, boosted my trust in him. Reynolds and Simmons were now truly figments of the past.

The dinner was outstanding, especially for someone like me, who had never experienced such luxury dining before. Our conversation started out light and fun, although Maude struggled at times to come down to our level. But after a while, I sensed there was more to it than that. She started to take some digs at Harry that were more disparaging than lighthearted. I began to wonder whether she might be growing unhappy with him, or he with her. As the evening progressed, and the drinks flowed, Harry bristled more obviously at her stream of remarks. By dessert, it was clear there was something seriously wrong with their relationship.

"Oh, by the way, Harry, I want to remind you that we have theater tickets tomorrow night. And please, don't be late. You know how I hate to make a grand entrance as the curtain goes up."

"Ah, Maude, I'm sorry, I forgot all about the theater. I have a dinner meeting with a corporate pension fund manager who's ready to sign an agreement to move a large chunk of his stock trading to Miller Investments. It's our first big break. And we can make a hell of a lot of commission money as this guy loves to trade."

Maude was clearly annoyed. "But Harry, you promised me a week ago when I got the tickets that you'd keep the date open. How can you do this to me? I ask you to do a simple thing as hold the date, and you entirely disregard my wishes."

"Now, Maude," he answered, "I didn't disregard your wishes; you have to realize business is business. I can't just walk away from an opportunity like this. He's a big-time fund manager, and he picked tomorrow because that's when he'll be in New York this month. It's as simple as that! Don't you understand I'm doing it for us?"

"You told me the same thing last week when we had tickets to the charity ball," she hissed, her annoyance hardening into anger. "You said you couldn't change your meeting with some wealthy client, and anyway, it didn't matter, because you wouldn't be caught dead in some ridiculous costume just to please me. It was an important charity ball which Al and I always came to New York to attend, and which he gave a lot of money to! You knew very well I had my heart set on it, but you had no intention of pleasing me, did you?" her face now flushed and eyes flashing angrily.

"Maude, I'm terribly sorry, but costume balls are not my speed, especially when I'm working day and night to make Miller Investments a success. As soon as I get the firm off the ground, we'll spend all the time you want together."

"How dare you feed me a line of crap like that, Harry! I wasn't born yesterday. You didn't want to go, did you? It was just another one of your excuses. You always have an excuse, don't you, Harry? It's one excuse after another, and I'm sick and tired of them all!"

"Maude, please! Don't start in front of Davey. I'll make it up to you, I promise."

Maude looked at me, her face beet-red to where I thought she was about ready to explode. I looked over at Harry, who was struggling to control his temper. "Maude," I said softly, "maybe you'll let me take you to the theater tomorrow night?"

She looked at me for a long moment, either trying to calm down or to overcome the embarrassment at getting an invitation to escort her from some young looking, wet-behind-the-ears, recent college grad. She leaned back in her chair and stared hard at me, still trying to regain her composure. Then, she quickly smiled, and with a warm appreciation in her voice, said, "Davis, I'd be more than happy to go with you tomorrow night. As for you, Harry, don't you play me for a fool! Let me remind you that a deal's a deal, and I expect you to hold up your end of the bargain."

Chapter Six

I remember that night like it was yesterday. The show was the latest Broadway revival of *West Side Story*. Maude and I arrived early and slipped unnoticed into our front row seats. The play was great, and Maude seemed to like me escorting her to the theater. She held my hand throughout the show and rubbed my leg with her foot under the table during our late evening supper.

We went back to her apartment, where she offered me a drink while she went to change her clothes. I looked out at the beautifully lit park, a vodka martini in my hand, wondering where all her attention was going to lead. I was pretty sure Harry wouldn't like it if I started having an affair with his benefactor, so I drank the last of my martini and prepared to say goodnight as soon as Maude returned. But my quick exit was stopped cold when Maude returned to the living room wearing a tightly wrapped, and very enticing, monogrammed blue robe.

I now had a pretty good idea where this was going, and I sure as hell didn't want to be caught in the middle of it. Either she wanted to have sex with me because she had an affinity for younger guys or wanted to have Harry discover us in bed when he came home. I was willing to bet my first month's salary it was the latter. Knowing Harry, I was very concerned about how he'd take my fooling around with his meal ticket. Standing there staring at her, all I could envision was my head joining Reynolds' and Simmons' on Harry's trophy wall after he finished with me.

"Maude," I said softly, trying to hide my nervousness, "I don't think this is a good idea. You know I'm Harry's friend, and I won't do this behind his back. Please understand. I had a great time with you this evening. The theater and late supper were, without a doubt, the best, but I had better go now."

She stared at me as if trying to determine just how crazy I was for not climbing into bed with her that very minute. Finally, she walked over to me, touched her face to mine, and whispered, "Davis, you're quite handsome, smart, and mature. Maybe you could instill some sense into your friend before he falls off a cliff."

Not sure how to answer, I stood there stuttering a bunch of words, hoping they'd come out right when suddenly, she put her arms around me and kissed me like I'd never been kissed before. I thought my reaction was quite reasonable, *I'm definitely staying the night, the hell with Harry!* But then that yellow caution light started flashing wildly. *What about your future? What about making all those millions? Don't be a damn fool! Get out before you do something really stupid and screw up a once in a lifetime chance to make it big.* Ignoring my own warning, I kissed her long and hard. She pulled away to catch her breath, and I, to regain my senses. Yes, what a fabulous night this could be, but was it worth the hell I'd pay tomorrow? I stepped back, brought the weakest of smiles to my flushed face, and then shouted 'goodnight' over my shoulder as I practically ran to the door, kicking myself every step of the way for giving all this up.

She shouted after me, angry and frustrated. "Tell your friend that he better live up to his end of the deal, or else he'll find himself out on the street and without the fifteen million after my lawyer gets through with him!"

As I dejectedly closed the door behind me, I could hear my mother telling me, "Always follow your intuition!"

****

In the office the next morning, I sat watching the ticker tape on the three growth stocks we'd taken five thousand share positions in:

Walmart, Disney, and Xerox. My buy was based in part on the bet that President Reagan's 1982 tax reduction bill would soon start stimulating the economy and that those three stocks would be prime benefactors as the market took off. Despite Xerox being down two points after a nice run-up last week, I was excited that Walmart and Disney were up smartly that morning in anticipation of positive earning reports coming out next week. I sat back feeling really comfortable that the three were going to make us some good money, and very soon. Just then, Harry walked in with what looked like a major hangover.

"You look awful," I whispered, believing his head would burst with any sudden loud noise.

"What a night, Davey! I learned something last night: Pension fund guys can drink anyone under the table. We met a couple of girls after dinner in some hotel bar that I can't even remember. We spent the night with them, and then he got up at 6:00 am to catch a flight back to Chicago."

"You missed a good show," I responded quietly.

Harry stared at me for a couple of seconds, then smiled knowingly. "So, did you have fun with Maude last night?"

"Yeah, it was fun. I really liked the show, the supper afterward was first rate, we had a drink at your apartment, and I was home before 1:00 am. I had a really great time."

"Maude said you stayed last night."

"What? No, I didn't!" I sputtered defensively, surprised she would do that to me.

"She said you did." His smile had disappeared, and his voice sounded colder with a tinge of resentment.

"Harry, she asked me to stay, but I didn't want to get involved. I was just trying to make it easy for you when I asked her to go to the theater. How could she say I stayed when I didn't?" I didn't like feeling caught between the two of them.

"Don't get upset, Davey; I believe you. I guess she just wanted to make me jealous."

I gave an inward sigh of relief that he understood I hadn't had sex with Maude. For a moment there, I was almost convinced Reynolds and Simmons would have to move over to make room for me on Harry's trophy wall.

"Davey, she's too damn possessive of me!" he shouted suddenly in anger or frustration or both. "I can't be running home every night after work to be with her. You should see how hard she tries to act twenty-four. But I only see a woman who's much older. Sure, she's pretty and smart, and definitely great in bed, but I just can't be tied down to her. I feel she's becoming an albatross around my neck." Harry studied my face as if I had the answer to a way out of his relationship. Realizing I didn't, he turned and began pacing back and forth. A few minutes later, he abruptly stopped and stared at me. I knew then he had found his solution, and somehow, it had to do with me. And sadly, I was right!

He gave me a beaming smile as he said, "Davey, my boy, you are going to help me out on this one. Maude really likes you. She said so in no uncertain terms this morning, and to the point where she implied she'd love to sleep with you. So, my friend, you have the distinct honor and privilege of being my surrogate when it comes to entertaining her."

"What! Are you kidding, Harry? Please! She's your partner in this deal, not mine! I'm only an employee, not a principal or the resident escort. Don't do this to me, Harry!"

"Davey, in my eyes, you are as much of a partner in this business as I am. So take a deep breath and smile at your new assignment to wine and dine Miss Maude."

"I'm telling you, Harry, you're asking for trouble, a hell of a lot of trouble, if you don't comply with what she wants. A deal is a deal, and you know it! And you're not living up to your end. Don't you realize she's got fifty-seven million to buy the best lawyers in New York? She'll make mincemeat out of you. Don't do it, please!"

"Let me be the judge of that, Davey," he replied stiffly. "The fifteen million is mine, all mine, she gave it to me, and I'm going to do what I think is best to make money with it. And she's not going to stand in my way!" He walked across the room and looked out onto Park Avenue, trying unsuccessfully to control his anger. Turning back to me, he exploded in rage. "She's not going to bury me under her obsessive need for a man in her life. Do you hear me? I won't let her! She'll get her half of the earnings according to our deal, but after that she doesn't have a case. Let her go to court all she wants, but I'll be damned if I'll climb into bed at her beck and call!"

"You're right, Harry," I responded softly, hoping it would help calm him down. "But you've got to recognize that she can still make a hell of a lot of trouble for you. It could end up costing you a bundle in lawyer's fees and maybe, ruin your reputation on the Street, or possibly with your Midwest pension fund friend. Look at the risk you're taking, Harry. There's no reward in it for you. Do what she wants for a while until the business gets off the ground, and then you can dump her, and the chances are the repercussions would be minimal."

"No! I'm done with her and all her demands. It's going to be your job to wine and dine her, and anything else she wants.

"Harry, listen to me, please! Stick with her until we make some money, or until your pension fund friend starts to produce some commissions for us. Then, you can kiss her goodbye. Right now, we have hardly any money coming in. You don't want to blow the fifteen million on lawyers…it's not worth the risk!"

"I don't care. I said she's all yours," he replied, his cold, heartless tone indicating that he was not going to change his mind.

****

I had no choice but to call. "Maude?" I said sheepishly. "It's Davis. I apologize for foolishly leaving so abruptly last night and would love to take you to dinner tonight to make up for it." I fully expected a screaming reply of *hell no*. But after a short pause, she answered positively, sounding genuinely warm and appreciative. Her response at first pleasantly surprised me, but then I wondered if she had an ulterior motive for saying yes. I thought about it all day.

Well, our dinner at Café des Artistes turned out to be wonderful. She accepted my apology most willingly; and, as an added bonus, rubbed her foot against my leg throughout dinner. The night was clear and reasonably warm, so we decided to walk over to Madison Avenue before grabbing a cab back to her apartment. She held my hand tightly, while enthusiastically telling me another story about the great Al Williamson. That brought the total to five so far that night. This one was where he made ten million in two weeks by flipping a Chicago office building. "I couldn't believe it when he told me," she said with loving admiration. "But he did, and I was so proud of him. Al was famous throughout the Midwest for his ability to sniff out these types of deals. Nobody knows exactly how he did it, but somehow, somewhere, he learned that a Fortune 500 company was interested in buying the building. So he bought it fast, then turned around and sold it to them for what they thought was a bargain price..."

Maude suddenly stopped talking and stood frozen, her mouth wide open and her eyes staring straight ahead in disbelief. At first, I couldn't figure out why. Then, I followed her gaze up the street. To my shock and amazement, Harry was coming toward us with a beautiful, young woman clinging to his arm, gazing up at him with adoring eyes while giggling at what he was saying.

"Please, Maude," I quickly begged, though knowing it was useless. "Please don't make a scene. I'm sure Harry has a good reason. He told me this morning he was taking out the daughter of the manager of a large mutual fund, hoping it would pave the way to get a meeting with her father."

Maude turned to me with her mouth still frozen open and then began furiously shaking her head from side to side as if to say, *Don't you feed me a line of BS like that!* She turned towards the approaching couple, sneering as she said, "She looks more like a hooker to me!"

Before I could back up my defense of Harry, she hissed, "He told me this morning that he was having dinner with a pension fund executive and would be home early. The lying bastard!"

Harry was too engrossed in conversation with the young woman to pay any attention to us. When they were about twenty feet away, Maude hysterically screamed, "You son-of-a-bitch!"

Surprised, Harry looked up to see who was yelling, then stopped in shock. His body tensed, and his eyes opened wide as his face quickly reddened, but he didn't say anything. My guess, he was frantically trying to come up with a story to tell her, hoping that she might believe it somehow. "Ah...Maude...Davey," Harry called out slowly in an undeniably guilty voice as they walked towards us. Stopping a few feet away, Harry's tone changed as he boldly introduced his young, sexy friend. "I'd like you both to meet Scarlet Higgins. I had dinner with her and her dad, an executive of a large Boston mutual fund, and I'm walking her back to their hotel. Scarlet, I'd like you to meet my business partners, Maude Williamson, and Davis Lowe."

Clearly, I had gotten Harry's story confused, but it didn't matter, as it wasn't even close to his story. I watched as Maude stood there listening to his obvious lies, her eyes filling with tears. Suddenly, the tears stopped, and she stared intensely at Harry before slowly turning her gaze over to Scarlet, who attempted to force a friendly smile. Turning back to a very nervous looking Harry, Maude's demeanor transformed yet again, to steaming mad and ready to go off any second.

I tried again to defuse the situation by saying to Harry, "Why don't you drop Scarlet off and meet us for..." when Maude stepped right in front of him. Turning first to give Scarlet a sweet smile, she then hauled off and smacked Harry with all the force she could muster from her small body. Harry's head spun far to the right, knocking him off balance. He recovered slowly, rubbing his cheek as he turned to face her. With a face flushed with pain, eyes narrowed in fury, and lips pressed tightly together, he was obviously struggling to hold back the words he wanted so badly to say to her. Knowing Harry, he was going to blow our future, and it wouldn't be pleasant. "Who the hell do you think you are?" he finally shouted in a voice filled with genuine loathing as he looked down at her. "No one has ever hit me…"

"You deserved it!" she cried out. "You made a deal, and the first thing you do is welch on it."

"Harry! Maude! Stop, please!" I tried to physically squeeze between them. "We're all partners. You can't do this just when we're getting started. Stop it, please! Don't let the business and its fabulous potential go down the drain!"

"I gave you fifteen million dollars," Maude screamed, her eyes blazing, mouth twisted in rage as she shook her finger right up in Harry's face, "and I damn well want it back since you failed to deliver on your end of the deal. You have until tomorrow!" She turned, and angrily started to walk away.

I frantically grabbed Harry's arm and pleaded, "Harry, don't end it now! Please! Be sensible, and don't forfeit everything!"

But it turned out Maude wasn't finished. She walked back to Harry, and after glancing at Scarlet, turned to him with eyes now aflame. "I trusted you," she said, shaking her head from side to side, her face twisted in disgust. "You gave me your word. Your solemn promise! Then what do you do? You find some floozy for a one-night stand. How could you do that to me, Harry? How?"

"How…how could I do it?" he repeated in a vicious mocking tone. "You're an old woman, Maude! And I'm much too young to spend all my nights with you!"

"Jesus, Harry! Stop!" I begged, not wanting to hear him tear her down like he did Reynolds and Simmons. I began to see Maude as the next trophy on Harry's wall.

Harry shoved me away, his eyes locked on hers as he coldly continued. "You think you still have all the sex appeal in the world, don't you, Maude? Well, let me tell you that Scarlet here can run rings around you. But you already knew that. That's why you bribed me with an additional five million. You were afraid I wouldn't want you because you're not twenty-four anymore. And you were right! You're never going to be loved again the way Al Williamson loved you, no matter how much money you spend on young guys like me. It's pathetic. You're a lonely, old woman, and I'm done with your desperate demands…deal or no deal!

Maude reached back to swing at Harry again, but this time he was ready and grabbed her wrist before she could hit him. With a sadistic smile, he squeezed it hard until she cried out in pain to let her go. As she stood there, rubbing her wrist, her eyes welled up with tears. She watched silently as Harry took Scarlet's hand, patted it lovingly several times, and started to walk away with her. After a half dozen steps, he stopped and turned back. Taking a long look at Maude, he said, "I'll be by later to pick up my clothes. And Davey, get her home before she makes more of an ass out of herself."

Chapter Seven

I'll never forget that cab ride home. Maude cried all the way as I tried to console her. She was heartbroken at how nasty, belittling, and downright humiliating Harry had been to her. Even knowing Harry, I still couldn't believe how badly he'd acted. How could he treat her that way after giving him such a fabulous start in the business? After all, he was the one who broke their agreement. But it was typical Harry. Nobody better get in his way when he wants something. I couldn't help but think he'd treat me the same way if we had a falling out. The thought was chilling.

When the elevator stopped at the penthouse, a sobbing and very defeated-looking Maude handed me the key to open the door. I put my arm around her waist as we slowly made our way into the living room and over to the sofa. She sat down, bowed her head, and just cried. The only thing I could think to do was put my arm around her, hold her close, and try to comfort her. After a while, she looked up at me still distraught, and between sobs asked, "Davis, could you make me a stiff scotch and soda? I need one badly." After taking a couple of quick sips and a deep breath or two, her tears slowly subsided. A few minutes later, they finally stopped. What replaced them surprised the hell out of me…a hard, steely look in those doe-shaped blue eyes of hers, which I immediately recognized as a need for revenge. Her mind was made up to get even with Harry. The drink was the needed catalyst to build enough courage to make her plans.

She started to excoriate Harry and kept this up for quite a while until we heard the front door lock turn and the door open. We silently watched Harry march across the living room toward the bedroom without even as much as a nod of recognition for either of us. After he slammed the door, Maude looked at me with her steely gaze and angrily shook her head as if to say, *I'm going to make him pay!*

She gulped down the last of her scotch and soda, then stood up and started walking to the bedroom to have it out with him. But I knew Harry wasn't the kind to be pushed around. She could say her piece, cry, shout, and call him names, but in the end, I just knew he'd turn it around to make Maude the loser. I didn't know how I was going to stop her, but I had to at least try. "Maude, please don't do anything rash. I know what you're thinking, as I've watched others try to do the same thing. But believe me, I know Harry better than you. He'll belittle you until you're a hollow shell of your former self, and he won't stop until he wins. And Maude, he's going to win! So please...please don't go in there!"

"Davis," she shouted over her shoulder, "he's nothing but a goddamn liar and a grubby little cheat who needs to be stopped. I'm telling you, I'm not going to let him get away with this. He's a heartless bastard who could care less about who he hurts. Just you wait, he'll brush you aside too, without any warning, and no regret."

"I know! But right now, I don't want him to hurt you any more than he already has. Please, Maude, don't go in there. He won't quit until he's won!"

"Take your own advice, Davis, and get away from him as fast as you can!" she yelled upon reaching the bedroom door. "When he turns on you, you'll find yourself out in the cold with not a thing to show for it!"

"I know that Maude," I answered softly, "but right now, my concern is stopping you from doing something foolish. Yes, he has said terrible things to you tonight, but please, I beg you, don't do something you'll regret. Let Miller Investments make money for you instead of putting the firm out of business. Otherwise, you'll be out the fifteen million, and I'll be out of a job!"

Maude stopped short. Turning slowly, she stared at me with cold disgust before whirling around to open the bedroom door. She stepped inside and slammed it behind her. When I heard the lock click, I was sure Miller Investments was finished. Finished before we even got started. I thought about her fifteen million disappearing down a rat hole. It wasn't much to lose when you had fifty-seven million left. But for me, I had nothing left. I needed Miller Investments...and badly!

I sat there staring out miserably at the magnificent nighttime view of Central Park. If Miller Investments failed, the embarrassment of my leaving the prestigious firm of Brown & Johnson for a little start-up would make it exceedingly difficult for me to find a decent job on the Street. Although I felt bad about saying what I did, I was also angry with Maude for being so naive. Here's a woman desperately seeking the love and adulation she once had, and willing to pay fifteen million to a much younger guy to get it back. The only flaw in her plan was to pick the wrong guy. I guess it's not hard to be naive when you think only with your heart and not your head.

I was still sitting there, lost in thought about how to salvage my financial career, when suddenly I heard shouts and screams coming from the bedroom, followed by the sound of objects smashing against the walls. The noise had reached a fever pitch when I heard several hard slaps and Maude crying out in pain. Complete silence followed for a minute or two as I sat frozen in my seat. Then I heard Harry beg in a loud, frightened voice, "Don't, Maude! Please don't do it! I'm sure we can work this out. It was just a misunderstanding. Please believe me, I know we can make this work. I beg you...please don't do it!"

Everything went quiet. Then Harry started begging some more, followed by Maude screaming, "Shut up!" Suddenly two shots echoed throughout the apartment. I heard a long, deep moan. Then silence. Realizing what had happened, I jumped up and raced to the bedroom door. Knocking furiously, I shouted, "Unlock the door, Harry! Maude! Please!"

After what seemed like an eternity, the door finally swung open, and Maude walked out with the smoking pistol in her hand, a wild look in her eyes, and her cheeks puffy and red. "It serves him right! The bastard deserved it!" she cried out, before crumpling to the ground.

I rushed into the room to find Harry lying on the floor by the bed, moaning loudly and bleeding profusely from wounds in his arm and side. I grabbed the phone, dialed 911, and told the operator to get an ambulance here, and fast! Harry fell unconscious while I tried to stop the bleeding.

Chapter Eight

I remember how much I enjoyed running Miller Investments while Harry was recuperating. It kept me so busy that I didn't have time to think about Maude after her trial. That was, until about five months later when I found a plain white envelope stuffed into my mailbox without a return address. At first, I hesitated to open it, but my curiosity got the better of me, and I slowly tore one end off, quite suspicious at what I might find. Inside there was a small piece of paper that said, *Please come visit me. MW.*

****

The rain intensified as the Metro-North train pulled slowly out of the Mount Kisco, New York, station. I sat in the second car watching a flurry of raindrops hit the window, then streak wildly down as if in a race to get to the bottom. That seemed to sum up my fears about this trip: *wild and unpredictable.* A trip that I had great trepidation about taking.

I soon grew bored watching the rain cascade down the window, so I began another game: betting how many minutes it would take before the conductor announced the next stop…my stop. I bet three minutes, believing it was that short a distance. But it was five and a half minutes later when the train door swung open, and against a backdrop of pouring rain, the conductor shouted in a deep baritone voice to the half-dozen passengers, "Station stop, Bedford Hills!"

The rain was coming down harder, if that was even possible, as I stepped out on the station platform to search for a cab. I soon spotted one and ran as fast as I could, holding a newspaper over my head with the hope that somehow it would protect me from getting drenched, but no such luck. I climbed into the back seat, soaked to the skin, and out of breath. I sputtered to the driver an embarrassed, "The Prison, please!"

He looked at me through his rear-view mirror, smiled knowingly, and said, "We get lots of fares visiting the prison all the time. Husbands, boyfriends, family, you name it, they come to see the inmates."

It was the word *inmates* that struck a sharp note of reality for me. This was the first time I had ever visited a prison. Like everyone else, I'd seen them from afar in the movies and on TV, but never firsthand. As we pulled into the parking lot a short distance from the fortress-like building's massive, gray walls, I realized this was going to be an eye-opening experience for me. Everywhere I looked, there were rolls of barbwire strung on the top of the high walls. I was surprised to see how narrow the windows were, like little slits with an iron bar across them. As I stepped out of the cab, I happened to glance up at the watchtower. Although I shouldn't have been, I was surprised to see a guard standing at the tower door peering down at me with what looked like a shotgun in his hand. I must have appeared clearly nervous about this visit because as I paid the driver, he gave me another understanding smile. "It happens to everyone the first time they come here. They see the walls, the watchtower, the barbwire, and get nervous as hell."

I thanked him over my shoulder as I dashed to the visitor's gate, again with my wet newspaper draped over my head.

****

The female guard behind the reception desk looked me up and down, taking in my wet suit, before asking for my name. She then searched the visitor's list for it. "Yes, here you are, Mr. Lowe," she said slowly and a bit suspiciously, as if I had brought a cake with a file in it. Looking warily at me and my soaking wet clothes, she asked, "You're here to see Maude Williamson, correct?" I nodded affirmatively. "I need some identification if you please."

I showed her my driver's license. She examined my picture at great length, then studied my face again, before nodding okay. "Sit down over there, Mr. Lowe," she ordered. "Williamson will be down in a few minutes."

I sat down, trying to grasp this new world of prison walls, barbwire, rules, regulations, and guards everywhere. I could only imagine the awful sense of hopelessness the inmates had from being locked up in this fortress with no way out. I began to wonder how Maude was dealing with this radical adjustment. After all, until now, her life had been glamorous and exciting, spent in a world where she could do anything and everything she wanted, since money was no object. Now, for the next five years, her life would be caged and controlled to the minute detail. What a bitter pill to swallow. I wondered, *Would she survive it?*

"Follow me, please," said the approaching female guard in a soft but firm voice. She led me down a long, silent, whitewashed concrete corridor to a double door with a sign that said, *Visitors*. As we walked, I remembered the devastating humiliation Maude had endured when every newspaper and TV station in New York sensationalized her story: Older woman makes desperate deal to back her twenty-four-year-old lover's investment business in exchange for his love and attention. She became a laughingstock, denigrated, and mocked by everyone. Her defense counsel tried to prove she had made a straightforward business deal. In fact, some newspapers even wrote that the jury seemed somewhat sympathetic to her story, particularly after hearing that Harry jilted her for a much younger woman. But when their verdict came in, they found her guilty of attempted murder and possession of an unlicensed firearm. The judge sentenced her to five years.

The guard ushered me into a large room divided in half by a floor to ceiling meshed metal screen. She pointed to a chair next to the screen where I was to wait for Maude's arrival. As I sat there on the cold metal chair in my soaking wet clothes, I felt the hard stare of the guard standing by the door. I turned to see her arms folded across her chest with her eyes glued on me. She so intimidated me that I thought one false move on my part, and she'd blow her whistle, and a slew of guards with guns would rush in immediately. The clamminess all over my body was no longer just from my wet clothes.

After ten minutes of waiting and frequent nervous glances at the guard, the door on the other side of the screen finally opened. A tall, older female guard led Maude to the chair opposite mine behind the screen and pushed her gently down into it. What a shock! This wasn't the Maude Williamson I had known. She was no longer the stylish blonde, hair perfectly coiffed and dressed in the latest fashion, an ever-present warm and ready smile on her face. I couldn't get over how thin she was, and how drawn, tense, and very pale her face looked. Her blond hair was now mostly brown with strands of blonde throughout. But what shocked me most was the intense anger in her eyes, which I assumed reflected her deep-seated bitterness at being here.

She sat there glaring at me for what seemed like minutes, her face flushing as I continued to look at her. It suddenly dawned on me that she was waiting to see whether I'd do what everyone else had done…ridicule and humiliate her. Her icy, penetrating stare flustered the hell out of me, but I forced a half-smile and managed a pathetically simple but concerned, "How are you?"

She didn't answer but instead turned away, struggling to control the tears now streaming down her face. Giving up, she shook her head despairingly from side to side, finally crying out, "How do you expect me to feel locked up behind these goddamn horrible walls and barbwire?" For another minute or two she fought to regain a semblance of self-control. Then taking a deep breath, she used her sleeve to wipe away her tears, and forced a weak, little smile. "I'm glad you came, Davis. As you can see, adjusting to this place has been hard for me. But I'm glad you came."

A lengthy pause followed as she battled another bout of tears. "Davis, I've often thought you're the only person…friend…I could turn to after all that's happened. All of my friends in Springfield and Chicago want nothing more to do with me. They can't believe how stupid I was for taking a twenty-four-year-old lover at my age, and on top of that, bribing him with fifteen million dollars to do it. They were right. I was stupid! Really stupid! And I regret it now more than anyone will ever know."

"Maude, believe me, I am your friend. And I want to be for a long time to come. But I have to join the chorus criticizing you for demanding Harry's love and devotion. How could you fail to recognize he wasn't the loving, loyal type? My God, you know as well as I do that he has only one ambition in life: To make himself rich beyond belief and do it before he reaches the age of thirty. He's out to prove to the world that he is the smartest guy on Wall Street, and he's never tried to hide it. Maude, you had to know that from the first moment you met Harry. You had to know he'd have absolutely no compunction using you and everyone else to reach his goal."

Maude's tearful expression suddenly shifted to one of suspicion. "Davis, have you had a falling out with Harry?"

"No, no, you've got it wrong, Maude. I'm still working with Harry. In fact, we're beginning to make some money in the market now that the economy is gaining speed."

Maude made a face that implied she couldn't care less about how the business was doing, but I sensed she did care…if only in relation to how it was affecting Harry. Her pale cheeks quickly reddened again, and her eyes hardened with resentment after I told her that Harry was doing fine. I should have realized the idea of him living high on the hog while she was languishing in prison wouldn't be well received. Clearly trying to control her anger, she responded in an irate, rasping whisper, "I'm glad you're making money, Davis. But I can't tell you how much I hate hearing that bastard is having one hell of a good time while I'm rotting in here!"

A long silence followed in which I didn't offer any defense of Harry, nor did I try to come up with the right words to console Maude. She turned away to look at the guard, struggling to rein in her anger. Finally, after a couple of deep breaths, she turned back, smiled weakly at me, and said, "Davis, I'm counting the days until I get out. My lawyer tells me that I could be up for parole, possibly in two years for good behavior. I can't wait to be free. You have no idea what *free* means!"

"That's really good news, Maude," I answered enthusiastically, wondering what she would do when she got out. "Any plans for when that happens?"

That hard, icy stare returned for a second or two, and then she gave me a devious smile. Half standing, she put her fingers through the iron mesh and squeezed the metal hard until they turned white. Leaning forward, so her lips were pressed against the screen, she hissed, "I plan to get even with that son-of-a-bitch! He destroyed my life after I gave him everything: money, me, my love."

"Maude, what are you saying?" I cried out in a loud whisper while motioning to her to sit down before the guard came over. "You're in prison for getting even with Harry! You have a chance to get out early and be free. Free from this place! No cell! No walls! No barbwire and no guard watching you every moment. Don't you get it? Forget Harry! Forget all about him and start a new life for yourself. You still have plenty of money. I'm sure some of your friends will forgive you. Go live wherever you want. Do whatever you want. You're still entitled to half the profits from the business…which I'm sure will piss Harry off no end. Use it towards starting over. Please, Maude, no more revenge! He's not worth another second of your time!"

Maude let go of the screen and slowly sat back down, her head lowered in an apparent sign of agreement. But when she raised it again to look at me, I was stunned to see the intense hatred that had reappeared in her eyes. There was no doubt she wanted Harry to suffer a hell of a lot more. All I could do was wonder at how badly this would end for everyone.

"What do you think I do here every day, Davis, sing to the inmates?" she whispered angrily to me. "All I do is sit in my cell and go over every detail of my relationship with that bastard. How he readily agreed to the ten million, then slyly negotiated for the additional five, making me believe he was happy that our relationship would work despite our age difference. What a fool I was, thinking he'd love and take care of me just like *my* Al did. Instead he lied and deceived me from the very beginning, knowing I was wearing my heart on my sleeve. He's a scheming liar who deserved to die!"

"Maude, you can't mean that!" I pleaded, fearing the worst. "Thinking that won't get you anywhere. You'll just end up back here again or worse!"

"No, I won't, Davis. You'll see!"

Chapter Nine

I looked up and realized that Monsignor Gerrity had stopped reading. Seizing the opportunity, Frank turned to me and asked, "So you knew Harry Miller. Why do you think most of us here today were so eager to buy into his 'pot of gold' story?" I started to answer, but he hadn't finished his question. "Tell me, what magical power did he have over us? Not just Millie and me, but over the whole town? We're a pretty smart bunch of people around here. Most of us are reasonably wealthy because we're smart investors. And everyone I know is financially conservative. We'd never let some Pied Piper come along and sell us a bill of goods since we all know the value of a dollar and what it can buy."

Frank paused to look up at the Monsignor again before continuing. "I know first hand that a hell of a lot of people in town look at a financial opportunity from every angle before investing their money. Why it's almost a badge of honor to tell your friends just how complete your analysis was before deciding to buy some stock or bond. So tell me, why should such a smart bunch of investors like us fall hook, line, and sinker for Harry Miller's scheme?"

"You know why, Frank, you just don't want to admit it."

He eyed me coldly before whispering contemptuously, "If I knew the reason, I wouldn't be asking you!"

"Okay, I'll tell you, Frank," I responded, a little miffed. "It boils down to two distressing failings each, and every one of us has: greed and fear. It's been that way ever since time immemorial. Both are embedded deeply in everyone's DNA. The first two, major financial panics recorded almost four hundred years ago, the German Kipper-und Wipperzeit Debasement of Metal Coins Bust in 1622, and Holland's Tulip Mania Panic in 1637, demonstrate my point."

Frank's expression changed to bewilderment. "What in the world are you talking about?" he blurted out. "Kippers and tulips, what the hell do they have to do with Harry Miller's scheme to milk us dry?"

"Greed, Frank! Unadulterated greed," I responded sharply. "It's human nature to be greedy. And if anyone understood human nature, it was Harry! He knew most people would find it hard to resist the chance to make a hell of a lot of money fast and easy. But what he did that was especially clever was to initially only offer his fund to a very select group of investors. He knew full well they would, in turn, brag to their friends, relatives, and everyone they knew about all the money they were making. So, by initially limiting the number of people buying in, he forced those kept out to drool with envy, and then ultimately convince themselves it was worth almost anything to buy in."

I paused to let this sink in before adding, "Frank, think of it this way: If John Smith was told he could be set for life with a much higher income than his current portfolio was delivering, and on top of that, have it guaranteed; and he also knew that his friends and neighbors were already reaping the rewards, do you think he'd waste time doing an analysis or investigation of the investment fund offering it? Hell no! He'd want to get in on that fabulous deal as fast as possible...no questions asked! After all, once word got around, who wouldn't want to jump onto this 'pot of gold' bandwagon? But in reality, deep down, everyone knows that if it sounds too good to be true, it's most likely not true...it's just greed.

Frank's expression went from disbelieving to defensive, as if to say, *That's not me at all. I'm not greedy. Not me!*

I couldn't help but smile. "Frank, there's a famous illustration of how financial greed works...maybe you already know it. Tulip Mania in Holland started out as a simple desire to grow beautiful tulips, and make some money selling them. The first batch of multi-colored tulips was quite beautiful, which produced an eager demand for the bulbs, and a willingness to pay a premium price for them. Word-of-mouth brought more people anxious to get in on this lucrative market. They soon realized that the more exotic-colored tulips bulbs brought higher prices and greater profitability. Season after season saw more and more Dutchmen develop their own uniquely beautiful tulip bulbs, then charge ever-higher prices, to the point where the country became obsessed with growing and selling tulip bulbs. Everyone believed with absolute certainty that their uniquely colored tulips were going to make a real killing in the market. Greed was rampant! Prices for bulbs climbed skyward, creating an ever-greater incentive to start growing them. Soon people who had never grown a tulip in their life invested in new exotic varieties to grow and sell at still higher prices, hoping to make an exorbitant profit."

Pausing, I noticed that Frank wasn't the only one enthralled with the story; everyone sitting around us appeared to be listening. "Then one fateful day in 1637, the bulb of the most extraordinary tulip ever seen was offered at an exorbitantly high price...and no one stepped forward to buy it. Growers quickly became alarmed at the thought of getting stuck with their less exotic bulbs. Greed suddenly turned into abject fear! Bulbs were dumped left and right on the market at any price as growers tried desperately to salvage any part of their investment. Panic set in. And before it was over, many, many people lost every guilder they ever had!"

Frank sat there, shaking his head. "Frank, history is filled with stories like this one. In Harry's case, he was selling financial security that was too good to be true, to the point where no one wanted to pass up the deal!"

"I'm not greedy," Frank said adamantly. "Never have been, never will be!"

"Then why did you buy into Harry's scheme?"

"Why...well...because it looked like a good investment. He was guaranteeing a fifteen percent return, year in and year out!"

"You just made my point, Frank. No one guarantees a fifteen

percent return on an investment year in and year out. You know that. There are years that exceed even the rosiest of expectations. Then there are years where nothing goes right. Portfolios contract, and can keep on contracting until people sell out in disgust. You've read enough prospectuses and financial reports to know there's always a qualified opinion to protect the writers from the unknown vagaries of the market. So, unfortunately, Frank, you were taken in by a master at selling greed!"

"Well, he paid me for five years straight, damn it! I got a statement and a check every month like clockwork. Although, one month he did send me a check amounting to a quarter of what I normally got. Claimed that the market took an unexpected dive, and he wanted to hold on to the cash to invest in the next upturn."

"Frank, what really happened was he ran out of new investor money coming in during the downturn and didn't have enough cash to pay investors like you, your guaranteed payment. It was a Ponzi scheme pure and simple. Take in money from new investors, turn around and pay out a portion to current investors, and then keep the rest for yourself!" Frank looked sheepish. "Tell me, Frank, how did you learn about Harry's guaranteed investment?"

"Well, I…ah…was playing golf with Dave Johnson and Ed Brown. Dave told me how he invested two million with Harry and was making three hundred thousand a year in income. And Ed said he bought in for a million and a half and was very happy with the two hundred and twenty-five thousand he was getting. Both of them told me it was by far the best investment they'd ever made! So I called Harry and asked to buy two hundred and fifty thousand dollars worth, but he told me he'd let me know. I waited a couple of weeks and called him again. He said his fund was closed at the moment, and he couldn't accept any new investments. He kind of hinted to me that my investment was really too small to be considered, so I went back and added a million more to my original number, and Harry agreed, although he still sounded kind of reluctant."

I nodded to him that proved my point, and turned to Millie, "And how did you decide to invest with Harry?"

"Well, I was playing bridge with Meg Dunn, who told me she had just invested a million dollars with Harry. Her reasoning seemed logical to me: Anyone who donated a million dollars to fix up the Town Hall and build the large annex, and could buy a twelve-room, ten-acre estate overlooking the ocean, must know what he was doing. So, I invested a million dollars my husband had left me, thinking he'd be so proud of me!"

I looked back at Frank, who was frowning at his gullibility, and hers too. "Harry was one slick operator, Frank," I offered as a small consolation. Based on his disgusted look and silence, I knew he was kicking himself for being taken in so easily.

I felt a tap on my shoulder and turned around to see a very suntanned man in a three-piece light brown suit with a muscular build and a very thick neck. With a knowing nod and grimace of *I got screwed too*, he whispered, "He took me for a million and a half!"

"Two million for me!" said the heavyset, gray-haired man sitting next to him.

A pretty, young woman with short blonde hair sitting in front of me spun around and said, "Three million, the son-of-a-bitch!"

I looked around to see if anyone else was going to chime in.

"A million for me," a woman across from me said despairingly.

"He suckered me for two million," snapped a well-dressed man behind me.

"All of his sweet talk cost me two and half million," the woman sitting next to Millie muttered.

"I know how you all feel," I said softly, "but unfortunately, there's no consolation for what he did to you. And I'm sorry to say it, but I think it'll be a long time before you get even some of your money back. I, for one, believe Harry was a master at this game and had no compunction whatsoever about taking your money. Unfortunately, you and all the others in town fell for his siren song of easy money and long-term security."

The Monsignor abruptly stopped reading. He turned to scowl at the group of us for talking so loudly, waiting until we were quiet before starting up again. But Frank was too enraged to stop. He took a breath or two, turned to me with fury in his eyes, and loud enough for everyone around us to hear, said, "No wonder someone put a bullet through the bastard's heart!"

A lengthy silence followed as we all tried to re-focus our attention on the Monsignor and his reading. However, it was clear the outpouring of anger emanating from our little group wasn't going away anytime soon. In fact, it didn't take long before Frank broke his concentration on the Monsignor, turned to me, and with flushed face and eyes on fire, demanded, "Tell me, how do you fit into all of this?"

"How do I fit in? I don't fit in at all! He took me differently ten years ago." But Frank wasn't convinced. As he continued to stare angrily at me, I realized he had already branded me a co-conspirator in Harry's Ponzi scheme. To him, I was guilty, no matter what kind of defense I offered. His mind was made up, and nothing was going to change it. I began to wonder if the others sitting around us agreed with him, knowing it's always easier to blame someone else for the mistakes you make.

I started to defend my innocence when the man behind me with the suntan and three-piece suit tapped me on the shoulder, and in no uncertain terms, demanded, "Were you or were you not working with Harry on this dirty dealing scheme?"

"I had nothing to do with Harry's scheme!" I replied over my shoulder in a loud, indignant whisper. "He forced me out of his investment firm ten years ago, well before starting this investment fund here!"

My answer received another disbelieving shake of Frank's head. That's when I lost control and angrily lashed out at him. "I don't care whether you believe me or not, Frank. But I'm telling you the truth! I had absolutely nothing to do with Harry's scam." But his incredulous expression said it all. He was definitely convinced I was lying through my teeth, and in fact, was sure I was Harry's conniving partner in screwing a hell of a lot of people sitting here today out of their millions. *Well, if he doesn't believe me, then the hell with him.* I turned to listen to the Monsignor. Still, his disbelief gnawed at me. He wasn't the first to try to link me to Harry's misdeeds over the years, but he was the first to accuse me of working with Harry to con people out of their retirement money. damn it! I can't seem to escape from Harry's shadow no matter how many times I try. It's always the same: a skeptical nod with an accompanying *sure* look...not believing a word I say. But to those willing to hear my side, I tell them in precise detail the exact day and time when we closed H.J. Miller Investments forever. The day: Monday, October 19, 1987. The time: 4:00 in the afternoon. That was the last time I had anything to do with Harry Miller.

****

It was a Monday, and has been and always will be locked in my memory, as it became a life-changing day for me. It was the day the stock market crashed, causing the worst one-day drop in financial history...worse than in 1929! Yet even with all the undeniable warnings on the previous three business days, there was Harry with his usual know-it-all arrogance, refusing to heed any of them. The world was ours then, and if he had only listened to me, we could have made it through with hardly a problem. But no, not Harry! The bastard wouldn't budge. *Buy! Buy!* That's all he could say, the hell with listening to anybody else. To hell with all the signals that were about to cause the crash! *Just keep on buying, and we'll make a ton of money when the market turns*, he repeated over and over again. Well...the Crash came that day, and it wiped out forty percent of the bull market's gain since it began in 1982. And did it in just four days! Forty percent! In four days! And there was Harry, fighting against this tsunami, insisting we'd come out of it smelling like a rose!

When I think about our start in 1982, I can only relish the fabulous run we had. Who could have imagined the Dow Jones Industrial Average climbing to a record high of 2722, up from a dismal 776 five years earlier? And boy, those were five fabulous years. H. J. Miller Investments made money hand over fist, and so did I. We were invested up to the hilt, but it didn't matter. We just couldn't do anything wrong. As the money rolled in, Harry made sure he spent his share of the profit, and Maude's too, as fast as he could. He bought himself an eight-room penthouse in Manhattan overlooking Central Park. Between the nightlife and the women, Harry was in heaven. I was too, although on a much smaller scale.

When the first shock wave hit on Wednesday, October 14, it scared the hell out of me. The Dow dropped a record-shattering 95 points, but Harry practically danced around the office, overjoyed at what he saw as the beginning of a great buying opportunity. "Keep on buying, Davey! We're going to make more money than we ever dreamed possible!" he shouted with glee, even though the value of our portfolio had just plunged dramatically.

The next day, the market dropped another 58 points. To Harry, this two-day drop was the signal for the start of a perfect market turnaround scenario. "Keep on buying, it's definitely going to turn, and we'll clean up!" was his ever-enthusiastic cry.

The following day, Friday the 16th, is when I knew the end was near. The bottom was nowhere in sight as the Dow slipped another 108 points, scoring another record fall. Still, Harry didn't even cringe, much less blink an eye. He was absolutely convinced this downturn was going to be short-lived, that if we were smart, kept our focus and courage, we'd make a bundle of money when the market turned up the following week. After the market closed that afternoon, we argued like hell over his strategy. He couldn't see the magnitude of the market falling two hundred and sixty-one points in three days! We nearly came to blows as I was dead set against risking all the firm's money, including mine, because of his bullheadedness.

That weekend was the worst I've ever spent. I knew that everything we had worked so hard for the last five years could disappear by Monday's close of business. And mine wasn't the only jitters; the financial community appeared close to panic, too. Of course, the only one *not* nervous was Harry. If he called me once, he called me ten times exhorting me to stay positive, and plan to keep on buying on Monday no matter what happened. *We'll clean up big time! You can bet the ranch on it!* We argued and argued, and I finally pleaded to wait and see how Monday started out before doing any more buying. "Don't be such a pessimist," he yelled at me. "You're like all the wimps on Wall Street! The first sign of a market pullback and you're ready to run for the hills like the rest of them! Well, I'm not doing that! We're going to buy. You hear me, buy!"

"Harry, let me get this through your thick skull. We're pretty close to getting a margin call. If the market keeps falling like this, we won't have any free cash left to cover our margin, so forget about buying! This is dumb, Harry! No, it's damn stupid! We'll lose everything we've made over the last five years if we keep on buying!" But it was no use...his mind was made up.

I remained nervous as hell the rest of the weekend, thinking how our portfolio could vanish in a heartbeat if we had to cover our margin. Five years of hard work down the drain. I remember running all the way to the office that Monday morning to get an idea of how bad the market's opening would be. Bad? That was an understatement. It was a disaster! The Dow opened down, way down, just as Harry arrived at the office.

"Buy! And keep on buying," he bellowed at me as he slammed the door. "We're going to make a ton of money on this pullback, Davey, a ton!"

But any fool could see this wasn't an ordinary pullback. It was extraordinary! The Dow was off two hundred points before we could catch our breath. Harry suddenly stopped with his rah-rah enthusiasm and stood there, looking shocked. At three hundred points, my body started shaking as if the world was coming to an end. I screamed at Harry, "You goddamn fool, we've got to sell now! This minute, or we'll lose everything! Don't you understand...everything!"

But he wouldn't, or couldn't, let go of all those years his overbearing, arrogant thinking had propelled him to unbelievable heights. Even now, with all facts clearly pointing to the obvious, he just couldn't admit he might be wrong. Instead, he shouted back, "Nah," but with a little less than his usual bravado. "Let's not. Maybe I'm the only one to think so, but there's still money to be made today, Davey! The market is going to turn! It's going to, I can feel it! You'll see. I guarantee it will happen before noon!"

At four hundred points down, I picked up the phone to start selling. The hell with Harry! I wasn't going broke too! "Hey, who's running this ship?" he yelled defiantly. "I'll make the decisions here, not you, Davey!"

"Harry, why can't you understand that there's not a dollar's worth of cash left if we get a margin call. If the market sinks another fifty points, we're done! We'll be sold out! Finished! Ruined!"

"Davey...Davey, my boy, you've got to keep the faith. This market has to turn real soon. The bottom is near. You can bet on it! And we'll pull through with flying colors. Just watch." But he no longer sounded so sure.

Throughout the late morning and into the early afternoon, we sat there mesmerized by the ticker tape. Then it happened. The telephone rang after the market fell another seventy-five points. I answered with great trepidation, as I knew my worst fears were about to be realized. It was our broker, demanding a check for ten million dollars in a half-hour or else he'd sell us out. Giving Harry an *I told you so* look, I wearily asked, "Well, Harry, do you have ten million right now to cover our margin? Yes or no?"

Harry appeared startled by the question. His face blanched as he looked at me with disbelief. How could this be happening to him? His aggressive, over-the-top style of doing things had always won the day. But the world had suddenly turned on him in a major, humiliating way. It was clear that this had never happened to him before, and he didn't know how to deal with it. I almost felt sorry for him, watching as he sat there, his face buried in his hands.

"Well, Harry? Do we pay up, or do we sell?"

Silence, nothing but silence. "Harry!" Now I was yelling, holding my hand over the receiver. "Answer me, damn it!"

With his hands still covering his face, he shook his head slowly from side to side. For the first time in his life, Harry was lost in defeat. Real defeat! And he couldn't deal with it. I probably should have shown some sympathy, but frankly, at that moment, I could have cared less, seeing how his arrogance had just ruined me too.

Mad as hell that I'd let him bamboozle me, I screamed into the phone, "Sell! Sell it all!"

There was silence on the other end. Then our broker said quietly, "Too bad. That's really too bad."

Harry and I sat there, frozen in fear for the longest time as we absorbed the shock. I tried to think of what, if anything, we could do to salvage H.J. Miller Investments, but it was pretty clear that the business was gone. We had risked millions betting on all kinds of stocks, and this sudden market collapse had brought us up short. We were essentially broke, and neither of us knew anyone on the Street who would loan Harry money, especially now. We were finished...really finished.

Harry still hadn't said a word, but as I got up to leave, he raised his head and looked up at me. His face was white as a sheet, but it was the look in his eyes that alarmed me. And for good reason, as he soon let loose a tirade of accusations and threats. "You screwed me...you screwed me royally, Davey. I trusted you to invest my money wisely, and what did you do, you bought a ton of crap stocks that would fall apart on any downdraft in the market. How could you have done this to me? I've lost everything. You've ruined me! You're fired, and I'm going to sue you for every dime you've got! Now get the hell out of here! I can't stand looking at your lying face!"

Realizing there was no reasoning with him, I didn't even bother defending myself and instead hurried out of the room. But it was a moment I'll never forget.

Chapter Ten

It's been ten years now, but I'm still not over Harry's firing and threatening me like that. I think about it almost every day. Five years of making real money. A supposed partnership, and then because of his pigheadedness, I'm financially ruined. But looking back, I only have myself to blame. After all, how many times did I tell myself that somewhere along the line, Harry would turn on me just like he did with Simmons and Reynolds and Maude? I should have been ready for it, but just like the three of them, I didn't see it coming.

I remember standing outside the Park Avenue office for a long time, trying to calm down from the shock of everything that had just happened. But all I could think of was I needed a drink, and badly. Hailing a cab, I headed uptown to The Carlyle bar to console myself.

I had just ordered my second double Dewar's on the rocks and begun to think about how much, and for how long, I had put up with Harry's crap, when I felt a tap on my shoulder. I turned and was shocked to see the angry face of Fred Simmons, the last person I thought I would ever see again! He was standing there with feet firmly apart and fists clenched, his pale blue eyes fixed on me, obviously anxious to get his long-overdue revenge. Knowing he wanted to have it out today, right this minute, was more than I could deal with. I smiled weakly and said, "Say, Simmons, please...come and sit down. Let me buy you a drink."

"No thanks!" he answered. "When I saw you sitting here, Lowe, I knew this had to be my lucky day. You know, I've been waiting a long time to catch up with Harry and you, and give you both something in return for what you did to me ten years ago. Harry ruined my life, Lowe! He made me into a laughingstock! Nobody would hire me. I spent over a year searching for a job with every brokerage firm on the Street. Nothing! They all believed I had contributed to Reynolds and Coleman's closing. I even stooped to hitting firms dealing in penny stocks, hoping for a job. Nothing! Not even a nibble. It took me a while, but I eventually learned Harry put the word out that I was a lousy stock picker. And they all believed him! Every last one of them!"

"Simmons, please, have one drink on me!"

"And you, Lowe, you hit me when I wasn't looking. I was going to beat the hell out of him, and you sucker-punched me. I've got to tell you, I've waited a hell of a long time to catch up with you too!"

"Come on, Simmons. Step up to the bar and sit right here!" I patted the barstool next to me. "I know just how you feel. As a matter of fact, today has been the worst day of my life. I just lost all of my money thanks to Harry's stupid arrogance, and on top of that, he fired me! Can you believe it? He wouldn't let me sell when I wanted to save the firm. Then he turns around and blames me for his lousy decision to keep on buying during this market collapse. After we had everything going our way for the last five years, blaming me was insane. And then to fire me! And to top it off, as I was walking out the door, he threatened to sue me for bad advice. Bad advice! Can you believe it? So, Simmons, that's why it's been a terrible day for me. Go on, have a drink! Have two!"

Calming down, Simmons gave me a *you got what you deserved* smile, apparently satisfied that I had got beaten up more by Harry than what he had been planning to dish out to me. "I still owe you one, Lowe. But I'll give you a pass today," he muttered condescendingly as he sat down next to me.

"I'll have a double Jack Daniels," he told the bartender. When he turned back to me, he was grinning from ear to ear, which I guess meant that he equated my getting fired and losing all my money as just punishment. Talk about bitterness! As soon as the bartender placed his drink in front of him, Simmons raised his glass in a toast. "You've now joined the list of Harry haters. Welcome to the club, Lowe!"

We both drank to that!

After sitting there for a few minutes, staring into our half-filled glasses, Simmons spoke up. "You know, Lowe, it's been my fervent hope that all of us who hate Harry will someday join together to collectively destroy him physically and financially. I guess we now have enough people to form quite a group, don't you think? He's ruined a hell of a lot of lives!"

"Definitely has, Simmons. He definitely has!" I answered, beginning to feel resigned to my fate as the scotch mellowed me into a more philosophical mood. That's when I began trying to rationalize Harry's actions. Maybe the Harrys of the world are born with an inherent aptitude for stepping on or over people in order to get ahead, along with an ability to not care about who they stepped on or over. It certainly would explain a lot. That, plus his over-the-top, overbearing arrogance in everything he said and did, which in his eyes always made him right and everyone else wrong. Well, whatever drove him may have worked all these years, but no longer! And to be honest, I'm glad. In my five years working for him, deep down, I'd always hoped that someday, somehow, he'd get his comeuppance. And what a day that would be! Well, today was that glorious day by God! But why did I have to end up being punished, too?

"Well, Lowe, now that you've gotten a taste of Harry's medicine, I'd be lying if I didn't tell you how much I'm enjoying your plight," Simmons said, sounding satisfied. "But if you think Harry is anywhere near washed up, you're kidding yourself! Guys like Harry always come up out of the sewer, smelling like a rose. He'll have another scheme before you know it, find some new gullible soul he can convince he can make lots of money for. You got to hand it to Harry...he does have a special knack for picking the right gullible people with money, doesn't he?"

"Yeah, he does, Simmons," I sighed. "Harry somehow draws in

moneyed people like a magnet. But after what he's done to me today, here's hoping he picks the wrong person to fund him. Someone who'll screw him just the way he screwed me. Or maybe, a member of our stepped-on-or-over club will decide to step up, and permanently stop him."

"Permanently? What do you mean by permanently, Lowe? That's a pretty strong word."

"True. But what about all the nasty, underhanded things Harry's done? Life-changing things, wouldn't you say, like destroying careers and financial security? Why wouldn't that push someone right to the end of their rope, causing them to do something drastic, like seeking revenge that ends up permanent?"

"Whoa...wait a minute, Lowe. I hate the guy too and would love nothing more than to see him get what's coming to him, but you're not serious, right?

"Just think about it, Simmons. Under ordinary circumstances, most people learn from their mistakes, bow their head in shame, then take a deep breath, and start over again. Never once thinking of doing bodily harm to anyone. But what about the person who believes their life has been destroyed forever because of someone else's actions and that becomes the driving force behind their irrational thinking: *You've destroyed my life, so I'm sure as hell going to destroy yours!* That's revenge, Simmons, pure and simple! And just how far someone pursues revenge...I think it rests on how convinced they feel their life has been destroyed. Obviously, there's a pivotal point where anger and desperation reach destructive proportions, where logic and reason no longer matter. The only motivation is to wreak ultimate vengeance on the person who ruined their life. But do you know what the real difficulty is, Simmons? It's determining the exact point when a person believes that's their only choice!"

For a few moments, he sat staring at me in wide-eyed disbelief as he registered the depths of my hatred for Harry, but then a look of fear quickly crossed his face, as if the thought had suddenly entered his mind that I might act on my plan of ultimate vengeance. I'd say that Simmons was definitely frightened to the point where he believed he was drinking with a potential murderer! But as I studied his face, I began to wonder if his fear was not really about what I might do, but what he might do! Maybe I'd put into words what his deep-seated hatred of Harry was all about, perhaps identified for him when permanent retaliation becomes justifiable, something he might have been seriously considering all these years.

To help break the tension, I ordered another round of drinks. We sipped them slowly, staring at each other, trying to guess whether the other was capable of committing the severest revenge. I finally looked away and finished my scotch. I had seen nothing that gave away the true extent of Simmons' hatred of Harry. But then again, I still believed there was a great depth to it. Raising his glass to offer another toast, Simmons gave me a weak smile, which I found most disingenuous. "Don't do anything I wouldn't do, Lowe. It could be detrimental to your health!"

He paused to let his words sink in, then finished his drink. "And Lowe, thanks for the drinks and your rather interesting philosophical analysis. Hopefully, we'll see each again and soon, under different circumstances."

"Thanks for joining me, Simmons, and letting me talk it out. You've helped me put Harry in a much better perspective. And frankly, you've helped me get through this disastrous day!"

Chapter Eleven

I felt a tug at my arm and looked up to find Millie leaning over me, whispering rather irritably, "Don't you know you should be standing when we sing the *Song of Farewell*?"

"Oh, sorry," I replied as I jumped up. "I was lost in thought about Harry and our parting company ten years ago. My apologies."

I turned to apologize to Frank, but to my surprise, he was gone. "Where's Frank?" I asked Millie, thinking he might have walked out of the service.

"He was very angry with you, and took a seat on the other side of the church."

At first, I didn't understand why. But then I realized it was probably because he didn't believe me. "Do you feel the same way, Millie?" I asked a little hesitantly.

"No, well...not quite. You seem like too nice a young man to be mixed up with the likes of Harry Miller."

"If that's an approval, Millie, I accept it!"

The service concluded with the sprinkling of holy water and a final prayer. The Monsignor closed his prayer book and then raised his hands for quiet before announcing that everyone was invited back to the church for lunch after Harry's burial. And for those staying, punch, cheese, and crackers were being served in the large room downstairs.

****

It appeared that almost every parishioner had decided to skip the burial from the size of the crowd heading downstairs. But the food and drink proved to be only a distraction, as the crowd's primary purpose was to grouse a lot more about Harry stealing their money, and how pissed off they were in believing they'd never get any of it back. As I pushed my way through the crowd to get something to eat, the bits and pieces of these angry conversations intensified around me.

I picked up some crackers, and a glass of punch, and walked to a quieter spot at the far end of the room to avoid having to listen to the litany of complaints. While munching on a cracker, I turned to observe the crowd and was surprised to see the suntanned man in the three-piece suit walking towards me. He was big, even bigger now that I saw him face-to-face, and tall, with very broad shoulders and an unusually thick neck, probably from playing football years ago. His eyes were large and brown, highlighting an aging, somewhat handsome face offset by a large crooked nose and thinning brown hair parted neatly down the middle. From his intimidating scowl, I had a sense our conversation wasn't going to be pleasant.

"Lowe...Davis Lowe...do I have the name right?"

"Yes, that's right," I replied, smiling weakly. "What can I do for you, Mr.....?"

"My name's Swenson, Tim Swenson," he answered, his tone rather hostile. I held out my hand to shake his, but he ignored it and immediately got to the point. "I was the one sitting behind you, and I was the one who said he lost a million and a half in Harry Miller's fund. That was a million and a half dollars, Lowe! A hell of a lot of money, wouldn't you agree?

"Yes, it certainly is, Mr. Swenson," I responded, now fully convinced this was going to turn out badly.

"I couldn't help overhearing your conversation with the white-haired gentleman next to you. Were you Harry Miller's silent partner in his Ponzi scheme?"

"No, for the last time, I was not Harry Miller's silent partner!" I exploded with anger, turning quite a few heads and stopping many conversations. "And if you heard all of my conversation with Frank Ellis, you'd know I haven't seen Harry in ten years. I can't tell you how sick and tired I am of being accused of a silent partnership with him! I'll repeat it again, Mr. Swenson: I had absolutely nothing to do with Harry Miller and his recent investment fund!"

Some in the crowd moved closer to listen to our conversation, ready for an opportunity to express their anger at losing their life savings. From the look on their faces, they had a lot to say. But Swenson appeared surprised by my vehemence, and changed to a more conciliatory tone, although I thought he still wanted me to admit I was Harry's partner. "Look, Lowe, Harry and I started out as friends. He was a fun guy to be with. And as two single guys, we spent a lot of time together. I guess you could call us drinking buddies who chased a lot of women here in town. Let me tell you, Lowe, that Harry was a helluva magnet for attracting the ladies. Frankly, I didn't understand why at first. But then I realized it was his money, and how he spent it...big time! Always bragging and showing off no matter who he was with, whether women or anyone we met at the bar, even our favorite bartender, and every waiter who ever served us. But ultimately, throwing around all of his money couldn't overcome that arrogance of his. It always drove people away. And Harry never let you forget how smart he was when it came to the stock market. Always boasting to me, and a helluva lot of others too, that he hadn't missed a market turn since opening his fund. Harry had a way of whispering loud enough so everyone around us could hear his forecast of when the market was going up...or coming down, and the stocks he liked. He was one helluva piece of work, Lowe! But when he made the wrong call on a stock he had bragged about, or his stock pick didn't deliver, he always carried on about how dumb his analyst partner was. That was you, wasn't it, Lowe?"

Before I could deny it again, he went on. "Somehow through it all, and as dumb as it sounds, Lowe, I grew to trust him. To this day, I still can't figure out why. Anyway, Harry kept needling me to invest in his fund. Kept telling me how his fund was making a ton of money for every investor. I finally gave in and bought into his story. He must have thanked me half a dozen times, always promising that I wouldn't regret it. And assuring me that I'd get my million and a half back before I knew it…plus a helluva lot more! But strangely after that, we got together less often, although when we did, his first question always was, *How did I like my fantastic return?*

"Well, it wasn't more than a month ago that it all began to fall apart. I got a letter saying the fund was temporarily paying only a quarter of the usual amount because of the market's downturn. I kept calling him to find out why, and was my money safe? But he never answered. The final letter came last Friday: *HJM Investment Fund regrets to inform you that the fund is closed permanently.*" Swenson was now shouting at me. "Closed permanently! Do you know what that means, Lowe? It means my life savings are gone! All gone! I'm left with nothing!"

I stared at him for a moment, trying to think of how best to commiserate with him, but all I could say was, "I'm sorry you lost your money, Mr. Swenson. But I lost all my money with Harry ten years ago and was left with nothing, too. I've been forced to work at a bank in New York for the last eight years. So believe me when I say I know what you're going through."

By this time, a sizable semi-circle of listeners had formed behind Swenson, ready to share their similar stories. As I looked at their angry faces, I felt surrounded and trapped, unsure of what would happen next.

"Look, Lowe," he said, sounding intimidating again. "I know you're the silent partner that Harry talked about. If not, then what's the point of your coming all the way up here to his funeral?"

Feeling nervous, but also frustrated, I tried again. "Swenson, as I told Frank Ellis, I haven't seen or spoken to Harry Miller in ten years. I assure you I've had nothing to do with him. I'm sorry he conned you into investing in his fund. But it had absolutely nothing to do with me. I am not now, nor have ever been, Harry Miller's silent partner!"

But any hope that I'd finally convinced him I wasn't involved in ruining his life was short-lived. "Stop trying to deny it, Lowe!" he hissed. "I know you were working with Harry. And since he's dead, it's you who's going to make things right. I want my million and a half back! Do I make myself clear? I want it back…now!" His eyes narrowed, his face reddened, and his bull neck stiffened as he threatened, "You have two days to come up with the money, Lowe. If I don't get it by then, I'd be real careful if I were you!" He turned and pushed his way past the semi-circle of sullen faces.

To say I was stunned by his threat would be an understatement. *Why won't anyone believe me,* I kept asking myself in utter frustration? Here I am, hating Harry as much as anyone for what he did to me, and now I have to prove to this guy, and I'm sure to all these people standing here, that I didn't help Harry to screw them all. I took a hard bite out of my cracker and gulped down some punch, trying to calm myself. But I was too pissed off at being painted as Harry's accomplice based on Frank Ellis' wrongful insinuation. And then this guy threatens me…just like that! All I could think of was showing him my W-2 to prove I worked at a bank. Nah, that won't help! But what the hell else can I do?

As I stood there contemplating my options, I noticed that a woman was working her way through the slowly dispersing crowd and heading straight towards me. *Oh, God, I hope this isn't another problem…I've had enough for one day!* At first, I didn't recognize her. But then I thought she might be the blond who had been sitting in front of me. From the way her eyes were riveted on me, I was positive this was indeed going to be another problem.

"You're Davis Lowe, aren't you?" she asked softly.

"Yes, that's me," I responded cautiously, expecting this highly attractive woman, probably mid-thirties, with sparkling green eyes, high cheekbones, and short blonde hair, was about to demand her money back, too.

"My name is Ellen Houser. I was sitting in front of you when you asked how much everyone had invested in Harry's fund. Remember,

I told you three million dollars?"

"Ah…yes, I remember you," I replied weakly.

"Since you knew Harry, and being his partner and all, I wanted to tell you how sorry I am he's dead…murdered, I mean."

"Ms. Houser, before you say another word, I was not Harry Miller's partner. I had nothing to do with his investment fund at all! I just told that to Mr. Swenson."

Taken aback by my reaction, she hesitated before continuing. "I am sorry he's dead as I knew Harry quite well. He was a complex man who, over time, I grew to have mixed emotions about. When I first met him a little over a year ago, I found him to be a loving, caring man, so much so that we developed a very close relationship. In fact, we were informally engaged earlier this year. No ring, mind you, but one always promised. I loved him, Mr. Lowe, very much…problems and all! And I was sure he loved me too. I thought we were a truly happy couple. Anyway, during this time, he kept asking me to invest my inheritance in his fund and telling me I'd make so much money I wouldn't know what to do with it. But every time I talked to my financial adviser about it, he warned me not to do it. My mother also urged me not to give him my money. But I loved Harry so much, and I wanted to show him just how much I loved him, so…" She paused for a moment to regain her composure. "Harry kept on pressing me to invest. I wanted so much to trust him. And to show him how much I cared for him even after the warnings about his investment fund. I believed we'd be happy together, but Mr. Lowe, I foolishly thought only with my heart. When I finally gave him the money, he told me it would be the best investment I'd ever make. How did he say it: *A cornerstone for our future together.* Well, we celebrated my investment by him taking me to Barcelona for two weeks. He also told me he was having an engagement ring made while we were away. Mr. Lowe, I couldn't have been happier!"

She turned her head to wipe away tears. When she turned back, those sparkling green eyes were now filled with hate. "After we returned, Mr. Lowe, I didn't hear from him for a whole week. My calls went unanswered. I became worried that something had happened to him. So I drove out to his house on Beach Drive and knocked on the door. When there was no answer, I was sure something was wrong. The door was unlocked, so I walked in. And there was the son-of-a-bitch, lying on the couch making love to another woman! Seeing me standing there, he calmly got up, put on his bathing trunks, and walked over to me. In the coldest, nastiest voice I've ever heard, he told me we were through, Mr. Lowe…through! That he didn't love me and never really had. A year together…and three million invested in his fund to prove my love, and he didn't care about me? He said it was only money, Mr. Lowe! Only money! I still can't believe it!"

She stopped to wipe away a flood of new tears. Clearly distraught and still hurting, she blurted out, "I'm so glad he's dead, Mr. Lowe. So very glad!"

I could only stare at her in disbelief, wondering how Harry, even at his worst, could have done something like that. She appeared to be so sweet and caring. But then I remembered that he had done the same thing to Maude Williamson, just on a bigger scale. Sadly, she too was now just another trophy on Harry's wall. I looked at the small group of people still standing around, sensing they also had their own horror stories to tell. I wouldn't be surprised if they'd also become more trophies hanging on Harry's infamous wall.

"I'm so terribly sorry about what happened to you, Ms. Houser. But I must tell you again that I wasn't Harry's partner. And I can't help you get your money back."

"Yes, I realize that now after what you said to that gentleman earlier," she answered, sounding quite disappointed.

"Then what do you want from me?"

"You knew him, I assume, quite well. So tell me…why would he do such a terrible thing to me, Mr. Lowe? I loved him! I gave him all my love and was always there for him. There were so many others who couldn't stand his arrogance. But I never let it get in the way of my being there for him or our happiness. So why did he do it to me,

Mr. Lowe...why?"

"Unfortunately, he did it to a lot of people before you, Ms. Houser," I replied softly. "All I can tell you is that what I believe; that Harry was driven by a lifelong, overriding obsession to make money. Enough money to satisfy his craving to be recognized as one of the richest and most successful investors on Wall Street. That's what he lived and breathed for! Money made Harry feel like the person he always believed he was meant to be. Being that rich would make people look up to him...respect him...and be in awe of him. His over-bearing arrogance was meant to block out anything that would prevent him from reaching that goal. Harry wasn't going to let anything stand in his way of achieving his dream...even if it meant stepping on or over people to get there."

"But my loving him and supporting his effort to build his fund...shouldn't that have meant something to him?"

"Yes, definitely! But Harry would never let that happen. He always believed the fastest steppingstone to success was to use people. History is filled with examples like Harry. Not caring about who or what was involved before taking unthinkable risks, always believing he'd succeed where no one else could. He'd show the world how far superior and smarter he was than everyone else! And he had no problem conning others to prove himself. But when he failed, it was always the same excuse...someone or something else was at fault, never Harry!"

She stared at me for a long moment absorbing what I had said. Hoping it would give her some consolation knowing she wasn't alone, I added, "Ms. Houser, Ellen, I hope it's obvious to you now that my knowing what made Harry tick was a result of his treating me the same way he did to you. He ruined my life! That's why I came to his funeral today...I was looking for some sort of closure. I hope you now believe that I was not his silent partner!"

She stared at me long and hard for a moment, then grudgingly nodded her head in agreement. Blowing her nose, she turned to make her way through the few remaining onlookers without saying a word.

My intuition told me she didn't really believe me, but at least she hadn't asked for her money back! I felt relieved but somehow knew it probably wasn't the last time I'd hear from her.

****

As I watched the despondent Ellen Houser walk away, I wondered if she would ever get over Harry. Poor woman! Putting her trust in a guy like that. Shaking my head thinking about it, it hit me that I had done the exact same thing! So many had fallen for Harry's siren song. And now it seemed we were all seeking some degree of revenge.

I finished my crackers and punch, still feeling depressed over Ellen's realization that her dream of love and happiness had all been a charade. Disgusted, I went to get another cup of punch. I was halfway there when I felt a hand touch my shoulder. *Oh God, not another anguished victim!* Very hesitantly, I turned to face a woman, I guessed somewhere in her mid-to-late forties, with blonde hair and gorgeous doe-shaped blue eyes, made-up to achieve what I thought was a youthful look, and in a dress to match. She smiled a knowing smile at me before saying a sweet hello. I smiled back, believing she had mistaken me for someone else, and continued to walk on. That's when she snarled, "Don't you recognize me, Davis?" I didn't and felt quite embarrassed about it. But she continued, "Well, either you want to avoid me, or have I changed that much, Davis?"

"Forgive me, but I don't know who you are," I answered, studying her face. Then I suddenly realized it was Maude. "Maude, it's you!"

"Yes...one and the same! The Maude who was Harry's original financial backer. And may I add, his first of many lovers. The same Maude who spent five years in prison. And the one you came to see. Remember me now?"

"Oh...I'm so terribly sorry, but it's been a long time. I didn't recognize you."

"Prison changes people, Davis. But I must say, you've changed too! You aren't the innocent choir boy anymore...are you?"

I let the remark pass and tried to respond diplomatically. "I'd say we've both changed a lot, Maude. My life hasn't been easy either since Harry fired me back in '87."

"Like it's been a bed of roses for me, Davis," she replied. "Being locked away for five years can make a person pretty angry. And it sure as hell brings out a lasting hatred for the person who put you there!"

I didn't know what to say to that, so I reached for her arm and steered us toward the punch bowl. At first, she pushed my arm away, balking at being directed, which I belatedly realized probably reminded her of prison and the guards. But she soon relented and smiled warmly at me as we started walking there together.

As I filled our glasses, I felt that same hard, icy stare I remembered from ten years ago at the prison. All I could think of was her wondering just how much that young, wet-behind-the-ears kid she had been ready to sleep with so many years ago had changed. After handing her a glass, I raised mine in a silent salute to her. Those blue eyes remained riveted on me. How angry she must be, I thought, with time treating her like this. Hell, time has passed me by too!

"Let's go somewhere we can talk without all this commotion," she directed in a take-charge voice.

"All right," I replied, wondering where this was going to lead.

She took my arm, this time without any hesitation, and we headed for the exit doors. As I pushed them open, a tall, heavy-set man with a large, squarish face and piercing brown eyes stopped us. He had brown hair, a bulbous nose that accented his shaggy mustache, and was wearing a brown tweed sports jacket and wrinkled gray slacks. "Are you Mrs. Maude Williamson? And you, Mr. Davis Lowe?"

"Yes," we answered in unison.

He flashed his badge and then handed us each a business card. "I'm Detective Edward Brantley of the Lymouth Police Department. I'd like to ask the two of you a few questions about Harry Miller's murder."

Chapter Twelve

Our surprise had time to wear off as we followed the detective upstairs into the church vestry, where he pointed out three chairs positioned under a large stained-glass window. As we sat down, he pulled out a small tape recorder from his pocket and placed it on his knee. After asking for permission to record our discussion, he clicked it on. He gave both of us a long, once-over that made me quite nervous. He then began by asking, "I understand that you both knew Harry Miller. When was the last time you each saw him?"

Neither of us answered; I guess assuming the other would first. His big brown eyes narrowed, indicating limited patience, so I jumped in. "The last time I saw Harry Miller was ten years ago. He had just closed H.J. Miller Investments on the day the stock market crashed in 1987. I haven't seen him since."

"Mr. Lowe, are you quite sure that was the last time you saw him?"

"Why…yes, I'm certain, Detective."

"Didn't you see him at a financial association meeting in New York, almost a month ago? I have a witness who attended that meeting with Mr. Miller, and remembers him speaking to you."

"Oh…yes! Yes, that's right! I completely forgot about that. I did see him there. I'm sorry, Detective. We said hello, but that was about it. We had nothing more to say to each other, and I left shortly afterward."

"Why was that, Mr. Lowe?" he asked, his voice matter-of-fact.

"Harry and I had a falling out the day the market crashed. He not only fired me that day but also threatened me with a lawsuit, blaming me for having to close the firm, even though he was the one who caused our losses. It was his fault, but Harry could never accept that fact."

"Did you know he ran an investment fund here in Lymouth?"

"I was aware he started one, but I knew nothing more about it until today when I talked to the people sitting around me and heard the large amounts of money they had lost investing with him."

"Where do you work now, Mr. Lowe?"

"In Manhattan. I'm an investment counselor at a small bank."

"How long have you been working there?"

"Oh…over eight years."

"You said you left Miller Investments ten years ago; what were you doing for those two years in between?"

"Well, I…ah…was looking for a job."

"I would have thought with your being in the investment business you could have easily found employment."

"Ah, no, Detective. You see, Harry went out of his way to make it impossible for me. He put the word out on Wall Street that I was the reason Miller Investments closed, that I was the one who pushed him into trading crappy, high-risk stocks. I became the villain who forced him to shut the firm's doors. But Detective, he was the one who caused the firm to fail, not me!"

He continued to stare at me with a questioning look, making me feel uncomfortable enough to try convincing him again. "It's the truth, Detective! He made sure no one on the Street would hire me! That was his payback to me. That was typical Harry!"

Brantley appeared surprised by my angry outburst. But in that same matter-of-fact tone, he asked, "Can you tell me where you were last Saturday night when Mr. Miller was shot, Mr. Lowe?"

"I was in New York at my apartment."

"Is there anyone who can confirm you were there, Mr. Lowe?"

"Well, I was in all evening but alone, mind you. So, no, Detective, I don't have any witnesses to confirm it."

"Do you own a gun, Mr. Lowe?"

"Why no, Detective!"

"Are you sure, Mr. Lowe?

"Yes, I'm quite sure!"

A look of doubt passed quickly over Brantley's face before he turned to direct his next question to Maude. "And you, Mrs. Williamson, when did you last see Mr. Miller?"

"I saw him over a week ago while shopping here in town."

Her answer totally caught me off guard. If Brantley noticed my surprise, he didn't let it show. Instead, he continued to question Maude. "Did you speak to him then?"

"No, I did not! I avoided him as often as I could. And when I was forced to speak with him, it was always very brief and unpleasant."

"Were you sure it was him?"

"Yes. I'd know that face of his anywhere."

"How long have you been living here?"

"I moved here in 1989."

"But records show that you were released from prison in 1987. Where did you live those two years in between?"

"I went back to Springfield, Illinois, to start my life over again. I did it for two years, but it didn't work out, Detective."

"Why did you move to Lymouth?"

"My husband and I liked to spend July here at the shore. We loved the ocean and the wonderful sailing. We had a forty-foot boat that we sailed up and down the coast. I thought I could recapture those happier days if I moved here."

"And you hardly ever spoke to Mr. Miller in all that time?"

"That's correct, Detective."

"Mrs. Williamson, did you attend the dinner last Saturday night honoring Mr. Miller for all the charitable contributions he made to the town?"

"Yes, I did."

"And you did not speak to him then?"

"I had nothing to say to him. I only attended the dinner because a friend of mine asked me, no…begged me to go with her. Otherwise, I would not have been there, Detective."

"So you're telling me, Mrs. Williamson, over the last eight years that you've lived here in town, two miles away from him, you rarely spoke to Mr. Miller?"

"That's true! As I said, Detective, I did my best to avoid him."

"Mrs. Williamson, I have a witness who said she saw you talking to Mr. Miller at the dinner party. In fact, from how the two of you were acting, she first thought you were arguing with him. But she said that you smiled and kissed him on the cheek before you walked away."

"That's not true, Detective! Yes, I did pass by his table. But as I did, he made a snide remark to me, and I told him to go to hell! Then I walked away."

"The witness said you kissed him, Mrs. Williamson."

"Well, I didn't!"

"Tell me, what time did you leave the dinner?"

"Around 10."

"Are you sure?"

"Yes! I got up and left, because frankly, Detective, I wasn't interested in listening to his self-congratulatory thank you speech."

"Are you aware that Mr. Miller was murdered at approximately 11:30 pm that evening?"

"I heard it was later that evening, but I didn't know what time. Anyway, I was at home getting ready for bed then, Detective."

"Do you hold a grudge against Mr. Miller?"

"No! I served my time for hating him."

"Are you sure? No one would blame you if you did."

"Yes, definitely! Very sure. But speaking of grudges, Detective, you should talk to Charlie Reynolds about his grudge against Harry. I saw him at the dinner that night."

"Who is Charlie Reynolds?"

"Harry put him out of business when I withdrew my money from Charlie's firm, Reynolds & Coleman."

Brantley reached into his jacket pocket, took out a small pad and pen, and wrote himself a note. "Why did you withdraw your money, Mrs. Williamson?"

"To invest some of it in Harry's start-up firm."

"I'm not sure I understand. According to our records, fifteen years ago, Mr. Miller was twenty-three or twenty-four. Why would you invest your money with someone that young?"

"Well, if you insist on knowing, he was my lover."

"Your lover?

"Yes, Detective, he was my lover!"

"How much money did you invest in Miller Investments?"

"Fifteen million."

Brantley's eyes widened in surprise. "Fifteen million!" he repeated slowly, trying to grasp the magnitude of the amount and the risk. "Ah...tell me, Mrs. Williamson, why did you break off your relationship with Mr. Miller?"

"I caught him running around on me."

"How do you know Mr. Lowe here?"

"He worked for Harry."

"Detective," I interrupted, "Harry got his start working for Charlie Reynolds. To climb the ladder fast in Reynolds & Coleman, he worked out a scheme to screw his boss, Fred Simmons, out of his biggest account. Harry made several substantial, unauthorized trades under Simmons' name that he knew would go sour. Simmons got fired for it. And, of course, Harry was promoted into Simmons' spot. I think this may help you see why Harry was not one to make friends easily, Detective."

"Fred Simmons? When did you see him last, Mr. Lowe?"

"Ten years ago, the day the market crashed. I happened to meet him in a hotel bar in New York that afternoon. And I haven't seen him since."

"And you, Mrs. Williamson, do you know Fred Simmons?"

"No, I don't."

"Mr. Lowe, would you recognize him if you saw him?"

"It's been ten years, but I guess I still would."

"Simmons. I'll check to see if he was at the dinner. But that name sounds familiar. Fred Simmons? We have a teacher in the middle school named Fred Simmons." Brantley scribbled something in his pad, then looked up at Maude. "Mrs. Williamson, before last Saturday night, when was the last time you saw Mr. Reynolds?"

"It was probably a few weeks ago when I passed him in town. I've had very little contact with Charlie since I moved here. He and my late husband had worked closely on some real estate deals in the late 1950s. After my husband died, Charlie handled my investments until about fifteen years ago, when I found out he was churning my account for the commission money, losing a hell of a lot of it in the process!"

The detective paused to look up at the stained-glass windows above us, probably trying to digest all he had heard so far. After a few moments, he turned back to us and asked, "Are you both aware that Mr. Miller died from a bullet through his heart?

"Ah…yes, Detective, I'm aware of it," I replied. "I heard it from the gentleman sitting next to me at the service."

"No, I wasn't," Maude answered coldly.

"Mr. Lowe, did you know he was found floating just off the beach near his estate?"

"I don't know any of the circumstances of his death, Detective."

"Well, let me fill you in. We believe Mr. Miller was not shot at the beach, but somewhere else at very close range by someone he knew well. He was transported to the beach, then dragged down to the water. We found bloodstains on the sand, confirming he was dragged into the water. The murderer must have thought the high tide would carry the body out to sea."

"Who else do you know, Mr. Lowe, that might hold a grudge against Mr. Miller?"

I found it difficult to hold back a laugh. "I would guess there's a roomful of people downstairs who have some very strong reasons to hold a grudge against him, Detective."

His brown eyes hardened, and I could see his back stiffen as he gave me a look of *don't be a smart ass*. "Mr. Lowe, I assume you drove up to the funeral today?"

"Yes, I did, Detective," I answered, almost apologetically.

"I would like you to please stay in town for the next day or two while we continue to conduct our investigation. And Mrs. Williamson, we'll need you to do the same."

"Detective, I really can't stay," I replied quite anxiously. "I need to be at work in New York tomorrow. I took the day off to come to the funeral."

"But why did you come here today, Mr. Lowe? Obviously, there was no love lost between you and the victim."

"Why? Well, to be honest, I was curious to see if there were others who felt the same way about Harry as I did."

I immediately worried that I might have just made myself Brantley's number one suspect. Still, all he said was, "Mr. Lowe, I suggest you find yourself a place to stay tonight, and we'll resume our questioning tomorrow at 10:00 am at police headquarters. We'll determine then when you'll be able to leave for New York. And Mrs. Williamson, we'll want to talk to you in the morning as well."

Clearly not expecting an argument, Brantley shut off his tape recorder and put it back in his pocket. He gave us one last questioning stare and then got up to leave. We watched him walk out of the room before turning to each other, visibly relieved. "I'm glad that's over," I said as I stood up to leave. Maude looked up at me with a warm smile and asked, "Why don't you stay with me tonight, Davis? I've got plenty of room, and we could spend the evening comparing notes on our mutual friend."

I hesitated at first, sensing a possible ulterior motive behind the invitation. But the convenience of staying with her clearly outweighed my spending time searching for a hotel room. "Thanks, Maude. I'll take you up on your hospitality. Why don't we go get lunch, and then on the way to your place, I'd like to stop and see Harry's infamous ocean palace."

Chapter Thirteen

The lunch following the service was a buffet. Once everyone was finished, the town selectmen got up one by one to laud Harry Miller's generosity, declaring the town would never forget his many contributions to bettering the community. I soon reached my limit of listening to Harry being praised and whispered to Maude, "Ready to go?"

She gave a quick and thankful nod, and we quietly made our way out. I followed her as she drove out to Beach Drive, a narrow, winding road with great ocean views between a few widely spaced mansions. Maude signaled she was pulling over, then stopped in front of a padlocked, imposing black wrought iron gate. Inscribed on a large white imperial-inspired crescent in the middle of the right gate were the giant initials, HJM. The gate was attached to stone pillars, which I'd guess were about twelve feet high, and were the beginnings of six-foot-high stone walls extending maybe a hundred feet on either side.

I got out of my car and walked towards the ostentatious gate and walls. My initial envy at the implied wealth quickly turned to anger and resentment. I peered down the long pebble driveway with manicured lawns on either side, but a barrier of tall hemlocks blocked my view of the mansion. Still, that didn't stop me from imagining what it looked like or thinking about what *my* mansion might have looked like if he had listened to me on those four fateful days. As I stood there dreaming my angry dream, I felt a hand softly touch my arm. "Davis, don't let it get to you. Think of it in more positive terms: You're alive, and he's dead! And appreciate the fact that he can't rub your nose nor mine in the dirt anymore."

With a faint smile, I nodded and said, "I can't deny it…my anger has never left me these last ten years, Maude. Frankly, I'm not sure it will ever go away, even with him dead and gone. Harry ruined my life that day, and I'll never get back what I lost." I paused, then blurted out, "I'm glad the bastard's dead!"

Maude appeared surprised to hear my true feelings but quickly recovered. "I'm just as glad as you are that the bastard is dead! He destroyed the best years of my life too!" We both gazed down the long driveway again, deep in thought. Finally, she grabbed my arm, and with a disgusted look on her face, said, "Let's go, Davis. This place only angers the hell out of me!"

We returned to our cars, and I followed her a couple of miles up the road where we drove into a long, pebbled, circular driveway. I got out of my car and stood admiring the imposing single-story, modern glass house. It stood on four massive, circular, shiny steel pilings perched high on top of a large sand dune overlooking the ocean below. Maude unlocked the front door, and I followed her into a spacious living room designed to capture the breathtaking view of the vast and shimmering ocean through thick floor-to-ceiling glass windows stretching the room's length.

"You know, Maude," I said slowly, shaking my head in admiration, "when I see this house and its magnificent view, it reminds me of the fabulous view you had of Central Park from your suite at the Plaza." I paused, unsure whether she wanted to talk about that night fifteen years ago. But what the hell, I thought, she'd tell me straight out if she didn't want to hear about it. "I'll tell you a secret…I've never forgotten that night I was going to spend with you at the Plaza. You forced me to make one hell of a tough decision. I assure you, it took every bit of willpower to walk out and leave you after you walked into the living room wearing that sexy blue robe. There was every reason not to leave, except one: I couldn't take a chance on Harry accusing me of taking advantage of you after he had given me that once-in-a-lifetime opportunity to work with him. And I hope you believe me when I say, I've regretted it all these years."

"Oh, I've often wondered if you remembered that night, Davis," she replied with a grateful smile. "But I must tell you, I thought you were a choir boy who panicked at the situation. How young you were then, Davis. I was young too! So full of life and spirit and convinced the world was mine. How I loved every minute of it! But those five horrible years in prison stole it all that away from me. Now, all I feel is old…with nothing to look forward to." She began to cry and turned way to try to compose herself. After a minute or so, she looked over her shoulder at me with a tearful smile, and sniffled, "I'm fifteen years older now, but it feels more like fifty! When I look in the mirror every morning, I curse every day I let Harry take advantage of me!"

We stood there, depressed as hell, realizing how much Harry Miller still dominated our thoughts and lives. Finally, Maude wiped away the remaining tears, blew her nose, and quietly asked, "How about a drink, Davis, I really need one about now. I can't aggravate anymore over what he's done to me, or to you. Let's think about something else. How about celebrating that Harry is six feet underground?"

"Great idea!" I practically shouted as I followed her over to the large mahogany cabinet in the corner next to a giant window.

"What will you have, Davis?" she asked, trying to sound lighthearted.

"Scotch would be fine."

She filled two large whiskey glasses three-quarters full, handed me one, then raised her glass in a toast. "Here's to the one who almost destroyed our lives. But thank God he's the one who's dead, and we're still alive and kicking!"

I smiled, nodding my full agreement as I raised my glass high, comforted in knowing our feelings were exactly the same about Harry. We each took a long, hefty swallow and immediately began coughing uncontrollably, a rush of tears flowing down our cheeks from the scotch burning as it went down. But we still kept grinning at each other, as if the drinks were the antidote to Harry's ruination of us. Soon we were both laughing at how lightheaded and suddenly energized we felt. As I watched Maude gaily laugh at our silliness, the years somehow seemed to disappear. And the more we laughed and drank, the more she became the spirited woman I had known fifteen years ago. All that anger and hate seemed to fade away. The change was remarkable! Watching the transformation, I couldn't help but wonder what I had missed that night with a sexy lady in a blue robe.

Well, it doesn't really matter, I thought. Everything in our lives is different now. All these years of anguish and disillusionment have changed us. I know I've certainly changed. Not because I'm a little paunchier or my hair has specks of gray, but because the spirit to do bigger and better things in my life has been sapped. I wake up every morning feeling devoid of hope or optimism. God, how these last eight years have been stifling, having to sit behind that little desk at the bank, explaining to customers how a 401k works, or how to conservatively invest money in stock and bond markets, when I should be down on the Street trading big-time for myself and living my life accordingly! But Harry took all that away from me and left me with nothing. No tangible success and nothing to be proud of. Eight years, and what do I have to show for it? Not one damn thing!

But as I gazed at Maude, I realized that what I've been through was nothing compared to how she's suffered. Life in prison had to be hell! I still can't believe she spent five years locked up. It had to have destroyed her life. Moments like these may bring back all her sexy, youthful looks and bubbly spirit, but will it last? Nah, I'm sure that before the evening ends, we'll revert back to our real selves: Two angry, bitter people cursing the day we ever met Harry Miller. Not even a large glass or two of scotch can change that.

"Are you married, Davis?" she asked, somewhat timidly.

"I was a few years ago, but it didn't work out. My wife loved New York, and the excitement of meeting the right people, going to dinners and benefits, and spending time in the Hampton's. My job at the bank didn't give me the means to give her any of that. Eventually, she met a guy who could."

I sipped my drink, not wanting to discuss any of the details. What purpose would it serve other than dredging up more of my anger and bitterness? I changed the subject instead. "I must admit, I was kind of shocked when you told Brantley you lived here. After all, it must have been pretty difficult to learn that the guy who jilted you out of love and money lived only a couple of miles down the road. So why did you decide to move here, Maude?"

She stiffened at my question but must have decided I could be trusted with the answer because she replied, "I've always loved Connecticut, Davis. And this house is wonderful. But truthfully, I wanted to be near Harry. I knew he had moved here, and had heard about his latest scheme, conning the people of Lymouth into investing in his fund, using that pseudo-caring and generosity spiel of his. I was positive it wouldn't take long for them to realize he was stealing their money just as he did mine. But I was wrong. As long as they got paid every month, they were happy. So I decided to sit back and wait patiently for the time I knew was coming when he found it impossible to pay that guaranteed income. I was sure that Harry would stumble. He just wasn't clever enough to keep attracting new investor money." Her face became flushed, and her doe-shaped blue eyes narrowed. "Do you understand, Davis? I had to be here. I had to see how his investors would react when they found out they had bought into a scam. It became a game with me, trying to predict the day and month when they'd uncover Harry's real intentions and how long it would take before their former hero went to prison. I wanted to see every second of it! I don't know, maybe, deep down, I wanted to see others hurt the way he hurt me. I know that sounds selfish, but I wanted them to hate Harry as much as I hated him. Most of all, I wanted to watch him lose it all!"

Maude's face was now bright red, and her eyes flashed angrily. "I was very patient and kept waiting for the day when his scheme would backfire. When I heard from friends in town that several of his biggest investors wanted to withdraw their money to endow a small college in the State, I knew it was the first clear signal the end was near. I could hardly contain myself! Then I heard through another friend that Harry didn't have the cash for a payout to them. When these investors learned they couldn't withdraw their money, they threatened Harry with a lawsuit. I was sure that would be the final blow. It made me almost giddy, thinking that the moment I had been waiting for so long had finally arrived. But then somehow, and no one knows exactly how…he paid them!"

Maude stopped and studied the remaining scotch in her glass before taking a last, long swallow, I assume trying to forget that frustrating memory. She then looked over at me and smiled. "Well, Davis, I can't tell you how fast the rumors began to fly in town. Everybody was asking the same question, *Was he out of money*? One of my friends told me the answer was definitely yes! I was ecstatic! Not long after, Harry's first letter came out, telling investors that their monthly payment was being cut in half for the next two months. Then the following month, he cut it in half again! The town's rumor mill went wild, claiming that he was desperate for cash. Many of his investors started demanding to get out, so Harry wrote a quick follow-up letter, swearing he'd restore everyone to full payment the next quarter because the stock market was moving higher. But they kept hounding him for their money back. Harry wrote again, this time promising to repay all the guaranteed income in arrears very soon. I heard he used every trick in the book…dirty or otherwise…to hold them off, hoping in the meantime to attract new money. But it was clear there wasn't enough cash coming in to pay everyone. Then the moment I had been waiting for all these years happened! Late last Friday afternoon, he sent out a final letter to investors stating his fund was now permanently closed. Those remaining investors lost their shirts! And Davis, we're talking about big money, in the multi-millions! You can't imagine how excited I was, thinking Harry was finally on his way to prison for a long, long time. And no one deserved prison more than Harry!"

As she stopped to take a deep breath, a look of disappointment crossed her face. "Obviously, as we all found out, someone had other plans for him. At first, I was so angry, thinking he didn't get to suffer enough. But then I thought…maybe this was better. Prison would have been too easy for him. He would have gotten out in five years, maybe less, ready to pull off another scam. That's when I realized his death was a more deserving punishment. Especially when you think of how many lives he destroyed. People who lost their life savings or were left dead broke, or just scraping by on Social Security, or whatever else they could earn in their retirement years. And think how humiliated they all must have felt at being so gullible to trust the scoundrel in the first place. Frankly, Davis, my only regret was his death should have been slower and more painful, just as my life in prison was!"

A long silence followed as we stood with glasses in hand, contemplating the magnitude of our collective bitterness towards this man. Maude finally forced a little smile and beckoned me to follow her to the sliding door that opened onto a large mahogany deck running the length of the house and extending out over the ocean below. The wind blew hard in my face as I walked over to the railing to see how high above the water we were. I guessed at least thirty feet above the waves crashing against the jagged rocks below. Between the height, the wind, and the wind-whipped ocean spray that nearly reached us, I suddenly worried that the deck might somehow be unsafe, and stepped back quickly. Maude saw my reaction and walked over to me, chuckling, "Don't worry, Davis, those steel pilings have been drilled down forty feet. It's safe, very safe! The house and deck won't collapse into the ocean during a storm or high wind. I have the builder's guarantee on that!"

I smiled weakly at her as I walked back to the table near the living room door. Maude followed. We stood huddled there, trying to avoid the brisk wind and taking fleeting glances at the ocean's glittering vastness and choppiness. After a moment or two, Maude looked up at me with a questioning expression. "Davis, what do you think made Harry tick? I mean, why did he have to take such advantage of people, even people like us? We liked and trusted him early on, and what did he do? He used us! In my case, it was getting his hands on my money with a little sex as a bonus. In your case, he used your brains for picking stocks until that day when he thought he was smarter at it than you. He destroyed Charlie Reynolds, whether for the fun of it or to prove what a big shot he was by making Charlie feel like a peon standing in his way."

I thought for a moment or two, then slowly replied, "My take, Maude? I think Harry was a born schemer who survived his early life by conning people with his over-the-top, positive attitude backed by an innate arrogance that bulldozed everyone into doing his bidding. Friendships, partnerships, and love affairs didn't mean a thing to him. He had only one objective in life: to make a ton of money, period! He didn't care about people trusting him with their money. They meant nothing to him. He'd sacrifice any friendship if it meant an advantage. It was all part of Harry's game to be a winner…a big winner at all costs! He never thought about losing…ever! Losing was for everyone else! I'll bet he never suspected that one day, one of his sacrificial lambs would become angry or distraught enough to take revenge."

Maude nodded in agreement. "I think you're right, Davis. He did have a low opinion of everyone he met, always believing he was the smartest one in the room. Well…of course until somebody decided otherwise." She smiled, seemingly pleased, before asking, "Would you like a refill, Davis?"

"Yes, please!"

The second scotch hit me quickly. My head felt light and about to spin as we walked back out onto the deck. The late afternoon ocean view of the sun sinking towards the horizon proved to be magnificent. A sailboat seemed to fly by, heeling way over in the strong wind with whitecaps splashing high over the bow. We waved enthusiastically to them, and they back to us.

After the sailboat disappeared, I looked over at Maude, wondering what we'd do next. She returned my gaze with a tender smile. I could see the drinks and conversation had revived that spirited youthfulness of hers. It was so positive, upbeat, and loving that I was enthralled, to say the least. Maybe it was too much scotch, or possibly the breathtaking beauty of a setting sun over a wild ocean that was causing my infatuation. All I know is her loving smile, and youthful glow had captivated me. Suddenly, I wanted to know what I had missed fifteen years ago. And I was pretty sure she was thinking the same thing.

Seeing the look in my eyes, Maude put down her drink in anticipation of my next move. Taking her in my arms, I kissed her with a passion I hadn't felt in a long, long time. She didn't balk or resist. On the contrary, she put her arms around me and kissed me back with fifteen years of stored up longing. After a few passionate moments, she broke away from my embrace. Stepping back, she took a deep breath and stared at me with the same aroused look I remembered from years ago. Taking my hand, she led me inside the house to her large bedroom just off of the living room with another fabulous view of the ocean. We fell on the bed and into each other's arms. While we kissed and struggled to undress, I could feel her become more aroused with every touch. This further excited me to where I felt like an enthusiastic twenty-four-year-old, anxious to enjoy the thrill of sex again. To recapture the feeling that the world was mine once more. Our sex exploded with a latent passion that neither of us believed possible.

As we rested, we held each other tightly, as if letting go would somehow awaken us from this wonderful dream. We kissed again and again until we were aroused once more, eager to enjoy the love and thrill of sex again. The second time was better than the first if that was possible. Maude smiled lovingly at me as she rested her head on my chest. "Davis, I never thought I would ever have sex again, much less enjoy it so much. It's helped me erase all those horrible memories. Suddenly, I feel young again! Full of energy and hope...and life! This is a brand new day for me!"

I started to reply, "I feel exactly the same way..." when the phone began to ring. Grimacing at the interruption, Maude walked around the other side of the bed to pick it up. *Got to say, she still looks good,* I thought. After saying an annoyed hello, she walked out into the living room. As I watched her leave, I wondered if this was the right moment to become involved with her. Setting aside the fact that she was quite a bit older than me, I had a feeling that the police had all but declared us prime suspects in their murder investigation. If our love affair blossoms, the police could easily conclude we had worked as a team to murder Harry. I didn't want to break off our relationship before it even got started, but damn…this could get complicated!

As I mulled things over, Maude came back into the room, bursting with anger. "That was Charlie Reynolds yelling and screaming at me! He demanded to know if I had given his name to the police. I told him I had, which made him go ballistic. He said he was coming over right now to discuss the situation. I told him definitely not, but he wouldn't take no for an answer. Claims he had nothing to do with Harry's death and knows nothing about it. But Davis, I think he protests too much!"

"He has a reason to be nervous, Maude. Harry told me the whole story over lunch years ago of how he destroyed Charlie in three days after making his deal with you. Just destroyed his business and him! Do you have any idea what he's been doing these last fifteen years?"

"No, not really. I had heard in town he tried to start another brokerage firm, but it didn't get off the ground. Then someone told me he'd heard that Charlie had set up an investment fund, just like Harry's. But it was obviously just talk, as I never heard anything more about it. There was also a rumor that he tried to work out some sort of deal with Harry. But I can't believe Harry was ever interested in working with him. The last thing I heard was that Charlie was running around town telling some of Harry's clients he was running a Ponzi scam, and they should get out fast!"

"Well, let's get dressed and see what Charlie wants to talk about."

****

Twenty minutes later, a car pulled into the driveway. We heard a door slam, followed by hurrying footsteps across the pebbles, then up the stairs to the front door. It flew open, and Charlie Reynolds burst into the room. He looked much different than what I had imagined. He was shorter and older, a fringe of white hair circling his balding head.

Maude stood in the middle of the living room, waiting with hands on her hips. Charlie immediately confronted her. "How could you do this to me? How could you involve me when you know I had absolutely nothing to do with Harry's death?" Then he spotted me over Maude's shoulder, standing by the bedroom door, and asked sarcastically, "Is he your latest stud?"

"Get out, Charlie! I don't need to take your crap!"

"I'm not going anywhere until I get some answers."

"Answers to what, Charlie?"

Ignoring her, he turned and stared angrily at me. "Does he have to be here?" he asked.

"Yes! He's Davis Lowe, Harry's former business partner. And he's here to protect me just in case you decide to murder me like you murdered Harry!"

"What did you say? You know I didn't murder Harry!"

"Then exactly why did you go to the dinner last Saturday night, Charlie? You knew they were honoring Harry. What did you expect to get out of being there other than him humiliating you some more?"

"Why I went is my business," he replied forcefully.

"You mean Detective Brantley's business!" she jabbed back with a sly smile.

"Well, I can ask you the same thing! Why were you there?

Maude hesitated, then replied, "I went because I wanted to see how he would soak up all that praise before he crashed back to reality."

Charlie stared at her, trying to decipher the meaning of her answer. After a few seconds, he shook his head and asked, "Look, I want to know what you told Brantley."

"He asked me if I held a grudge against Harry. I told him not anymore. But I said you might, after what Harry did to you years ago."

"You told him that! How the hell could you do that to me?"

"Well, it's the truth, isn't it, Charlie?"

"That was fifteen years ago...I got over it! I haven't held a grudge against him for a long time. Somebody else did, but not me. We were working on a deal together."

"You were what?" I exclaimed incredulously.

"That's none of your damn business!" He started across the room towards me, a ready-to-do-battle look on his face. "Hey, big shot, what kind of problem did you have with Harry?"

"Lately...none at all!" I answered, standing my ground. "I haven't dealt with Harry in ten years."

He stopped just a few feet from where I was standing. "So then why are you here?"

"I came because I read about Harry's murder."

"Curiosity is a weak alibi, Lowe. You're going to need a hell of a better one than that." He pointed his finger in my face. "You know, Maude, this guy here is probably Harry's killer."

I was too stunned to ask why he was accusing me, but Maude didn't hesitate. "How can you say that, Charlie?"

"Because I bet he's not as innocent as he claims. I never heard Harry talk about a partner. And now he suddenly shows up at his funeral? I'm sure the cops are going to be interested in finding out why."

"What are you talking about? Davis wasn't here last Saturday night. He was in New York at home. You know, Charlie, this is one of the reasons why I never trusted you. You were always making things up...or lying...or blaming someone else. That's why I took all my money out of your brokerage house."

"Really, Maude? Wasn't it for your new lover?"

"Charlie, they don't come any lower than you," she replied acidly.

Reynolds spun around to face a combative Maude. "You're not

little Miss Innocent either! Who the hell gets out of prison, then moves two miles up the road from the person who put you there? And then to be seen at Harry's dinner? All I can say is you've given the police plenty of ammunition for charging you with the murder!"

"Worry about yourself, Charlie, and I'll worry about me!"

There was a long pause while the three of us stood glaring at each other. Then Charlie shrugged his shoulders, and with a look of disgust on his face, turned to leave. "I'll see both of you tomorrow morning at police headquarters," he said, opening the front door. "We'll see then who's the murderer." He walked out, slamming the door behind him.

Chapter Fourteen

The sun had just broken through the early morning ocean fog as I followed Maude down Beach Drive to the police station. I parked between two police cruisers while she parked at the end of the lot next to the town hall. We met and walked together to the colonial brick building's front entrance. As we climbed the three steps, it dawned on me that our arriving together was a dumb idea.

Detective Brantley met us at the door. He eyed the two of us a little suspiciously, but his only comment was a gruff, "Good morning." We followed him into a large open room where he led us past several police officers sitting at gray metal desks filling out forms until we came to an opaque glass door marked Conference Room. As we walked in, we saw Charlie Reynolds sitting at a scuffed metal table looking quite nervous. But it was the person sitting next to him that shocked the hell out of me. It was Fred Simmons! It had been ten years since I'd last seen him. He'd aged gracefully, I thought, only a few flecks of gray in his red hair, and looked in as good physical shape as the day he was ready to beat the hell out of me at the hotel bar.

The detective took his time, giving each of us a long, careful look, as if he was memorizing our faces before saying, "I think you all know each other."

Maude piped up. "I'm sorry, but I don't know the gentleman sitting next to Charlie."

Brantley was surprised. "I thought you knew Fred Simmons?"

"No, I've never met him before," she replied.

Simmons leaned across the table with his hand out. "Hello," he said cautiously, as Maude shook his hand.

"I've heard about you from Davis," she said.

"I'm sure nothing good," was his antagonistic reply, looking squarely at me. "The last time I saw Lowe was at a bar ten years ago, where he was trying to calm down after being fired by Harry. Two drinks later, he's telling me his plans to get rid of Harry...permanently! I got the hell out of there and haven't seen him again until now."

"Wait a minute, Simmons! If I remember correctly, you're the one who talked about still wanting revenge on Harry from when he got you fired from Reynolds & Coleman!"

"I don't remember firing you," Charlie interjected from across the table. "Tell me, what exactly did Miller do to you?"

Everyone turned to Simmons, who was trying unsuccessfully to control his anger, his face now matching his red hair. It was obviously still a vivid memory even after all these years. In a voice shaking with rage, he answered, "Miller bought two stocks without my authorization. Not only were they dogs, but they were a step away from bankruptcy. My client lost his shirt! You blamed me right off the bat, and before I could even accuse Harry of double-dealing, you fired me! You fired me right there on the spot in front of everybody! You never gave me a chance to explain what happened, you just kept screaming at me to get the hell out! Everyone in the office was shaking their heads at my supposed stupidity as I walked out the door. I'll never forget it. It was the day you and Miller destroyed my career in finance!"

Charlie's expression said it all: not only didn't he remember, I'd also bet he could have cared less.

"Please!" Brantley interrupted, sensing the growing hostility in the room. "I want you all to take your seats now," pointing to chairs on the right side of the table for Maude and me. He waited until we were seated, then said, "As you know, I've been asked to lead this investigation. I'm sure you're all aware that Harry Miller was a prominent person in this town. That's why the town council, including the first selectman, has given the police commissioner and me the authorization to use every means possible to quickly solve this case. I also want to tell you that this case will be my only focus until Harry Miller's killer is found. Does everyone understand that?"

Everyone nodded in agreement. We understood the pressure he was under. What worried me, though, was he seemed to believe one of us was guilty. And from his tone and intensity, he was determined to find out which one by starting with the assumption that we were all guilty until he proved us innocent! Looking around the room, I saw varying degrees of fear on every face...and knew I was no exception. Brantley had noticed, too, as he pressed his lips together and nodded slightly, clearly satisfied he had made his point. I suddenly had a sickening feeling that this detective might not be above offering one of us up as a sacrificial lamb based on weak circumstantial evidence if it helped to close the case quickly.

Brantley looked slowly around the table, then pointed to Sergeant Brock, who stood by a small window covered with iron mesh. "That is Sergeant Brock. He will be working with me on this case." They each took their seats at either end of the table while Maude and I faced Reynolds and Simmons. Brantley pulled out a small notebook from his pocket, opened it, and placed it in front of him. Then Brock set a tape recorder on the table and turned it on.

The room remained still, very still, as we all nervously watched Brantley study his notes, writing a few things down before finally looking up. Focusing on Simmons, he began his questioning. "Let's start with you, Mr. Simmons. When did you move into town?"

"A little over six years ago, when I got the teaching job here at the Middle School."

"Why this town, Mr. Simmons?"

"Well...the job was open, and I wanted it."

"What were you doing before that, after you said Mr. Reynolds fired you?"

"I looked for a job on Wall Street for close to two years. When that didn't pan out, I spent the next six years getting my teaching and master's degrees, then looked for a teaching job."

"Are you married?"

"No, not ever."

"Why did you go to the dinner last Saturday night?"

"I was curious, Detective. I wanted to see if anyone in town who didn't like Harry Miller showed up.

"Did you talk to him?"

"Yes…he cornered me, so we talked.

"What did you talk about?"

"Nothing really. He was surprised that I came to his dinner.

"Anything else?"

"I told him that he never thanked me for promoting him from runner to my assistant at Reynolds & Coleman."

"Do you own a gun, Mr. Simmons?"

"Ah…yes, I do."

"What kind?"

"It's an old .22 Colt pistol. I use it for target range shooting, but I haven't been to the range in a long time. Why?"

"We would like to test it."

"Oh, okay."

"Tell me, what time did you leave the dinner last Saturday night?

"Just after the town's first selectman finished his speech honoring Miller, I guess around 10 o'clock.

"You didn't stay to hear Mr. Miller's thank you speech?"

"No, I didn't."

"Where did you go after that?"

"I went home. Watched a movie."

"Do you remember the name of it, Mr. Simmons?"

"Not offhand, Detective, but give me a couple of minutes, and I'll think of it."

"Mr. Simmons, Sergeant Brock, will call you this afternoon before he stops by your home to pick up your gun. Oh…and Mr. Simmons, I want to check your car trunk before you leave today."

"Certainly, Detective!"

Brantley next turned to Charlie Reynolds. "Now, Mr. Reynolds, just how long have you been living here in town?"

"A little over twelve years. I came up here three years after I closed my business in New York."

"Why did you pick this town?"

"I liked the idea of living close to the ocean, and thought I could make a fresh start here."

"Did you know that Mr. Miller had moved into town about around the same time?"

"Not at first, Detective, but then I saw him around town."

"Did Mr. Miller work for you at one time?"

"He did, yes. And I fired him too!"

"Wasn't Mr. Miller the reason you closed your business?"

"No! No, he wasn't. It was the lady sitting across the table who suddenly decided to take all the money I'd made for her out of my firm. She invested it with Miller after she began sleeping with him."

"How dare you say that, Charlie!" Maude practically threw herself across the table, jabbing an angry finger at him. "You know damn well I caught you red-handed stealing my money with all of your commission churning on stocks going nowhere. I want you to know, Detective, I lost over three million dollars with him! That's why I left!"

Reynolds glared at her. "Come on, Maude, tell him the truth! You left because you found a young stud who was willing to trade sex for your investment in his start-up firm."

"Detective! Harry was a horrible person, but he knew how to pick stocks. Not like Reynolds here, who never, ever, picked a winner for my account!"

"Please! Enough of this! Let's move on," a clearly frustrated Brantley said testily.

"Tell me, do you own a gun, Mr. Reynolds?"

"No."

"Are you sure?"

"Well...I did years ago. But frankly, I don't know where it is."

"What was the make and model of your gun?"

"I don't remember exactly. I think it was a .38, but I bought it so long ago, and then stuck it into a drawer and forgot about it. I probably got rid of it when I moved to town."

"Mr. Reynolds, I would like Sergeant Brock to go to your house with you after we finish here today to see if you can find it."

"Well, of course. But I assure you, Detective, I don't have it."

"There's no harm in looking, now is there, Mr. Reynolds? Also, before you leave, I'd like to inspect your car trunk too."

"Certainly," Charlie quietly replied.

Brantley looked down at his notes for a couple of seconds. When he looked back up, he appeared confused. With a slight shake of his head, he turned to Maude and said, "Mrs. Williamson, I have most of your history. But I'm still puzzled as to why you would move two miles up the road from Mr. Miller and yet rarely speak to him all these years. It sounds almost impossible, especially in a small town like this."

"I bought the property because of the beautiful ocean view, Detective. I had no idea who lived on Beach Drive then. I became aware of Harry after I moved in, but frankly, I had no reason to speak to him after all that has gone on between us. Yes, I saw him in town over the years, but I always made it a point to keep away from him as best I could. But after I left you yesterday, I got to thinking about the last time I spoke to him. It must have been over six months ago when I bumped into him in front of the bank. We were both surprised. He became quite angry and told me that he didn't want me living here in no uncertain terms. He said it was his town, and I wasn't welcome. And he said he told Charlie Reynolds the same thing when he found out Charlie was living here."

Before Charlie could deny it, Maude went on. "I was quite taken aback. I told him that I had been living here long enough that it was my town, too, and that Charlie had been living here just as long as him. He just gave me a little smirk. In typical Harry fashion, he had to make sure I knew all about his wealth and importance in the town. Then he proceeded to tell me how Charlie was hounding him about a deal for a 40-acre piece of property where the two of them could make a fast five to ten million. Charlie needed five hundred thousand dollars to close the deal and was chasing him for the money. Typical Harry, he said he just laughed in Charlie's face. Told him *no* in no uncertain terms, then demanded that Charlie get the hell out of town, and out of his life."

"She's lying!" Reynolds cried out, rising halfway out of his chair. "After I told Harry about this real estate deal, his eyes lit up. He said he was interested, but told me it would have to wait because he needed help raising four hundred thousand dollars that would return a guaranteed five million! His deal sounded interesting, but when I asked him about the details, he just hemmed and hawed. I told him I wouldn't help him until I knew what the deal was all about. It took about a week before he came back with hat in hand, again asking for my help. And if you knew anything about Harry Miller, Detective, that was totally out of character. Nobody, but nobody, ever saw Harry Miller beg! He was an arrogant son-of-a-bitch who took advantage of every person he ever met. But now he was apparently desperate for money, and willing to beg for it!"

"What was the deal, Mr. Reynolds?"

Charlie sat back and looked across at Maude with a smug, *I'm in charge* expression. "Well, Detective, there was a very wealthy woman in town who had fallen for Harry's infectious charm. She agreed to invest five million in his fund if he assured her that she'd get her money back, if…and that *if* was key, his fund had any problems that jeopardized her investment. The four hundred thousand amounted to his buying an insurance policy to protect her from any possible losses."

"Why did Harry Miller come to you, Mr. Reynolds?"

"Obviously, Detective, he thought I had that kind of money, or could get it."

"And did you lend or get him the money, Mr. Reynolds?"

"No! I tried to raise it for him, but there were no bites. Then I thought about the person who lived a couple of miles up the road from him who could write that large a check."

"That's a lie, and you know it, Charlie!" Maude shouted.

"Is it, Maude? I know for a fact that Harry came to see you after I couldn't raise the four hundred thousand. He told me so. He said you laughed in his face at first, then cursed him out. But in his conceited way, he told me how he turned on the old Harry charm, took you out for a couple of dinners, and spent a couple of nights with you."

"You're a damn liar!"

Ignoring her, Brantley asked, "What happened next, Mr. Reynolds?"

"Maude here stipulated a certain condition for loaning him the money. Harry had no choice but to agree as his fund was heading towards disaster. After she gave him the money, he swore up and down to me that he'd never fulfill her condition."

"That's just another lie! I never made any deal with him. Never!" Maude cried out. "I'd never make another deal with that bastard, ever!"

"Do you know what Mrs. Williamson wanted, Mr. Reynolds?"

"Why yes, Detective. Harry told me."

"What was it?"

"She demanded they pick up where they left off fifteen years ago."

"How can you listen to these disgusting lies, Detective?" Maude demanded, practically shaking with anger.

The room remained silent while Brantley absorbed this new information. A frantic and despairing Maude turned to me, pleading for help to get her out of this trap. I sat there sympathetic to the core, but too stunned at the accusation to know what to say or do. I looked at Brantley to see how he was grappling with the question of who was lying and who was telling the truth, but he seemed as confused as me. Glancing across at Charlie, I noticed a little smile at the corners of his mouth, signaling he thought he had won this round.

We all sat there watching Brantley, waiting for his next move.

Anticipating the worst, Maude kept turning to me, desperate, and silently pleading for help. I could feel her fear and anxiety, but I didn't know how to help her. And here she thought I was her friend...or more. But at this moment, I was useless!

Several more minutes passed before Brantley looked up. Sighing deeply, he gave a slight nod, indicating he had reached a decision. Staring hard at Maude, he asked, "Mrs. Williamson, did you give Harry Miller the money? And did he perform his side of the deal? Remember, it would be very unwise of you to lie to me."

Maude's face had turned chalk-white in abject fear as the nightmare of her five years in prison had come back to haunt her. She spun around to face me, tears streaming from her eyes, pleading for help. But what could I do? After all, Harry was the lover she had coveted since her husband's death, and she did invest fifteen million in him. Yet the more I thought about Charlie's allegations, the more they seemed based on hearsay. *There's nothing there,* I concluded. Unable to watch Maude cry anymore, I turned back to Charlie. There he sat with a self-satisfied smile on his face, waiting patiently for Maude to confess. His smile reminded me of a Cheshire cat's smile after swallowing the canary, which irritated the hell out of me! I knew he was lying, but why? I started to go through his story again. Why would Harry ask Charlie for money in the first place? It didn't make any sense, as Harry Miller would never ask anyone he had screwed over for help. His over-the-top arrogance wouldn't allow him to be so humble, no matter how much money was involved. And other parts of Charlie's story just didn't jibe, especially the part where Maude demanded Harry revive their love affair in return for the four hundred thousand. There was no way that was true! Not after what she'd been through because of him. No, Charlie was just blowing smoke to confuse Brantley.

I looked over at the detective. He was still gazing intently at Maude, waiting for her answer. A moment later, he gave a quick little nod to indicate her time had run out. "Well, Mrs. Williamson? Is Mr. Reynolds telling the truth?"

"No, Detective! He's lying through his teeth!" she answered belligerently through a new flood of tears.

Brantley's face tensed. He stared coldly at her for a few seconds, then said, "Well, Mrs. Williamson, I warned you about the consequences. It's clear to me that you were anxious to renew your relationship with Mr. Miller. You could easily write a four hundred-thousand-dollar check and thought you could hold it over Mr. Miller's head that the only way he was going to get the money was to agree to your demand. But this time he didn't agree, so in a fit of anger, you killed him! Mrs. Williamson, you leave me no choice but to arrest you for the murder of Harry Miller."

Upon hearing this, Maude buried her face in her hands, crying hysterically. I sat back in my chair, shocked. Could Brantley arrest her without any real evidence? Right now, all he was going on was Charlie's word. There was no proof whatsoever that Maude had given Harry any money. And even if she had, why murder him? *I must be missing something.* What could possess Brantley to charge her like this? Maybe he thinks pressuring her would force her to confess without needing incriminating evidence? Could that be it? After all, he'd be the town hero for solving this major case in less than a week. And how often does a case like this fall into the lap of a small-town detective? Once in a lifetime…maybe? I glanced over at Simmons, but he clearly had no intention of getting involved. As for Charlie, his satisfied smile had broadened into an enthusiastic grin. He'd obviously gotten the retribution he'd wanted from her all these years.

I had to help Maude, but how? If I tried speaking in her defense, Brantley might claim that I was her co-conspirator in Harry's murder. *My God, I'm not on anybody's side except my own!* Then again, Brantley can turn my story of how Harry unceremoniously fired and threatened me ten years ago into the reason I conspired with Maude to murder him. And Simmons would back him up on it! But I'll be damned if he's going to throw both of us to the wolves! Just then, Brantley stood up. I watched as he reached into his back pocket for his handcuffs and slowly walked towards Maude to cuff her. It was now or never. I couldn't let him destroy the last vestiges of her self-respect, life, and maybe mine too! I could feel myself shaking as I warily asked, "Detective, don't you think Mrs. Williamson is entitled to speak to a lawyer before you arrest her? I mean…isn't she entitled to know what evidence you have other than the hearsay you've just been told? I really don't know much about the law in this situation, but I'm…er…not sure what you're doing is legal."

"Mr. Lowe, who the hell are you to tell me about the law!" Brantley bellowed at me while opening the handcuffs. "I represent the law, Mr. Lowe! Do you understand that?" He was about to put them around Maude's wrists when he stopped and glared at me. "And may I also remind you, Mr. Lowe, you're a prime suspect too, as Mrs. Williamsons' accomplice in the murder of Harry Miller!"

Although I had suspected it was coming, his accusation still took my breath away. But I wasn't going to let his threats railroad the both of us. "Ah…Detective, please, I'm not trying to tell you how to do your job, but where's the evidence to support Reynolds' story? Where's the check for four hundred thousand dollars supposedly written by Mrs. Williamson? No one knows that at this moment. With all due respect, Detective, right now, this case boils down to a 'he said, she said' standoff."

Well, that really pissed him off! I knew I was going to get it…with both barrels! Brantley slowly turned to stand over me with his open cuffs and an aggravated *stay out of my business* look on his face. I thought for sure he was going to cuff me first. Instead, he stared at Maude and me for what seemed like minutes. Maybe he was deciding what to do with us, but then I realized he was trying to figure out how he could extricate himself from what was turning into a potentially career-threatening situation for him. He pressed his lips hard together, then turned to stare across the table at Reynolds. Forcing as calm a voice as possible, he asked, "Mr. Reynolds, can you prove your statement about the four hundred thousand and Mrs. Williamsons' deal with Mr. Miller?"

Charlie froze. His winning smile was gone, replaced by a frantic look as he struggled to come up with an answer to Brantley's question. But he regrouped fast and did what slick politicians do when caught without an answer…he deflected. Wagging his finger at both of us, he shouted, "Don't you see Detective, these two are in this together. They've been sleeping together, so naturally, Lowe's going to defend her. His story about coming up here from New York because he was curious about Harry's death is garbage. Pure garbage! There's another reason, Detective, I'm sure of it!"

"I told you, Mr. Reynolds, I'll ask the questions here!

"Okay, but…"

"No buts, Mr. Reynolds!" Brantley yelled at him in frustration. "Now, do you or don't you have proof that Mrs. Williamson wrote a check to Mr. Miller for four hundred thousand dollars?"

"Er…no, I don't, but I'm sure the bank has a record of it."

Clearly embarrassed by his rush to judgment, Brantley moved to cover his tracks. Without apologizing, he practically mumbled, "Well, I'm going to get to the bottom of this check business. I'll get a warrant to search your bank records, Mrs. Williamson." Not waiting for her reaction, and wanting to forgo any further embarrassment, he asked, "Do you own a gun, Mrs. Williamson?"

"Ask her about the gun she used to shoot Miller the first time, the one that put her in jail for five years!" Charlie yelled across the table.

Maude gave Reynolds an icy stare. "As I just told you, Detective, I don't own a gun."

"Mr. Reynolds," Brantley said irritably, "how many times do I have to remind you that I ask the questions here?" He turned back to Maude. "Mrs. Williamson, I've changed my mind about arresting you until we find out about that check. But understand this: You are still the key suspect."

Maude nodded that she understood.

"And Mrs. Williamson, I will still need to check your car trunk."

"Detective, you're most welcome to check my car trunk anytime," she replied, clearly anxious for the conversation to be over.

But Brantley wasn't quite finished. "Yours too, Mr. Lowe."

"Of course, Detective."

"And none of you plan on leaving town any time soon."

Chapter Fifteen

We all followed Brantley and Brock out to the parking lot and handed them our keys. Then we silently watched as the two of them opened each trunk to check, I assume, for any incriminating blood stains or other clues. In the first three, they found varying amounts of ocean sand, beach chairs, and typical odds and ends. In mine, they found several bundles of my bank's financial pamphlets and application forms. But there were no bloodstains anywhere. A furious Brantley hissed to Brock, "Get that forensic expert over here now! Have him check for blood and hair in each trunk."

Brantley appeared shocked that his theory about the murder occurring elsewhere was now debunked. We all knew this was just the beginning of his wrath. Yet I couldn't help but wonder if he actually believed the murderer would leave such incriminating evidence to be found so easily. Brantley turned around and led us back into the police station, clearly angry and frustrated at not finding a quick solution to his case. He was back to square one, and still faced the baffling question: which one of us murdered Harry?

****

We returned to the police conference room, took our respective seats, and waited silently for Brantley's next move. He took his time scrutinizing each one of us, likely trying to decide who was his best choice to be the murderer. When he finally spoke, there was a threatening tone to his voice. "I will find out very shortly which one of you murdered Harry Miller. And when I do, that person will spend the rest of their life in prison."

We all grimaced at the thought. He then whispered to Brock in a voice loud enough for us to hear, "Get over to Judge Bernstein's chamber and get him to sign the warrant to search Williamsons' bank records. Hopefully, he hasn't gone fishing. Then find out if she wrote that four hundred-thousand-dollar check and if Miller cashed it. Also pick up Simmons' Colt before heading to Reynolds' place to see if he can find his pistol." A sly grin spread across Brantley's face. "Oh…by the way, Mr. Lowe, you better call your office and tell them you're under suspicion of murder and won't be coming in for a while."

Well…that sucked the air right out of me. *There goes my job!* But I wasn't going to let him think he'd gotten to me. I turned to Maude, whose expression confirmed my thought: *What a bastard!*

Brantley waited expectantly for my reaction. But the only thing he got was a nonchalant nod indicating I'd make the call. His grin faded quickly, replaced by a stern expression as he announced that we were free to go and that our next meeting would be back here tomorrow at 10:00 am sharp. We looked around at each other, wondering what was in store for us, then stood up and walked out of the station.

****

Maude and I were standing in the bright sunlit parking lot, trying to decompress when she suddenly burst into tears. I wasn't surprised, figuring it was just relief at not being marched off in handcuffs to a cell in the back of the police station. Hell, I was definitely relieved that Brantley hadn't slapped the cuffs on me for standing up to him. I took her in my arms to comfort her. After a minute or two, she slowly smiled up at me, and I knew then and there what we both needed, and badly. "Say, I think we both could use a drink."

She nodded approvingly through a wet smile. "There's a nice little restaurant half-hidden in the corner of the nearby shopping center where we can get a drink and some lunch."

"Let's go! After spending the morning with Brantley, I damn well need to steady my nerves!"

We drove separately to the restaurant, parked, and walked in together. The dining room was not quite semi-dark at noon, and it was already noisy. There was a large, three-sided bar dominating the place with tables spread around it. We sat down on the right side near the back, where it was a bit quieter, and ordered two vodka martinis from a hovering waitress. Maude leaned her head back, took a deep breath, and tried to relax. I took a slow look around at the worn nineteen sixties décor, including some interesting artifacts on the walls. After viewing it all, I turned to her and abruptly asked, "Will Brantley find a canceled check for four hundred thousand in your bank records?"

"If he does, it'll be news to me!"

"That's good! In fact, very good!" I replied, very relieved. "I was quite concerned this was going to be a major problem for you…and us. I'm so glad it's not! But what I don't understand is why Reynolds took such a chance in accusing you of writing it."

"You have to realize, Davis, that Charlie was never very clever at anything. I can attest to that based on what he did with my portfolio."

I smiled at her comment but was still perplexed. After mulling it over for a few minutes, I said, "The only reason I can think of why he'd take such a ridiculous risk was to get even with you for putting him out of business fifteen years ago."

"That's reason enough, Davis! And it suits him perfectly. He certainly had Brantley believing it. But you know what really scares me, Davis? It's Charlie's willingness to do something like that without caring about the consequences to himself. I'm afraid there's no telling what else he'll do to get even."

Her point was well taken. I was still wondering about Charlie when the waitress came by with our drinks. After she left, I smiled and raised my glass to toast Maude. "Thank God we're not behind bars right now!" Maude barely smiled back as we downed our martinis. Maybe we were hoping the vodka would wash away this morning's memory of our close brush with the law. But we both knew full well there were many more Brantley threats to come.

Our little celebration continued as we ordered another round of drinks. I sat watching Maude as she scanned the lunch crowd sitting around us and across the room. She suddenly appeared startled at something she saw and leaned back to think about it.

"What happened? What's wrong?"

"Your friend Fred Simmons is having lunch with Lucy Grimes. I didn't realize he was Lucy's Fred."

"Who is she? And what do you mean that Simmons is 'her" Fred?"

"Fred was the love of Lucy's life before Harry came and swept her off her feet," Maude replied. "And she's the one who was going to invest five million in Harry's fund."

"Really! How do you know that?"

"Davis, in a small town like this, gossip flies faster than you could ever imagine. She inherited an awful lot of money and likes to show it off."

"Maude, you know gossip usually ends up being wrong. Are you sure she's the one?"

"That's what my sources tell me," Maude replied defensively.

"Was Harry seeing her?"

"Seeing her? She was the one he was about to marry last Sunday! I heard he even gave her a seventy-five-thousand-dollar ring! And if you turn around and take a look at her, you'll notice that she's not exactly the eye-catching type; she doesn't fit in with the beautiful women Harry was known to romance. My understanding was the only reason he was marrying her was to get his hands on her money!"

That didn't really surprise me as I thought about Ellen Houser's ill-fated romance with Harry. After Maude, Ellen, and now Lucy Grimes, I guess Harry's typical move to ensure financial survival and maintain his lifestyle was to propose marriage whenever he needed money. It didn't take long for my curiosity to get the better of me. I slowly turned around to get a first-hand look at Lucy. Surprised, I tried to visualize Harry exuding his charm on wooing this woman, but I couldn't picture it.

"And why is she with Simmons?"

"Well...that's an interesting story too, Davis. It seems that Fred and Lucy were practically engaged until Harry burst onto the scene. In his usual persuasive style, he swept Lucy right off her feet, leaving poor old Fred in the dust. According to my friend, this was the second time Fred had a run-in with Harry over Lucy. The first time, Fred begged Lucy not to fall for Harry, and it worked. This time, she couldn't help herself. She fell for Harry...head over heels! The marriage was to be at Lucy's house the day after the dinner honoring Harry. Well, with Harry dead, poor Lucy was so devastated that she ran right back into Fred's arms. And as you can see, he's very quick to forgive!"

"It seems odd that she went back to Simmons after jilting him like that. And that Simmons was so willing to take her back given his history with Harry."

"Well, you have to understand Lucy Grimes. She's a spoiled, rich girl who never left home, someone who always got everything she wanted. But she's always depended on having someone take care of her. When Harry came along, he filled that need perfectly. For Lucy, it was a match made in heaven. Not only did she catch a handsome guy, but she could rely on him for everything. The gossip was Harry introduced her to his crowd, and although Lucy loved being part of it, she was way over her head. I was told that Fred was definitely more her speed, but she was madly in love with Harry, and wouldn't listen to anybody. The only time she listened to Fred was when he insisted that she insure her money before investing in Harry's fund."

"Harry must have been pissed at that!"

"More than you think! The way I heard it, the two of them actually came to blows, at least that's what my friend told me."

"Who won?" I asked offhandedly.

"It wasn't Harry!"

The waitress came over, and we ordered lunch. But I couldn't stop thinking about their fight. It brought back memories of that dinner at

Harry's at Hanover Square fifteen years ago. Harry lost then and lost a hell of a lot more now. I turned around again to stare at the two of them, still trying to visualize Simmons punching out Harry over Lucy. He must have felt me staring at him as he turned in my direction. Looking surprised, he said something to Lucy, got up, and walked slowly to our table, never taking his eyes off me. When he reached us, he sneered, "Lowe, you're lucky you got away with what you did this morning, but rest assured, Brantley will nail you. He's tenacious as hell!"

"You know, Simmons, you of all people should be very careful. I'm sure Brantley would love to hear how you and Harry fought over your rich girlfriend over there not once...but twice! Now that has all the makings of a fascinating story, don't you think?"

He glared at me, making up his mind as to what to do next. Typical Simmons, it took a moment before he reached down, grabbed me by my shirt, and pulled me up so he could take a swing at me. Knowing what was coming, I threw the first punch. It surprised the hell out of him, and everyone sitting near us.

He hit the floor hard, his nose bleeding profusely, shocked that I'd actually taken the first swing. Grabbing a napkin from a nearby table, he pressed it against his nose while mumbling some garbled curse words at me. I reached down to pull him up, then eased him into my chair. Simmons glared at me as he sat there, trying to clear the cobwebs from his head and pressing the napkin against his nose. I brought over a nearby chair, sat down, and then looked over at Maude. She just sat there, mouth open and wide-eyed, unwilling to believe what she'd just seen. "Maude," I explained, "Fred here has had this unrelenting urge to punch me out these last fifteen years to get even with me for knocking him down to protect Harry after he hit Harry for getting him fired."

The restaurant manager rushed over to see how Simmons was doing, shooing away a growing crowd of onlookers. He indicated he was all right. By now, Maude had recovered enough to ask, "Would you like a drink or some ice for your nose?"

Simmons whispered, "Some ice, please!"

I was beginning to feel a little guilty about punching him out that way when he looked me straight in the eye and said, "Lowe, it's not over between us. I'll settle the score soon, very soon! And trust me, you're not going to like it!"

I couldn't let the opportunity go by. "You know, Simmons, for someone as persistent as you, how'd you let Harry steal your girl?" I watched as he tried to get up to come after me, but clearly, I'd left him in no shape to move. Instead, he just glowered at me, likely planning his next get even assault.

We stared hard at each other, eyes locked until Maude broke the silence with a friendly hello to the approaching Lucy Grimes. Simmons looked up at her and smiled, indicating he was okay. The look she gave him back, however, bordered on disgust, which made me wonder as to how Simmons' love affair was going.

"Won't you sit down and join us?" Maude said sympathetically while pointing to me to find another chair.

Lucy sat down, still looking at Simmons and the bloody napkin covering his nose. Hissing at him as an angry mother would do to a child, she said, "You and your awful temper. It serves you right! You're always ready to fight someone. How many times did you fight with Harry? Was it two times or three? You know, I felt like I was dealing with two fifteen-year-old boys. Well, now that Harry's gone, maybe you can grow up and act like a man!"

I tried hard to stay out of it but just couldn't resist. "Yeah, Fred…maybe you can grow up and stop trying to punch me out all the time!"

To say Simmons was pissed was an understatement, but just who he was mad at was unclear. He stared at me with hatred in his eyes, but his angry, "I'll see you later," whisper to Lucy seemed to settle it. Everyone on this side of the bar watched as he got up slowly, still a bit wobbly, and walked out.

"Please let me apologize for Fred," Lucy said soothingly to me. "You must understand he's not himself, nor am I frankly, after

Harry's murder. He and Harry never got along. I don't know why. I tried so hard to have them make peace with each other, but it never worked. They just didn't like each other; it was that simple!"

Maude nodded her complete understanding, saying, "Men always seem to push their animosity towards each other to the limit. Especially those who think they're far superior to the other. And it always ends in trouble, my dear!"

I was about to challenge Maude's all-encompassing statement but figured it wouldn't serve any purpose. Instead, I turned to Lucy and said, "I was sorry to hear about your loss on the day before your wedding."

Lucy immediately welled up with tears. "I know Harry was no saint, but I loved him and wanted to be his wife. Everyone warned me against him, even you Maude, but I didn't care, I loved him so much!"

Well...that was unexpected! Why hadn't Maude mentioned her conversation with Lucy to me earlier? My mind started racing with questions, the primary one being, *Had she renewed her friendship or more with Harry?* My trusting answer, *No, she couldn't have!* Then my distrusting answer, *How could she not have, living just two miles up the road from him?* Leaving me wondering, *Weren't we going to be very honest with each other?* I looked at Maude, but she just looked back at me with a pleading expression as if to say, *It's not what it seems!* Okay, maybe I shouldn't jump to conclusions...yet.

Meanwhile, Lucy had stopped talking and was staring at me. Seeing this, Maude jumped in, sounding a little embarrassed for not introducing me earlier. "Oh, Lucy, this is Davis Lowe. He worked with Harry years ago in New York."

Lucy continued to stare at me, and I squirmed a little, not knowing why. Then out of the blue, she declared, "Don't I know you? Yes...I do! I'm sure I saw you in town recently!"

"Umm, I don't think so. I'd never been here before until I came up for Harry's funeral."

Lucy shook her head, disagreeing vigorously. "Well, I don't forget handsome faces, and I know I saw yours a couple of weeks ago. Yes…I'm positive! But where? Oh, yes, I remember now! It was at the ice cream stand. That's it! I remember watching you order a double scoop of butter pecan, and the top scoop almost fell off. I started to laugh at how you kept juggling the cone to save the ice cream. It sounds silly, I know, but it was you, definitely you!"

"I'm sorry, but I'm sure you're mixing me up with someone else. I work at a bank in New York, and didn't take time off to drive up here for ice cream."

Sounding suspicious, Maude asked, "Well, Davis, is it true?"

"You surprise me, Maude, jumping to such a quick conclusion. I was not here two weeks ago, nor was I standing in line to buy a double scoop of butter pecan, so I couldn't possibly have juggled two scoops of ice cream. She's got it all wrong, and is confusing me with someone else."

Lucy shook her head profusely, indicating to Maude that she was right. Maude appeared perplexed and a little hurt but smiled a weak *thank you* to Lucy. Noticing Maude's distress, Lucy realized that something unpleasant was happening between us. Somewhat embarrassed, she stood up quickly. Practically stammering, she said, "Well, I better see about helping Fred," and then left.

Maude's sudden coldness was reflected in her steely stare at me. I stared back, thinking *I don't want us to part company right now…we need each other.* But how do I convince her that I wasn't up here before the funeral? That penetrating stare of hers meant I'd better have a seriously good story. "Maude, why don't you call my office and ask if I was working all that week, two weeks ago? Oh, and by the way, what was it you told Lucy about Harry? I seemed to have missed you telling me what that was all about."

She didn't answer, and instead we kept staring at each other, trying to make up our minds whether to believe the other was telling the truth. Finally, she gave me a small smile and said, "Davis, we need to stick together. It's the only way to keep Brantley off our backs."

That certainly sounded reasonable, but it left me wondering…did she say it because she had something to hide? And have I now become her protector in case Brantley goes after her again? What if I don't protect her, will she get Lucy to tell Brantley I was here in town for ice cream two weeks ago, and my alibi was, therefore, a lie? Well, I guess sticking together does have its advantages.

"Say, Maude, why don't we order another martini to toast our bond of unity. A friendly drink always works well to seal an agreement, don't you think?"

She smiled and nodded agreeably as I signaled our waitress for two more drinks. I returned Maude's friendly smile, still wondering if our agreement would stand up to a full-blown crisis. It seemed that the only thing I was sure of was the trust we'd developed in bed last night was clearly gone.

The waitress placed our drinks and lunch in front of us. We picked up our glasses and clinked them together as I toasted, "To our partnership!" We downed our martinis, smiled approvingly at each other, and began to eat.

****

We lingered long after lunch, enjoying some wine while trying to re-establish the feelings and trust we had before Lucy Grimes appeared on the scene. We talked about the old days, about the thrill I had felt making so much money so young and spending it as fast as I could in those early 80s boom days with Harry. About Maude's exciting life in New York, enjoying the theater and clubs before and at the start of her relationship with Harry. We lost track of time until the late afternoon bar crowd began filtering in, filling up seats on our side. Maude looked at her watch, "Davis, you won't believe it, but it's almost 5 o'clock! Why don't we go back to my house to freshen up, watch the sun go down, and decide where to eat tonight?"

I paid the bill, and we walked out to our cars. I followed Maude through town to Beach Drive, where we drove slowly along the twisting road, the spectacular ocean views shimmering in the fading light. Reaching Harry's seaside mansion, I stopped in front of the large, black wrought iron gates while Maude drove on. Standing there with my hands wrapped tightly around the bars, I peered down the long driveway, taking another look at what I should have had. All those good times I had just told Maude about, and all those anticipated good times I never got to have flashed through my mind. My reaction was to curse Harry out long and loud for what he did to me, still not understanding even after all these years why he had fought me tooth and nail against selling out our portfolio that infamous day. How could he have not seen that we would have survived unscathed and oh so rich! I knew arrogance and ego were the answers, but I still couldn't believe he had been so willing to risk it all because of them. Feeling thoroughly angered, I mumbled a few more curse words through the gate and headed back to my car. I drove off, trying to overcome my funk by stealing glances at the fading light over the ocean when suddenly I glimpsed a car racing up behind me in my rearview mirror. I watched as it slowed, staying no more than a few feet back as I rounded a sharp bend to the straight stretch of road ahead. After several seconds, the driver sped up alongside me. I glanced over, wondering, *Who the hell was playing games on this narrow, winding, two-lane road?* But the driver was hidden behind tinted glass. Was he drunk or just crazy? I pulled over to the far right, giving him plenty of room to pass me. Instead, he just maneuvered closer, almost hitting my car as if playing some kind of crazy game of chicken.

My instinct was to race to the next bend, hoping to lose him. But he threw caution to the wind by remaining parallel with me, traveling on the wrong side of the road. Suddenly he slammed his car into mine, forcing me half off the road into the brush. This was no longer a game! I had to get away...and fast! I jammed my foot down on the gas pedal, kicking up sand and rocks as my car shot out way ahead of his. For a moment, it looked like I had lost him, but then I caught sight of him in my rearview mirror, racing to catch up. It was clear he wasn't giving up. As he approached, I swung into the middle of the road, blocking him from passing me. But that didn't stop him; he shot around me, not caring about driving over the brush, sand, and small rocks lining the roadside. Once he got ahead of me, he slowed, then drifted back next to me. The next thing I knew, he slammed hard into my car, forcing me half off the road again.

By now, I was frantic with fear. Was this guy trying to kill me? All I knew was I had to get as far away from him as possible. I slowed my car down to a crawl, my heart racing. It took the other driver a couple of seconds to realize what I was doing, at which point he jammed on his brakes, shoved his car into reverse, then burnt rubber to get back even with me. When he was almost parallel, I slammed my foot down on the gas pedal, shooting well ahead of him and back into the center of the road before he could shift back into drive. My speedometer read sixty as I thought I had gotten away. But he must have hit ninety, as he pulled right up behind my car and began maneuvering from side to side looking for an opening to pass me. Watching him in my rearview mirror, all I could think was, *Who the hell is he? And why is he trying to kill me?* Then I stopped thinking and became intent on blocking his every move until I lost sight of the upcoming bend and drove off into the brush.

Swearing out loud that I wasn't going to let him get ahead of me, I jammed the gas pedal to the floor, kicking up sand and rock everywhere. I bolted back onto the road, smashing into the side of his car. The momentum pushed his car way off to the left, giving me time to retake the lead. But not for long! He came roaring back, pulled even, then hit my car hard, which forced me back into the brush. Each time I tried to get back on the road, he smacked into my car's side, trying to push me deeper into the brush and rocks. Then for some reason, he stopped and let me get back on the road, albeit next to him. Out of the corner of my eye, I suddenly didn't see any tinted glass on his front passenger side. Instead, I saw a pistol pointing straight at me! Between instinct and fear, I ducked down as he fired four shots. I thought I was finished as I lost control of the car and slammed into a tree with a deafening sound.

The impact, the shots fired at me, the sudden pain in my back, and the airbag whacking my face and chest before enveloping me, left me dazed and scared. I heard the other car drive away, tires squealing. I knew my car was totaled, and I knew I had to get out, but I was worried about moving for fear of being badly hurt. It took several minutes to assure myself that I was okay and to regain a modicum of composure. I didn't think anything was broken, so I started to push the airbag far enough away from me so I could move. After several more minutes wrestling to break free from the airbag, I was able to kick open the door. I got out, stood up very slowly, and reached behind my back where I felt a lot of pain. I discovered that my jacket had ripped open, and felt warm, sticky blood on my hand. My ribs were sore, and my right arm throbbed from getting caught in an awkward position when the airbag burst open. I then noticed the three bullet holes in the rear door and the shattered driver's side window. I slowly sat down near the car and started to shake, realizing just how lucky I was to be alive. It was a while before I tried to stand up again. I staggered around to the front of the car to examine the damage. When I saw how badly the car was twisted and mangled, I started to shake all over again. Hurt, bleeding, and distraught, I managed to walk over to a large rock near the road where I sat down to wait for someone to come along to help me.

I don't remember how long I waited before I heard a car approach. When I saw it was Maude's car, I stood up slowly and painfully and gave a little wave. She stopped short, jumped out, and ran to me. Throwing her arms around me, she kissed me again and again. All those kisses proved enervating, to say the least, and I found myself smiling, despite all the pain. She then stepped back to look at me and immediately cried out, "Let's get you to the emergency clinic and fast!" With that, she put her arm around me, only to quickly pull it away when she felt blood on her hand. Wiping it off, she put her hand under my elbow, and we walked slowly to her car. As we drove off, I kept asking her, "Why would someone want to kill me?" Each time, she started to answer and then just shook her head. But the question kept me occupied until we reached the clinic.

****

I left with a tightly wrapped bandage covering twelve stitches across my back and a pain killer prescription in my hand. Maude drove me first to the pharmacy, then back to her house. On the way, we saw a police car's flashing lights. She slowed, then pulled over, and we watched as a tow truck hoisted my car up onto its flatbed before driving off. Arriving at her house, she struggled to help me out of the car, into the house, and then to the living room sofa, where I sat down very slowly and carefully. As I tried to get comfortable, I couldn't help but ask her again, "Why would someone want to kill me, Maude? It doesn't make any sense."

"I don't know what to tell you, Davis, except maybe it was the same person who shot Harry?"

"Why would Harry's killer be after me? I have no idea who killed him. And why would anybody believe I did?"

"Well…somebody must think you do, Davis. But thank God whoever it was missed you!"

Fear bubbled back up inside me. For a second, I wondered, *Could she have tried to kill me?* But why would she want to do that? She needs me! Or does she? God, how I'd like to get the hell out of here and back to New York! But could I run fast enough, or far enough away, if somebody was out to kill me?

"Davis, I'm going to call Brantley and tell him what happened. Then I'm going to make us some drinks, and we'll go sit out on the deck and watch the sunset."

"With that kind of medicine, Maude, maybe I can stop shaking."

She disappeared into the kitchen, making it difficult to hear more than snatches of her conversation with Brantley. After hanging up, she made a beeline to the bar, poured two double scotches, and led me slowly out onto the deck.

We sat and watched the setting sun, its vibrant red color

- 140 -

reflected across the becalmed ocean and then magnified into a light pink sky everywhere along the horizon. I raised my glass and said appreciatively, "Well…here's to you, Maude! Many thanks for helping me."

****

About fifteen minutes later, the doorbell rang, announcing that the police had arrived. Maude jumped up from her seat to answer it. She soon returned, leading Brantley and Brock out onto the deck. I thought about standing up, but given how the pain medicine and scotch had started to kick in, decided against it. Brantley stood facing me with the red sun silhouetting his tall, heavyset frame. He slowly looked me up and down; I'm sure to determine how my wound was affecting me. When he saw the half-empty glass of scotch, I swear there was a glint of disappointment in his eyes. "Well, Mr. Lowe, it looks like you're a fortunate man! Whoever shot at you was a lousy shot at close range." I stared at him, wondering what he really meant by that. "I think you can now appreciate what this case is all about. Murder is a serious crime, Mr. Lowe. It requires honest answers from everyone involved. And I'm ready for your honest answer. Tell me the truth, Mr. Lowe, why did you come to Harry Miller's funeral yesterday? I know it wasn't just out of curiosity."

"But it was, Detective! As I told you, I hadn't seen Harry in ten years. When I heard he was murdered, my curiosity brought me here to see what it was all about. And then today, someone tried to kill me! Why me, Detective? That's what I don't understand! I knew nothing of Harry's financial difficulties with his investment fund. Nothing at all! So why in the world would anyone want to kill me?"

Brantley stared at me for a moment and then leaned over so we were almost face-to-face. Ignoring my question, he said, "Your answer doesn't hold water, Lowe. I know for a fact that you were seen in town several weeks before Miller's death. It's better that you tell me what you were doing here, as I'm going to find out one way or another."

I sat there stunned! I looked at Maude, hoping for help…any kind of help. But all I got was a frown and raised eyebrows. I could feel Brantley's breath on me as he stood there, waiting for my reply. I began to feel clammy all over, not knowing whether to stick with my story or tell the truth. Avoiding Brantley's suspicious stare, I answered as innocently as possible, "Look, Detective, I took a ride up here to get out of New York and into the countryside. I had no idea about Harry's problems or even knew that Mrs. Williamson lived here. It was just a pleasure ride, nothing more!"

By the look on Brantley's face, it was clear he wasn't buying it. Straightening up, he said, "Don't lie to me, Mr. Lowe, I wasn't born yesterday. I expect the truth from you tomorrow or else!" He then motioned to Brock they were leaving. Stopping at the door to the living room, Brantley turned back. "In the meantime, I'm going to find out who took a shot at you and why. You see, Mr. Lowe, even in a small town like ours, we have the ability to arrest shooters and murderers, then send them to prison for a hell of a long time. I will plan on seeing you both tomorrow morning, 10 o'clock sharp. Feel better, Mr. Lowe. Good night, Mrs. Williamson."

Maude and I stayed out on the deck for a while longer, watching the bright red sun sink below the horizon. But I felt anything but calm as I replayed in my mind what Brantley had said, positive he was going to do everything possible to make me his sacrificial lamb. At one point, I looked over at Maude, but from her wary expression, I could sense that she was backing away from me. So, between the pain in my back and my growing paranoia, I felt trapped, and at a loss as to what to do about any of it.

****

I was up early the next morning, having spent a restless night in Maude's spare bedroom. Feeling groggy from lack of sleep and the probably unwise mix of drinks and painkillers the night before, I went out to the deck, hoping to clear my head. As I waited for the sun to peek through the thick ocean mist, I kept coming back to the question that had kept me up all night: *Who would want to murder me?*

Maybe I could find an answer, or least a clue, by going over the possible suspects, but where to start? How about with Fred Simmons? He's made it crystal clear he's wanted to get even with me for the last fifteen years. And now I've gone, adding insult to injury by humiliating him in front of Lucy Grimes and even Brantley. But humiliation is one thing; attempted murder is a hell of a lot different! For some reason, I just can't picture Simmons as the type to risk murder, unless maybe he thought I knew something or saw something that could pin Harry's murder on him? Would that be reason enough to take a shot at me? Perhaps, but I haven't a clue as to what that reason could be!

The mist began to fade away as the sun broke through here and there, casting a sparkling yellow and white reflection across the water. As I admired the view, I thought back to how Charlie Reynolds had come rushing into Maude's house that beautiful morning so outraged and defensive. Could it be him? Maybe he was looking for a way to kill two birds with one stone: get rid of someone he obviously dislikes...me...and then somehow blame Maude. Nah, there's no way Charlie Reynolds could drive a car like that while shooting at me at the same time. Well, I guess I'm back to Maude. Maybe she began a relationship with Harry again, and then he dumped her when he thought it would be a hell of a lot easier to snare Lucy's five million. But how do I fit in? Murdering me wouldn't solve her jealousy problem. She could have figured out a way to make me the fall guy for her murdering Harry, but that seems too clever by half. Who else? How about Tim Swenson? Underneath that Florida tan and those out-sized shoulders and bull neck was a real hothead. And he definitely has a strong motive...getting back the money he thinks I owe him. Maybe shooting at me was his way of warning me. But any of his random shots could have killed me, and then he'd never see his money. And then there's always Lucy Grimes. After all, she was the one who told Brantley I'd been in town two weeks before Harry was killed. Did she think I came up here to plan the murder of the man she desperately loved? Possibly, but it was hard to imagine her behind the wheel and lowering the window to fire four shots at me. I guess she could have hired someone else to do the shooting. Or had Simmons do it. *My God, I'm really getting paranoid!*

I gazed up at the sun as it moved higher in the sky, flooding the ocean with a blinding reflection that was mesmerizing. After a few minutes, I reluctantly came back to my list of suspects. Ellen Houser...what could her motive be? Well, she wanted her three million back and felt jilted by Harry. But wouldn't Harry have been the one she would have murdered if she had the chance? And it was hard to picture her firing a gun at me during a car chase.

I was at a dead-end and knew it, but the question still gnawed at me. Suddenly an idea popped into my head. Suppose it was someone seated near me in the church who'd been taken in by Harry's scheme? They could have convinced themselves I was Harry's silent partner and decided to wreak their revenge on me instead. As a motive, it seemed pretty far-fetched, but I wasn't ready to rule it out. After all, there were a lot of people in that church who had lost millions. Frank Ellis had moved to the other side of the church because he thought I'd been working with Harry and didn't want anything to do with me. Yet how could anyone believe I was Harry's silent partner when he'd destroyed my life too? And why in the world would I show up at his funeral, sit among people who could potentially hate me, and give a lecture about a centuries-old market crash to explain their inherent greed and fear if I had been involved in Harry's scheme? It made no sense at all! Wait...what if someone thought I'd been mocking them for being stupid enough to invest their life savings in Harry's fund in the first place? Could that have inspired enough anger and resentment to seek revenge, to want to murder me?

Just then, Maude came out on the deck carrying two cups of coffee. She handed me one, then sat down and stared out at the ocean for a few minutes. When she finally turned to look at me, she appeared quite frightened. Practically stammering, she said, "I'm scared, Davis. Really scared that whoever shot at you is not going to stop until they kill you. And since you're staying with me, they could easily believe we're working together. I know it sounds crazy, but I don't feel safe." She took a sip of her coffee, her hands shaking. "All night, I wondered if you were being honest with me. Please tell me the truth. Do you know why someone tried to kill you?" When I didn't answer right away, her eyes widened in fear. "I...I can't be involved in this. I didn't murder Harry! And I don't know who did. I served my time for shooting him once, Davis, I can't go back there again!"

"Maude, believe me...I didn't murder Harry either! And I feel terrible that I haven't been entirely truthful with you. Yes, I did come up here two weeks ago. I came because I was curious to see the kind of life Harry was living. I wanted to know if he was still on top of the world while I was trapped in a dead-end job. I hoped his fund was failing; that would have pleased me very much. But I swear I didn't kill him! Would I have loved the chance to beat the hell out of him for what he did to me? Yes! But I never wanted him to die for it."

Maude nodded sympathetically. "Davis, when I shot Harry, I felt the same way you do, so I understand completely. Sitting alone in my prison cell, I often wondered why I hadn't been able to control myself that night. But I eventually realized it was because I just hated him too much. Still, I honestly believe with all my heart, I never wanted to kill him. All I was hoping to do was take that damn ego of his down five or ten pegs. But never, ever kill him!"

"I believe you, Maude. What I don't understand is why someone would want to kill me. I've been sitting out here since sunrise, trying to figure it out. What would they gain...what sort of satisfaction would there be in murdering me? I had absolutely nothing at all to do with Harry or his fraudulent fund." Maude didn't answer. Instead, we sat silently, watching the sun climb higher in the sky as the dark ocean water turned a brighter, lighter blue. Finishing my coffee, I looked at my watch, then turned to her. With a slight smirk, I said, "We better go. We can't keep the good Detective waiting."

Chapter Sixteen

Maude drove slowly and silently down Beach Drive towards town. She frequently glanced out the window at the ocean, presumably finding in its vast beauty a way to calm her nerves ahead of the morning's interrogation. Following her cue, I tried to control my growing anxiety by watching the sun's vibrant reflection move across the still water, but truthfully, it didn't make me feel any better.

Entering town, we made our way towards the police station. I looked over at Maude and wondered if we'd be facing another barrage of erroneous accusations that would end in our both being arrested. The thought gave me a sense of foreboding that this meeting had all the earmarks of being led into a snake pit.

With great trepidation, we entered the police station and met Sergeant Brock, who greeted us with a quick nod and a frigid, *Good morning.* We followed him into the conference room where Charlie Reynolds and Fred Simmons were already seated. As we took our seats, Maude leaned over to whisper a little nervously, "Davis, they look ready to murder both of us right now."

I looked across the table to see the two of them glaring at me. "You're right," I whispered back. As I continued to watch them, I began to wonder if behind that anger, they had some sort of plan to pin Harry's murder on me. *God, I am getting paranoid!* I whispered to Maude, "Get ready for some fireworks from them. They look out to get me…and maybe you, too!"

Before she could respond, Brantley entered the room, the door slamming shut behind him. Without looking at any of us, he strode quickly to his seat at the head of the table, took out a notebook from his pocket, opened it, thumbed to a specific page, then nodded to Brock to start the tape recorder. He gave us all a quick once over, then looked back at me with a suspicious stare that made me squirm. "Well, Mr. Lowe," he said icily. "I can tell you that our investigation into who shot at you last night is proceeding. We've found some initial evidence, but we still have a long way to go." Forget the way he said it; I was so shocked to hear he was actually doing something positive for me that I didn't care whether he elaborated or not. All I could think was...*thank God he's doing something!* Brantley then turned and gave Maude a withering stare. Shaking his head, he said, "Mrs. Williamson, your checking account shows you wrote a check for four hundred thousand dollars to Mr. Miller on the Tuesday before he was murdered. You lied to me, Mrs. Williamson. Why did you lie to me?"

"I didn't lie to you! I never wrote a check for four hundred thousand dollars, Detective. Honestly, I didn't! I don't keep that much money in my checking account. Tell me...when was the money deposited into my account?"

Brantley glanced down at his notes. "The deposit was made the same day. The check was made out to Harry Miller, and was signed by you."

"No, it's just not true, Detective. I never deposited that much money into my account, and I never wrote a check to him. I would never give Harry Miller a dime!"

It was clear that Maude was not backing down. Brantley hesitated, seemingly not sure what to say or do next. Then his face flushed as he pressed his lips tightly together, signaling, I thought, his readiness to charge her again with Harry's murder. *Well...what choice do I have but to help her?* Treading lightly, I said, "Detective, if you don't mind my asking, how was the deposit made into Maude's account? Was it by check or wire transfer?"

"By wire transfer!" he shot back furiously.

"Ah...can you tell me from what bank and by whom?" I asked

quietly, knowing I had just raised his anger level three or four notches.

He started to sputter a response, then stopped abruptly. It was clear he wasn't sure of his answer, and clear he didn't want to make another mistake. He glanced at Brock for help, but he just shrugged his shoulders, not knowing the answer, then looked away, refusing to meet Brantley's enraged glare.

Taking advantage of Brantley's embarrassment, I tried to ask as tactfully as I could, "Isn't it possible, Detective, that someone knew Maude's investment account number and was able to wire the money into her checking account? Then they went to the bank that Tuesday, and being well acquainted with the teller or bank manager, asked for several blank bank checks? It probably wasn't too difficult to forge her signature on the bank check, and I assume, deposit it in Harry's account. Ah…it was deposited in Harry's account, wasn't it, Detective?" Before he could answer, I exclaimed, "Maybe Harry did it! After all, we know he had one hell of an incentive since he desperately needed the four hundred thousand dollars to get the five million to keep his fund going. It makes sense, wouldn't you agree, Detective?"

Brantley didn't answer. Instead, with growing fury, he walked around the table to come face to face with me. "Lowe," he sneered, "who the hell do you think you are making up a story like that? First of all, how would anyone get Mrs. Williamson's account number?"

I struggled not to be intimidated by his withering glare, but still ended up almost stuttering my reply. "Well, I don't know exactly how, in this case, Detective, but it's definitely possible! Remember, I work in a bank!"

"Used to work in a bank, Mr. Lowe, used to work!" Brantley gloated. "I believe that is a more accurate statement of your current employment status. And as to your theory, well, frankly, I don't believe a word of it!" He then stepped back, seeming to reconsider what I had said. After a moment, he grudgingly shrugged his shoulders, recognizing I might have a point. "But we will find out, Mr. Lowe."

Surprised, I just stared at him, wondering how in the hell he became a cop. But my thoughts quickly turned to something far more critical: *How in the world do I handle his ongoing hostility towards me?* I can't keep sticking my foot in my mouth every time he's about to arrest Maude. Next time, I'm certain he's going to slap the cuffs on me too.

Shaking his head angrily, Brantley walked back to his seat, still clearly agitated at my interference. He flipped over a couple of pages in his notebook before finding what he was looking for. He read the information slowly to himself, I assume buying time to regain his composure, then looked up and turned to face Simmons. "Mr. Simmons, we found that your weapon was fired recently. Tell me where and why?"

"I told you yesterday, Detective, I used it for target practice. It's a hobby of mine."

"Exactly when was the last time you were at the range, Mr. Simmons?"

"I don't remember offhand, Detective. Ah…maybe a couple of weeks ago…maybe a month. You can check with the gun club where I'm a member."

"You know, Mr. Simmons, the bullet that killed Harry Miller was fired from a Colt .22, just like yours. Whether it came from your gun or not, we're still determining."

"Look, Detective, I swear I didn't murder Harry Miller. Oh, we had our differences years ago, but…but I was never at the beach that night. And I've never used my pistol for anything but target practice. Believe me, that's the truth!"

Brantley just shook his head. "Well, Mr. Simmons, all I can say is it's lucky for you that right now, there are a lot of Colt .22 pistols out there using the same ammunition that you use."

Furious at being under suspicion, a red-faced Simmons looked over at Maude and me, then stood up and jabbed his finger in our direction, shouting, "Detective, why don't you ask those two about being on the beach after the dinner last Saturday night?"

Startled by his accusation, Brantley fired back. "Mr. Lowe claims he wasn't here and Mrs. Williamson swears she left the dinner early. In any case, how would they know Mr. Miller was going to the beach after the dinner? Was it to meet you, Mr. Simmons?"

Caught off guard by the question, Simmons stared fearfully at Brantley, then across the table at me. In a voice bristling with anger, he said, "Who says Lowe wasn't in town last Saturday night? Why couldn't he have met Miller down at the beach?"

"Who told you that Mr. Lowe was here before yesterday, Mr. Simmons?" snapped Brantley.

"Well, it has been talked about around town."

"Tell me who said it, Mr. Simmons."

"Ah…I don't remember."

"Was it Lucy Grimes, Mr. Simmons? Remember, this is a murder case! We need to know about every possible witness."

As Simmons hemmed and hawed, Charlie Reynolds spoke up. "Why don't you ask Lowe himself, Detective? That curiosity of his could have brought him up here before last Saturday night. And say…it was easy to learn about the dinner honoring Harry: every store in town advertised it in their window. Knowing what a curious guy he is, it was a perfect time to be here, especially for someone who hated Harry as much as he did."

"How do you know that?" Brantley shot back.

"Well, didn't Simmons here say that Lowe talked about revenge, I think he called it "permanent revenge," when they met at a bar years ago the day Harry fired him? Now he's having an affair with the lady across the table who has already shot Harry once before. It's obvious they both hated Harry and wanted to see him dead. And the beach was a perfect spot to murder him!"

"Again, Mr. Reynolds, how do you know all that?"

"Wasn't he murdered there, Detective?"

"That's a theory."

"Well...someone must have heard the shot!"

"We're investigating that too, Mr. Reynolds."

Brantley moved slowly around the table to where Reynolds was sitting. Leaning over to face him, he asked, "Speaking of guns, Mr. Reynolds, Sergeant Brock didn't find your pistol, but he did find your holster. So, where's the gun?"

"I told you, Detective, I lost it years ago. But I was the one who found the holster and gave it to the Sergeant."

"I thought you told me yesterday that you owned a .38?"

"That was the gun I lost when I moved to town years ago."

"Well...if you owned a .38, your holster is too small to hold it. A Colt .22 would fit much better. Do you own another gun, Mr. Reynolds?"

"I don't, Detective."

Brantley stood up and stared off into space to consider the answer. Then he leaned back over again and looked Reynolds straight in the eye. "If you lost your .38, why did you bother keeping that holster in your house?"

"Why? I have no idea why, Detective. But say, why don't you ask Maude what caliber pistol she shot Harry with the first time. I remember reading it was a Colt .22. Maybe she still has that gun."

Brantley stood back up, looking surprised. He turned to Maude and demanded, "Is that true, Mrs. Williamson? You shot Mr. Miller with a Colt .22?"

"Yes...yes, I did," she answered nervously.

"Do you still have it?"

"I told you before, Detective, I'm not allowed to own a gun."

"That doesn't mean she doesn't have one!" Reynolds practically shouted.

Ignoring him, Maude answered, "Detective, I'm telling you, I don't have a gun."

"She's lying, Detective, and you know it."

"I'll be the judge of that, Mr. Reynolds," Brantley snapped. He walked back to his chair, shaking his head, apparently flummoxed by what he'd just heard. The room fell silent as we all watched him decide what to do next. After a few minutes, he stood up and slowly walked around the table to where I was sitting. Seemed my paranoia about being his whipping boy was not so far-fetched after all. Looking down at me, he said, "Mr. Lowe, we know you were here in town at least once prior to the dinner. Were you also here last Saturday night? And don't you lie to me, Mr. Lowe. If I find out that you were, I'll book you for murder so fast your head will spin!"

His question wasn't new, but his threat came as a shock. How could he accuse me without a specific witness or any circumstantial evidence to back up his allegation? *My God, he's really desperate!* But still, why pick on me? Why not Simmons or Reynolds? They have just as much of a motive to murder Harry as he claims I have. Same with Tim Swenson, Ellen Houser, Lucy Grimes, or even Maude. So why only me? Pissed as I was, I tried to answer as calmly as possible. "No, Detective. I wasn't here last Saturday night. I was in New York as I told you before."

Shaking his head, Brantley replied, "Mr. Lowe, I don't believe you. And the only reason I'm not going to book you right now is to first check on whether you own a gun. Oh…I know you said you don't, but I'm not satisfied with your answer."

"Detective, I told you the truth, I don't have one!"

"I don't buy it, Mr. Lowe. We're going to get a warrant to search your apartment. Sergeant, get the Judge to sign a warrant."

"He's out, and won't be back for a couple of days," Brock answered nervously.

Brantley didn't look happy. "Damn it, he hasn't gone fishing again, has he?"

The two of them moved to the side of the room to figure out what to do, while I tried to keep from exploding at Brantley's insinuation and avoid saying anything that would give him a reason to slap those cuffs on me. That's when I noticed two faces grinning at me from across the table and realized it was high time to shift the focus elsewhere. "Detective, don't you think those two over there have provided you with more than enough evidence to be key suspects? Both of them have strong motives for revenge...and have the right to carry a gun. Why not investigate one of them?"

Before Brantley could reply, Simmons and Reynolds jumped up from their seats and raced around opposite ends of the table, apparently determined to give me one hell of a beating...whether in police headquarters or not!

I got up too fast and felt a sharp pain from pulling on the stitches in my back. Pushing my chair away, I readied myself as best I could for their attack. But suddenly Brock, closely followed by Brantley, came running to my defense. Grabbing both men, they pushed them back around the table and down into their chairs as Brantley bellowed, "Next time either of you does something stupid like that, I'll slap the cuffs on both of you!"

I looked over at Maude, who nodded back with a knowing smile, believing Brantley would now have to focus as much attention on the two of them as us. Well, that turned out to be wishful thinking when he turned and, eyeing us threateningly, said, "Don't think either of you is home free. Do you get my gist, Mr. Lowe? Mrs. Williamson?" Then seemingly overwhelmed by every aspect of the case, he returned to his chair, where he leafed through some pages in his notebook. *He's definitely confused*, I concluded. Sounding defeated, Brantley said, "Well...we've got more testing and checking to do before we have you all back in here again. Everybody should remain in town, including you, Mr. Lowe. It will take us a day or two to complete our work." He paused, then looked directly at me and added, "Let me emphasize to all of you again, if you value your freedom, don't leave town!"

Chapter Seventeen

Maude and I walked quickly out of the police station and down the stairs, stopping only to collectively breathe a sigh of relief. "Let's get out of here!" she cried out. "I can't take any more of this drama and all these accusations. I need some fresh air!"

I nodded my head in agreement. Looking up at the clear blue sky, I realized it had turned out to be a magnificent day. "Say, Maude, I have an idea. Why don't we buy some lunch, pick up a cold bottle of wine, and head to some secluded beach where no one can bother us. I'd like to feel the soft, warm sand under my feet and take a refreshing walk in the ocean. It's guaranteed to work wonders!"

Maude smiled, nodding enthusiastically. As we hurried to her car, I heard the sound of running footsteps. I spun around to see Simmons and Reynolds charging straight at us. My first thought was, *They couldn't be serious about attacking me here in the police parking lot,* quickly followed by my desperately wondering, *How the hell do I take on the two of them with these stitches in my back?*

Simmons stopped just a couple of feet away from me, his flushed face surpassing his red hair. It reminded me of how he looked just before he punched out Harry that night at Harry's at Hanover Square. "You dirty bastard," he shouted at me. "You're not getting away with accusing me of Harry's murder! This time, I'm going to teach you a lesson you're never going to forget!" With that, he cocked his arm back, intending to throw one punch to flatten me. Lunging forward with his easily telegraphed swing, he again proved why he should stick to school teaching, as I simply stepped back, causing him to miss badly. The force of his swing threw him off balance, enabling me to throw a hard counterpunch. It landed on his left cheek with a resounding thud, dropping him to the ground, disoriented and dizzy. I let out a loud groan as pain radiated throughout my back.

When Reynolds saw how hard I hit Simmons, he stopped in his tracks. He must have realized that fighting a much younger man would be quite detrimental to his health. Instead, he did the next best thing and launched into a litany of curse words covering subjects and areas that I'd never heard before. As he rambled on, I couldn't help but give him the sort of smile you give when you know that your opponent is afraid to challenge you to a fight. Ignoring me, he continued his tirade until Maude finally screamed at him, "Charlie, why don't you just shut the hell up!"

He immediately stopped and stepped back. He glanced at me to see if I was going to hit him, then bent down to help Simmons up. But a groggy Simmons wasn't quite ready to get on to his feet. Seeing the state Simmons was in, Reynolds turned to me and snarled, "I'm going to get you, Lowe, if it's the last thing I do. You're not going to pin Harry's murder on me...or Simmons here!"

"Look, Reynolds, I'm not trying to pin Harry's murder on either of you. But I'll be damned if the two of you try to railroad me, or Maude, into prison. So stop attacking us!"

"I know you murdered Harry. I'm convinced of that, and I'll prove it too! If Simmons here wants to work with me, we'll both see you behind bars!"

I just shook my head at his phony indictment, knowing a case could easily be made against either of them. As I started to reply, Maude grabbed my sleeve, pointing to Sergeant Brock hurrying towards us.

"Mrs. Williamson," he shouted as he came closer. "I'd like to come out to your house this afternoon to look for that old pistol of yours. I'd rather not get a search warrant...say...what's going on here? Why is Mr. Simmons on the ground?

"He wanted to prove a point, Sergeant," Maude replied casually.

"And there's no need for a search warrant. I'm happy to let you search my house. I have nothing to hide."

"I'll be there at about 3 o'clock then, Mrs. Williamson."

Chapter Eighteen

We stopped in town at the deli and liquor store, then drove out to Beach Drive. A mile or two down the road, we turned off just past an old mailbox and onto a potholed lane that stretched about half a mile, ending in a small parking area. Maude took a blanket out of the trunk, and I carried the food and wine. We walked down a path that cut through two tall dunes covered with dune grass and opened onto a small but beautiful beach. I was immediately struck by the soft, fine sand, and the spectacular, glittering reflection of the sun across the ocean. After admiring the view for a few minutes, we started to walk towards the water when Maude suddenly stopped. Gasping, she turned away to compose herself. I looked over to see what had upset her so. There, on the right side of the beach near the water, was a plot of sand surrounded by yellow tape printed with the words, *Crime Scene Do Not Cross.*

"So this where Harry was killed," I muttered, quite taken aback at having stumbled onto the murder scene.

Maude didn't respond but kept looking at the closed-off area with a frozen stare. Her face had turned a chalky white, and she looked as if she was about to faint. I quickly put my hand under her elbow to help steady her. Ignoring me, she continued staring at the yellow taped area. I was puzzled by her reaction, as it seemed at odds with what she had told me earlier about hating Harry and wanting to see him suffer. Was she still in love with him, I wondered, or simply surprised at seeing where he had died? I couldn't figure out which, and I didn't want to stand around trying. I thought I'd break the spell by putting my arm around her waist and walking over to the other side of the beach. But she refused to budge, obviously still hypnotized by the yellow tape and Harry's death there. I let her stand there for another minute, and then forcefully pulled her away, which earned me one long, nasty look.

We walked down to the water's edge, where I spread the blanket out and sat down to take my shoes and socks off. I waited for her to join me, but she just stood there, gazing across the beach. I thought, *The hell with waiting* and rolled my pants up above my knees and walked towards the inviting water. As I stepped in, I turned back to shout, "Relax, Maude. You're the one who told me he's dead and you're alive. Remember?"

That seemed to break the spell. She nodded slowly and gave me a weak smile. "I did say that, didn't I. Well, Davis, I guess it was easier for me to vent my anger when I hadn't seen the spot where Harry was killed."

I shook my head and continued into the water. It was just what I needed. I walked the length of the beach and back in the shallow water, hating to get out. Making my way back to the blanket, I started to wonder why Harry had been here that night. As I sat down, I asked, "Maude, why do you think Harry came down to this beach at that hour of the night instead of celebrating at some bar or restaurant in town? Was he meeting someone? Was it a payoff? Or maybe to tell someone off?"

"Who knows?" she replied, shrugging her shoulders and turning to gaze at the yellow tape again with a sad, distant look on her face.

I was left wondering if, despite all her denials, there'd still been something between her and Harry before he was killed. But what had it been? And how far did it go? Believing the answers could be important, I decided to try asking her, hoping not to sound like Brantley. "I know I'm guessing here, Maude, but I'd say Harry was quite short of cash to cover all his personal and business debts, and I'm pretty sure he knew he was about to face criminal charges for his Ponzi scheme. So I have to believe he was getting ready to leave town before the roof caved in on him. That's why I've got to ask…why didn't he use his irresistible charm on someone who once loved him dearly, and who was in a position to write a check for four hundred thousand that would enable him to get his hands on Lucy Grimes' five million? Maude, isn't it possible you met Harry down here after the dinner?"

Maude appeared startled by the question. She stared at me for a moment or two, trying to make up her mind whether or not to answer me. She finally replied, "Yes, Davis, you're right. He did ask me at the dinner to meet him down here for old times' sake. I knew what his intentions were. They were always the same. He'd start by seducing me, then pledge his undying love, and after I had succumbed to it all, ask me for money." She gave me a knowing glance. "I knew how his mind worked, Davis. But this time, I slapped his face, refusing his offer. And he got mad as hell and swore he'd get even with me."

"Oh, come on, Maude! Brantley told us he had a witness who said you kissed Harry at the dinner. You didn't slap his face, now did you? Maude suddenly looked fearful, realizing she had walked into a trap. It was obvious she didn't know what to say. "Damn it, Maude…I want the truth!"

She stood there hemming and hawing until finally she sighed and said, "All right…I'll tell you. Harry showed up at my house the Tuesday morning before Saturday's dinner. He was beside himself; no trace of the arrogant, overbearing man I'd known. He told me how his dream of building a major investment fund would be destroyed forever if I didn't help him right then and there. I couldn't believe he thought that I, of all people, would help him. But what really shocked me was how nervous and frightened he was…and for good reason! People in town were after him, demanding their money back. And Harry desperately needed money to keep his fund afloat."

A strange sort of smile appeared on Maude's face. "This was the moment I had waited for all these years, Davis. And I wasn't going to make it easy for him. When he saw I wasn't moved by his plea, he started into a long-winded apology for the way he had treated me, ending with him begging me to start over again with him. Even after I told him he was crazy, thinking I'd go back to him, he kept on pleading with me, insisting that he still loved me, and promising over and over again he'd be there for me every day as I'd always wanted. He even got down on his knees and begged me. Can you imagine, Davis, that kneeling before me was Mr. Arrogance himself, begging until he actually began to cry? I shouted at him to get off his knees. Something must have snapped because when he stood up, he started to scream that he wouldn't leave until I gave him the money. Like that, he'd gone from begging me to threatening me. I tried to throw him out, but he refused to go. He was like a wild man! I told him I'd call the police, but he didn't seem to care. Davis, I was terrified he was going to hurt me, and just wanted him out of my house and my life. So, I offered him a deal; I'd give him the money if he swore to leave me alone, leave town, and never return. And he agreed. As he was walking out the door, he gave me a winning smile as though he'd won the battle. I called my broker that afternoon to wire the money to my account."

"How much did he ask for?"

Maude paused before answering nervously, "He demanded four hundred thousand with the promise to be gone after the dinner honoring him Saturday night."

I jumped up from the blanket, not believing what I'd just heard. "He asked you for what? You gave him four hundred thousand?"

"Yes."

"But you told Brantley that you didn't give him the money! So it's true, Maude. You lied again."

"I had to give it to him, Davis! He threatened me!"

"You gave him the cash he desperately needed to get Lucy Grimes' five million," I repeated, still in shock at her confession. As I grappled with the fact that Maude had lied to me again, I suddenly thought about what Brantley would do to the two of us if he found out. I started panicking, realizing how much I was caught up in her lies. *God, I'll never get out of this!*

"Why? Why, Maude?" I shouted at her. "Why did you lie to me and to Brantley about the money?"

"Because I was afraid! All I could think of was that prison."

"You gave Harry the money, enabling him to skip town and leave his investors in the lurch. And that's the reason why you're so upset at seeing the yellow tape? Just tell me, how does that work, Maude?"

She fumbled for an answer, finally replying in a low, tremulous voice, "It's because, well, it's because I once loved him!"

I stared at her in disbelief. *My God...he destroyed her life, and she's still talking about love!*

"So you did kiss him at the dinner!"

"Yes...yes, I did! I don't know why, Davis. And I know that sounds ridiculous. But every time I saw him, he reminded me so much of *my* Al, who I loved so dearly. I know, I know...you don't have to tell me how crazy I am, but Harry was everything I wanted in my life except without his arrogance and self-centered soul. I just couldn't help myself."

I stood there feeling like the wind had been knocked out of me, incredulous at what she had done. "So you let me not only make a damn fool of myself by believing in you, but you made me...us...Brantley's prime suspects?"

"I'm sorry, Davis, I truly am. But all I could think about was going back to that goddamn prison."

"Now, there's a good chance we'll both end up there!" I answered, enraged at her duplicity.

"No, I'm never, ever going back there!" she practically screamed at me.

I closed my eyes for a moment, trying to calm myself. "Did you murder Harry? Tell me the truth, Maude. Did you?"

"No! I swear I didn't murder him!"

Her eyes, her expression, pleaded for me to believe her, but I was too pissed off to accept her answer at face value. She clearly was too good a liar. *So good, that I'm now deeply embedded in her lies.* How in hell am I going to get out of this? I looked out at the becalmed ocean, thinking how boxed in I was. If I tell Brantley that Maude gave Harry the four hundred thousand, he'll probably leap to the conclusion that I was breaking up our partnership after we murdered him, and lock us both up on the spot. And even if I told him nothing right now, it's not going to be long before he learns the money came from her bank account at her request. What the hell was I going to do? A desperate, harebrained idea popped into my head: *Find Harry's murderer*! But me, a detective? Out of the question…except really, what other choice did I have?

I sat back down and started thinking about who could have met Harry at the beach that night. I quickly realized the list was long, and everyone on it had a strong motive to confront and murder him: Fred Simmons, jealous over Harry stealing away his one and only love; Lucy Grimes, possibly learning that Harry was leaving town without marrying her; Charlie Reynolds, wanting one last chance to get even with him; Tim Swenson, looking to get his million and a half back; Ellen Houser, angry over him taking her money and then dumping her; and then there's Maude, who I cannot leave out, still loving him no matter what she told me, and not wanting him to end up in someone else's arms. *My God, where do I start?*

Just then, Maude reached over and took my hand, asking most innocently, "Davis, how do we get out of this mess?"

I could feel my face flush as I pulled my hand away. Gritting my teeth, I hissed at her, "How the hell do I know! You got me into this mess with your lies! You figure it out!"

Startled by my anger, she began to cry. "Don't you understand? I had no choice. Brantley was going to arrest me. And I swore I'd never, ever go back to prison. Do you hear me! Never!" With tears running down her cheeks, she got up and walked down to the water. She stood there for a while, very still, gazing out at the calm, vast ocean. When she finally walked back, she was no longer crying. She stood at the edge of the blanket and gave me a cold, hard look. The same one I saw when visiting her in prison. But frankly, she could stare all she wanted; I wasn't going to be intimidated after she had jeopardized my life and my future. Unable to hold back my anger anymore, I shouted, "How the hell could you have done this to me, Maude?"

But that steely stare didn't waver as she silently shook her head, indicating she wasn't going to answer me. We faced each other for quite a while just staring, neither of us talking until finally, she looked away. "I'll ask Lucy if she gave Harry the five million. And by the way, Davis, let me tell you this, I needed your help, and I thank you for helping me."

"I can't even say you're welcome, Maude. You've put me front and center as a prime suspect for a murder that I had absolutely no part in." Then I added sadly, "I just can't trust you anymore, Maude."

"You have no choice now, do you, Davis?" she replied coldly. "We've got to stick together and concentrate on getting out of this mess before Brantley arrests us. Or both of us will end up in prison for the rest of our lives!"

"Tell me about it!" I shot back. Yet despite my anger, I knew she was right. Sticking together was going to be tough, though. Then again, what choice did I have? Still, it took some time for me to cool down enough to grudgingly accept her offer. "Okay, Maude, but no more lies. It won't work unless I can trust you."

She nodded her head in agreement. "No more lies, Davis, that's a promise,"

"Okay. Now for the hard part, Maude. We've got to find out who met Harry down here that night."

"You got any ideas, Davis?"

"Ah...no, not yet."

"So we're off to a lousy start, aren't we?"

Seeing that this wasn't getting us anywhere, I decided to offer some possibilities, hoping to get us thinking in the right direction. "Let's start with Harry using your four hundred thousand to get Lucy's five million."

"Sure, why not," she replied sarcastically.

"Well, knowing Harry, after getting Lucy's five million, he probably was back to his usual arrogant self. I wouldn't put it past him to have asked Lucy to meet him down here to cancel their wedding...and to say goodbye. Naturally, she'd agree to come without knowing why in advance."

"So then how could she have planned to shoot him?"

"Well...she couldn't have, could she. But maybe after Harry gave her the bad news, she cried on Simmons' shoulder, and he, in turn, shot Harry for her and to get even himself."

"But when would she have told Simmons?" Maude interjected.

"Good question. Maybe instead, he followed her down here and heard Harry tell her. A possibility, don't you think?" She rolled her eyes in disbelief. I had to agree...my logic was all desperate pie in the sky. Feeling a little defeated, I hesitated in posing my supposition about Charlie Reynolds, but figured, what the hell. "We know Charlie had a deep-seated grudge against Harry for destroying his business and life dreams. Suppose he got wind that Harry was planning to back out of the deal he and Charlie were working on and skip town, leaving Charlie holding the bag and his last great opportunity to make a lot of money destroyed. When Harry tells Charlie to meet him down at the beach, Charlie decides to kill two birds with one stone. Murder Harry, and blame you. Why not? That revenge would be a sweet one!"

Maude appeared frightened by that scenario, I guess fearing it could come true. Her eyes quickly filled with tears as she sputtered, "Davis, I'm so sorry I got you involved in this. Harry was such a bastard, but I couldn't help myself...and he knew it!"

I didn't answer her. I was too busy visualizing Brantley slapping the cuffs on us. We were back to square one with no leads and no idea of what to do. I tried to calm myself by gazing out at the still ocean. When I turned back, I forced a weak smile in a vain attempt to signal to her that somehow everything would be all right. She seemed surprised, but the frown that followed indicated she didn't believe me. Discouraged, I was at a loss as to what to do next. I looked out at the ocean again, and then by chance over at the yellow tape. Something about it sparked my curiosity, so I decided to take a closer look.

****

The tape was laid out in almost a T-shape, I guess to account for Harry's body leaving two impressions in the sand; the first from where he fell from the killer's bullet, and the second from where he was dragged down to the water. I stepped closer to the tape, but only a mishmash of indistinct footprints was visible around where he was shot, presumably made when the police were investigating, and probably destroying any evidence of the murderer's footprints.

I walked around to the other side to see if I had missed anything, but it looked the same. I decided to follow the deep concave shape that Harry's body had left in the sand as he was hauled down the twenty or so feet into the water.

"Did you find anything, Davis?" Maude questioned timidly, approaching from the other side of the tape.

"No, but what's strange is there are no footprints from when he was dragged down to the water. They must have been erased by his weight. I'd say that whoever did it had to be pretty strong to pull Harry down so far. Although with the tide going out, the sand would have been fairly hard, so dragging him out into the water might have been easier. But then again…maybe he had to be dragged further out to catch the outgoing tide so his body would drift out to sea. And if the ocean had kicked up that night, it would have been a hell of a lot harder to haul him far enough out. Damn it, if we only had the murderer's footprints, that could have been a really good lead!"

"Who do you suppose did it, Davis?"

"Seems obvious, doesn't it? A man."

"I guess that eliminates Lucy as the possible murderer."

"Lucy could still be a co-conspirator, Maude."

"You think Fred Simmons did it?"

"Possibly. Or Tim Swenson…he looks pretty strong to me. Even

Charlie Reynolds, at his age, could be strong enough to drag the body."

I stood there wondering who Harry had met down here and why, but the answer kept eluding me. Frustrated, I cried out, "God, if we only knew who met Harry down here, Maude, we'd be out of this mess!"

"What do we do now, Davis?"

"Beats me!"

I stood there conjuring up possible next steps until Maude suddenly shouted, "Oh my god! It's 2:45, Davis! We better get back to my house before Sergeant Brock arrives."

"Do you think Brock knows that it was your signature on the check Harry deposited?"

"God, I hope not!"

"If he does, you're in really deep trouble, Maude."

"What should I do?"

"Hold off running, and just pray that Brantley hasn't gotten clearance from Judge Bernstein to examine your bank account yet. Because knowing the way he thinks, if he finds out you lied to him about writing the four hundred-thousand-dollar check, he'll leap to the conclusion you've lied about not owning a gun."

"But I don't have a gun!"

"Are you sure?"

"Yes, I swear I'm telling you the truth…I don't have one."

Chapter Nineteen

Sergeant Brock was sitting in his police cruiser when we arrived at Maude's house. We both tensed up at the sight. Maude walked quickly up the stairs to open the front door while I walked over to him.

"Have you been waiting long, Sergeant?"

"No, Mr. Lowe. I got here a couple of minutes ago."

I breathed a sigh of relief that he wasn't about to arrest me. "Well... why don't you come on in, Sergeant."

Maude stood waiting at the door, her face pale as she handed me a note that had been stuck between the door and the frame, obviously bad news. But I didn't know how bad until I read it: *Lowe, I'll be back later this afternoon to pick up my money. You better have it ready, or you and your lady friend will face a lot of trouble.* I shook my head in disbelief, thinking now I had to deal with Swenson, on top of everything else.

Brock took one look at my distraught face and asked, "What's going on here? What's that note about?"

"One of Harry Miller's investors thinks I was his silent partner in running his fund. He's demanded I pay him his million-and-a-half-dollar investment back by this afternoon, or else."

"Or else what, Mr. Lowe?"

"Your guess is as good as mine, Sergeant."

"That's an awful lot of money, Mr. Lowe."

"It certainly is."

"Were you his silent partner, Mr. Lowe?"

"Of course not!" I replied indignantly, handing him the note to read. When he finished, he eyed me suspiciously and said, "I'll show it to Detective Brantley, and we'll follow up on it."

Somehow his words did little to relieve my anxiety. I looked at a frightened Maude, who, in turn, gave Brock a quick, nervous smile. "Please come in, Sergeant."

Brock spent the better part of an hour searching the house. Maude went everywhere with him, opening drawers, cabinets, closets, and her desk. Then he spent some time alone rechecking. Maude and I ended up standing in the middle of the living room, anxiously waiting his return. At some point, her nerves got the better of her, and she grabbed my hand and squeezed it hard as if anticipating his finding some incriminating evidence.

We stood there for what seemed an interminable amount of time before Brock reappeared. He didn't say a word to us but kept looking around to see if he had missed anything. Maude tightened her grip while we waited for him to say something, anything! He finally turned, and looking coldly at Maude, opened his hand to show us five .22 caliber bullets. "Where's the box these shells came in, Mrs. Williamson?"

"Those aren't mine!" Maude cried out. "Where did you find them?"

"Are you sure, Mrs. Williamson?"

"Yes, Sergeant, I'm positive! My gun and bullets were confiscated when I was arrested and used as State's evidence against me…I never got them back."

He eyed her for a long moment, clearly not believing her. Turning to me, he asked, "Is there a basement or attic in this house?"

I was about to answer that I didn't know when Maude replied sharply, "No, Sergeant! I've shown you the entire house. It's all on this floor." Before he could ask another question, she added, "As you can see, Sergeant, there's no pistol in the house. And you know very well that I can't buy another one."

Brock nodded doubtfully. He took a long and final look around the living room, then said, "I hope you're telling me the truth, Mrs. Williamson."

"I am Sergeant! You've checked everywhere, and there's no gun. I have no idea where those bullets came from…but they're not mine."

Brock studied Maude's face intently, then glanced over at me to see if I had any reaction. Seeing none, he shook his head in apparent disbelief and walked out the front door.

Maude and I stared at each other, fearful of what would happen next. I finally couldn't hold back my anger any longer and shouted at her, "Why in God's name do you have five bullets? Don't you realize your gun held six shells, and the missing one becomes circumstantial evidence against you? I'm begging you, for once would you tell me the truth…did you shoot Harry?"

"No, I did *not* shoot him! How many times do I have to tell you that, Davis?" She reached out to hold my hands, pleading with me to believe her.

I pushed her hands away in disgust. "How can I possibly believe you, Maude? You just lied to Brock. And you've been lying to me all along."

"Davis, please! I swear I forgot I had those bullets. It's been so long since I've thought about them. And I didn't tell Brock they were mine because what good would that have done? I didn't shoot Harry!" She started to cry. "Davis, please don't give up on me. We've got to work together, or we'll never get out of this mess."

"You promised me, Maude…you promised you wouldn't lie to me again."

"I haven't lied to you, I swear! You've got to believe me!" she sobbed, throwing her arms around me.

It seemed impossible to believe her after all her lies, but in the end, did it make a damn bit of difference? Even if I walked out the front door right now, Brantley was still going to come after me. I pushed her away and walked out onto the deck. I had a decision to make: *Do I stay, or do I go?* The quiet, peaceful-looking ocean proved no help in calming me down. If I go, she might try to blame me for the murder, which would make Brantley very happy. If I stay, then I'd have to trust her. But can I after all that she's done?

Maude followed me out on the deck, still in tears. As she walked towards me, looking very apologetic, I glared at her, thinking, *I can't believe she lied to me again. How can I possibly trust her?* I guess my scowling face really scared her. She stopped, not sure what to do next.

Sighing to myself, I said, "Maude, let's just have a drink and watch the sunset." I forced a weak smile.

She breathed a small sigh of relief, then ran inside to pour two scotches. A couple of minutes later, she carried out the drinks and handed me one with a warm smile. I stared at her as I sipped my scotch, wondering how long the two of us could run before Brantley caught us. *Could she run without me? More importantly, could I make it alone?* I quickly concluded neither of us would get very far...alone or together! I gulped down the remaining scotch, cognizant of the risk I'd be taking in trusting her. But what other choice did I have? I felt trapped. It was like being squeezed into a smaller and smaller box with no way out. Looking out again at the ocean, I thought, *There's got to be a way out of this box I was in without having to run and hide.* I looked over at Maude. She was studying my face intensely, waiting for my answer. I felt another flash of anger that, because of her, I was out of options. Still, all I could do was nod and give her a fleeting smile, cementing our partnership...hopefully not to a bitter end.

"Davis, you know I'm not going back to prison under any circumstances...right?"

"I know, Maude," I answered. "But understand the risk involved in staying here. Brantley would love nothing better than to indict you...and me."

"True," she replied softly. "Maybe we should run, Davis. How would you feel about that?"

I smiled gamely at her. "Sure, like Bonnie and Clyde. Although that didn't end very well for them, now did it?"

Chapter Twenty

We sat quietly, watching the pink sky brighten behind the deep red sun as it neared the horizon. A second scotch proved to be an overpowering tranquilizer for both of us. When Maude reached over to hold my hand, I squeezed hers in reply. As the sun dipped to the horizon, we heard a car pull into the driveway. We both jumped up, believing the worst was about to happen. We ran into the living room to look out the window to see if it was true.

Lucy Grimes stepped out of her car, looked around quickly, then walked briskly to the front door. Before she could ring the bell, Maude opened it and smiled warmly, waving for her to come in. She frowned the moment she saw me standing there, then shrugged it off with a perfunctory smile.

"Maude, I'd like to talk to you."

"Of course, Lucy. Do you have a problem if Davis sits in? We were having drinks…would you like one?"

"Yes, thanks. White wine would be good," she replied, staring at me with some trepidation.

While Maude went off to pour the drink, Lucy and I walked out on the deck, where we sat and watched the sun fade away. After a lengthy silence, she cautiously spoke up. "You know I told the police about seeing you in town two weeks before the dinner…and Harry's murder."

"Yes, I know."

Suddenly her eyes filled with tears. "Did you murder *my* Harry?" she sobbed.

"Absolutely not!"

"I'm not sure I believe you!"

"Believe me, it's true," I replied, hoping she'd stop crying.

Just then, Maude stepped out on the deck with a glass of white wine. Seeing Lucy crying, she glanced at me with a questioning expression, wondering if I was the cause of her tears. She said softly, "Please don't cry, Lucy. I know how devastated you feel, but crying won't help."

"Oh, Maude, I loved him so. He was everything I'd ever wanted!"

"I know, dear," she replied sympathetically.

Lucy pulled out a tissue and wiped away her tears, then blew her nose. When she was done, she gave Maude a hard look and asked, "Why did you go down to the beach after the dinner to meet Harry?"

"Why do you ask?"

"Well…Harry had asked me to meet him there after the dinner," she replied, her voice cracking a little. "But he said to wait an hour because he was meeting someone there about business first. I thought he was planning a romantic date for us, so of course, I told him I would come down later." Lucy stopped for a moment to regain her composure. Taking a deep breath, she continued. "I went home to change my clothes, and came down to the beach about an hour later and parked in the lot. It was pretty dark when I got out of the car, as the moon had just passed behind some clouds, so I turned on my flashlight. As I walked up the path between the two dunes, I heard loud voices, then a shot, followed by a loud groan and then silence." Lucy stopped to wipe away some tears. "I ran as fast as I could towards where I thought the shot and groan had come from. That's when I saw the light from another flashlight bobbing up and down as someone was running away, taking the long way around the furthest dune to the parking lot. I stood there watching the light disappear before I ran towards the sound of the shot, shining my flashlight everywhere, searching for him, hoping against hope that he wasn't dead. Finally, I saw him lying there…so very still. I ran to him, screaming and begging him to answer me. But he was dead!

My Harry was dead!"

She began sobbing uncontrollably, causing her to spill the wine on her skirt and fumble the glass, which ended up on the deck. Totally distraught, Lucy covered her face with both hands as Maude jumped up to console her. She held her tight for some time, until Lucy's sobs slowly diminished to whimpers, then stopped. Wiping her eyes, she looked up at Maude with a grateful, wet smile.

"Were you sure he was dead?" I asked as gently as possible.

"Yes…yes, of course, he was dead! There was blood all over his shirt, and…and he didn't move. I called out to him a hundred times, begging…pleading with him to answer me, but he was gone!"

"What did you do then, Lucy?"

"I ran back to my car and drove as quickly as I could to the police station to get help!"

"Who did you speak to there?"

"I don't know, some officer at the desk."

"Did he send someone to immediately investigate?"

"I don't know…I didn't go back to the beach. I went home. Don't you understand? *My* Harry was dead!"

"Yes, I understand. Do you have any idea what time it was when you saw Harry lying there?"

"I don't remember. Twelve-thirty maybe? Why are you asking me all these questions the police already asked me?"

"Was it a woman's voice you heard arguing with Harry?"

"I don't know…I was too far away. All I heard were loud voices the moment before the shot. Please stop asking me these questions!"

"Sorry, I just need to ask a couple more. When you were driving away, did you see anyone? Possibly the person with the flashlight?"

"No, I didn't see anyone. Now stop it!"

"Last one, I promise. Did you give Harry a check for five million dollars?"

A long, suspicious pause followed before she slowly answered, "Yes, I did. He said he was going to deposit it in his investment fund after he gave the insurance company four hundred thousand dollars to protect my money. He planned to do both on Monday, just before we left on our honeymoon."

"And you believed him?"

"Yes! Why wouldn't I? He was going to be my husband. And I loved him!" Lucy screamed at me before burying her face in her hands, sobbing again.

Maude gave me a rather nasty look, then reached over and hugged her, before asking softly, "Can I get you another glass of wine, Lucy? It will help."

"No, thanks, Maude. I'm so sorry I've made such a spectacle of myself. I think I'll go home now."

****

The pink sky had disappeared, and as the darkness deepened, I looked over at Maude, whose sadness reflected my feelings too. I depressingly stated the obvious: "No husband! No love! And nothing to protect her five million from disappearing down a rat hole. And your four hundred thousand with it."

Maude winced at my choice of words. "She's so unlucky. This was her one real chance for love after spending so many years searching for it. Now it's all gone."

"Well, I'm not so sure of that," I said sarcastically.

"What do you mean?"

"She has a fallback guy waiting, and I assume rather impatiently too."

"Well, yes…you might be right. Fred doesn't have any competition anymore, now does he?"

"No, he does not," I replied emphatically. "And maybe that's what he told Harry just before shooting him."

"Don't be so crass! Fred doesn't seem like that kind of person."

"Well…why couldn't he have argued with Harry, then shot him, and when he started to run away, he saw someone with a flashlight coming up the path and hid, wanting to see who it was. When he heard

Lucy screaming for Harry to wake up, he waited to see what she would do next. When she ran back to her car, he knew there was enough time to drag Harry's body down to the water, haul it out to sea, and hope it would take days before anyone discovered it."

"But why Fred, Davis? Why couldn't it have been Charlie Reynolds or Tim Swenson?" Maude rightly argued.

"True! Either one of them could have done it."

We both stared out at the darkened water for a while. I finally broke the silence to ask, "What do you think Harry did with your and Lucy's checks?"

"If I had to guess, knowing Harry, he'd use Lucy's five million as his get-out-of-jail ticket to run and hide from the police at some faraway luxury resort until things quieted down. There was no way he was going to give your check to the insurance company when he had a five million dollar one in his pocket." I thought for a moment. "You know, Maude, I don't think Harry would have wanted to carry those checks around if he was running from the police. What he needed was cash, and lots of it, not those two large checks. He'd have to deposit them somewhere and then wait days for them to clear before he could draw on them. And whatever bank he used, they'd probably be suspicious, thinking it might be drug money, especially when he wanted to make big cash withdrawals."

"Well, you're the banker…what do you think he did?"

I got up and walked over to the deck railing to look out at the moonlit sky. After thinking for a minute or two, I turned around and said, "Harry knew it would be difficult, probably impossible, to turn those checks into cash as fast as he needed to. And even if he could somehow do it, to carry all that cash in a suitcase on his honeymoon was both unrealistic and dangerous. He was smart enough to know that he had to convert those checks into something equivalent to cash that was easy to carry and difficult for the police to trace. My guess…he exchanged them for negotiable certificates."

"Wouldn't the police still have a trail to follow if he used them?"

"Maybe. But negotiable certificates are usually a lot harder to trace unless, of course, they're spent foolishly, which Harry was known to do. Since he was leaving on his honeymoon on Monday, and I'd bet anything he wasn't coming back, he probably had planned on taking those certificates with him. Do you know where they were going?"

"Lucy told me it was to some Caribbean island, but I forgot which one."

"There are lots of small banks throughout the Caribbean, any one of which would be a perfect place to stash the certificates. Don't forget, bribes go a long way there!"

"Even if he was planning to take them with him last Monday, what do you think he did with them from Tuesday until Sunday?"

"My guess is he probably kept them in a safe at home. Wait, a money belt would have been even better. That way, he could keep them close, really close, until he could rent a safety deposit box at a Caribbean bank."

"Davis, are you saying he had the certificates on him when he came down to the beach last Saturday night?"

"Yeah, probably. And maybe whoever Harry met at the beach knew he had closed his investment fund that Friday and was leaving on his honeymoon on Monday. And just maybe, he had a deal going with that person and wanted to terminate it. They argued, and that person shot him! He could have quickly searched Harry, found the money belt just as Lucy came running up the path between those two dunes, and when she ran off to tell the police, he dragged Harry's body down to the water, hoping it would drift out to sea before dawn. A lot of supposition, I know. But still possible."

Maude mulled it over. "If what you're saying is right, then it's got to be either Charlie Reynolds or Tim Swenson. I'd guess Charlie was most likely to have had a deal going with him. But Swenson could have confronted him about getting his money back. He could also have been the one who shot at you."

"Maybe." I thought more about it. "You know, Maude, I just hate to leave Fred out. Although I doubt he was involved in any deal with

Harry, he certainly had every reason to want to get rid of him."

"Davis, I just don't see Fred as the murdering type."

"Well...I don't know about that. I think he had a damn good motive: marry Lucy, and gain access to her money. Then start living a lifestyle that's nowhere feasible on a schoolteacher's salary. On the other hand, maybe he demanded that Harry give back Lucy's money, knowing his investment fund was closed. Harry refused, and Fred shot him. He found Harry's money belt, took it from him, then dragged him down to the water."

"I hadn't thought of it that way, but maybe you're right."

"So," I asked rhetorically, "who else would have a reason to meet Harry down at the beach that night?"

Maude instantly glared at me. "What are you implying, Davis?"

Shrugging my shoulders, I said, "I'm not implying anything. I'm just wondering how difficult it would have been to drag Harry's body those twenty or so feet down to the water, and push him out to sea."

"You think I murdered Harry and was strong enough to drag him down to the water? Well, let me tell you...I didn't!"

"I believe you, Maude," I replied softly.

She continued to glare at me. "If you're looking for suspects, Davis, why don't you add your name to the list? You hated Harry for destroying your Wall Street career. You spent eight years at that bank detesting every minute of it and despising him for making it happen. That sounds like someone wanting revenge to me!"

Surprised at her vehemence, I quickly pointed out that she had forgotten one crucial thing. "But Maude, you know I wasn't here last Saturday night."

"Well...maybe you were!"

"Come on now, you know I wasn't here. Anyway, I thought we were working together now."

"Well, then don't accuse me, Davis!"

"I wasn't accusing you. Look...why don't we call a truce." We sat staring angrily at each other until I finally said, "Are we, or are we not still working together?"

"We are, okay!"

We sat in silence for another couple of minutes until Maude said thoughtfully, "Should we add Lucy's name to the list?"

"Why? I thought a moment ago, you felt sorry for her."

"I can change my mind."

"Okay…but why add her name to the list?"

"Well, I was thinking, she might not have listened to Harry and came down to the beach early."

"That's possible, although Harry did tell her to wait an hour before coming to meet him. He was obviously meeting someone else."

"Suppose he hadn't yet met with that person when Lucy showed up. Maybe in a fit of anger, he told her the wedding was off. Furious, she went home, got her gun, came back, waited until that person left, and then shot him."

"You could be right," I said, surprised at her deduction. "Lucy definitely had a strong motive if Harry balked at marrying her. You know…this sounds exactly like what happened to Ellen Houser. She gave Harry her money, believing he was going to marry her. Then he ditched her to go after Lucy's money."

"Do you think Lucy owns a gun, Davis?"

"Maybe we should find out."

Chapter Twenty-One

At some point, we gave up trying to figure out what had happened at the beach the night of Harry's murder and instead sat in silence until Maude got up and said, "Let's go inside, it's getting chilly. The wind seems to be picking up, probably bringing a storm with it. And when the sea gets rough around here, the spray flies right off the top of those whitecaps, right on to the deck. But more importantly, it's a good excuse for another drink."

We pulled our chairs close to the house as we went inside. The living room warmth was unexpected, as I hadn't realized how chilly it had gotten outside. We walked over to the bar, where Maude poured two scotches, then we took our drinks over to the sofa. Just as we were about to sit down, the wind started howling, followed by the loud rumbling of waves crashing against the rocks below. I was beginning to feel a little edgy when suddenly, a torrent of raindrops pounded against the floor-to-ceiling windows. The ocean now had my complete attention. I stood there staring out into the darkness, wondering what kind of trouble we'd be in if one of the pillars supporting the house was to collapse. I started to say to Maude, "Have you ever been in a storm...," when another giant wave roared in, followed by the sound of water smashing against the pillars and then gurgling up the underside of the deck.

My edginess had turned into full-blown anxiety. I looked over at Maude sitting on the sofa, looking at me with a big grin on her face. "This is not funny!" I yelled. I stood there anxiously anticipating the sound of the next wave. I tried to look out at the ocean again, but to my surprise, a blanket of white foam covered the windows. My anxiety rose exponentially. By this point, Maude had her hand over her mouth, trying to control her giggling. "Not funny at all," I yelled nervously again. The wind's frightening roar, accompanied by crashing waves, made my imagination run wild. All I could think of was the terrifying force of those giant waves smashing against the steel pillars, knocking them over, and the house tumbling down onto the rocks below. As the wind increased, the roar of the waves against the rocks grew even louder, which spun my imagination to visualize more death-defying images. I gulped down the rest of my scotch, as Maude said, laughing, "Davis, this isn't the movies, the angry sea isn't going to crash against the defenseless beach house, causing it to crumble and destroy everyone in it!"

"Thanks, Maude, for that dire description."

"It will never happen, Davis. Trust me on that!"

Since my trust in her was currently in short supply, I seriously considered leaving before one of those waves wreaked havoc on the pillars. But after taking another look at her amused face, I decided if she didn't think it was a problem, why should I? Sitting back down, I said, "How about a refill, Maude? I've never experienced a storm like this before, so I'm going to require a hell of a lot of additional support!"

Still enjoying my alarmed state, Maude walked over to the bar and poured me another scotch. Just as she handed the glass to me, the front doorbell rang, followed by a loud, persistent knocking. It surprised both of us, as who'd be out in a storm like this? She moved hesitantly across the living room to the front door, pausing before opening it cautiously, as if ready to shut it fast before the person could force their way inside. Her concern was well-founded, as Tim Swenson pushed the door wide open, shoving her out of the way to step inside, dripping wet.

"How dare you force your way into my house!" she shouted at him.

"I didn't come to see you!" he answered, slamming the door

behind him. "I'm looking for Lowe. Ah...there he is!" he shouted, sounding menacing.

"Get out of my house, do you hear me!"

"Lady, I'm not leaving here until I finish my business with Lowe. I heard in town he was leaving tonight, and I want my money...all of it!"

"Who told you that?" Maude demanded.

"A friend who knows just how devious he is."

"Sounds like Charlie Reynolds has been whispering in your ear."

"It doesn't matter who it was. All I want is to finish my business with him." He pushed her aside, eager to face me.

Swenson was a big man...extraordinarily so! And he was looking mighty angry to boot. His eyes narrowed to an ominous squint as he started to slowly cross the living room towards me, ready for a fight. From the look of his unusually broad, overly muscled shoulders and arms, and his bulging bull neck that made his soaking wet jacket look three sizes too small, it was clear he knew all about fighting. But it wasn't until I saw his large hands opening and closing, just itching to take me on, that I was convinced he meant every word about getting his money...right here and right now!

Swenson stopped about a dozen feet away from me. Before, he had appeared to tower over me, but now that he was closer, I saw he was about my size...it was his width from shoulder to shoulder that made him appear so immense. He stood there with feet apart, glaring at me, waiting for me to hand over his money. When I didn't respond, he leaned forward and stuck out his hand, palm up, and in a low and threatening voice said, "Did you hear me, Lowe? I want my million and a half dollars now before you skip town."

"I'm not going anywhere," I replied as calmly as possible, wondering how in the world I was going to fight this bull of a man, and with twelve stitches in my back. "Who told you I was leaving?"

"No stalling, Lowe. I want my money now, damn it!

"And I want to know who told you I was leaving tonight!"

"What does it matter to you? Just give me my money."

I put my glass down on the table next to the sofa, then stepped back closer to the floor-to-ceiling windows, hoping it would give me a little more room to maneuver if needed. I tried to stay calm as I thought of how to stop him from attacking. Only one thought came to mind, and not a very encouraging one at that: stall for more time until I could think of something, anything to deter him.

"I don't owe you a dime, Swenson!" I shouted as bravely as possible, hoping he'd keep his distance. "You're the one who bought into Harry's scheme, and you were the one who got screwed in the process. It had absolutely nothing to do with me. I'll say it again; I was never Harry's silent partner. And if you'd listen to me for a minute, you'll learn that he screwed me worse than he did you. I lost millions of dollars. Harry destroyed my career, my future, and my life! So, what right do you have to come in here and demand I pay you back your million and a half dollars?"

If I had thought I was getting through to him, I was sadly mistaken, as he resumed moving closer. His hands were now tightly clenched into fists. Those glaring eyes were the focal point of a face burning with anger. "Look, Lowe, I know for a fact that you were Harry's silent partner."

"Who told you that? Was it Charlie Reynolds?"

"Maybe."

"Well, he doesn't know what the hell he's talking about. Swenson, Harry was a con man, someone whose only desire in life was to be a rich Wall Street player even though he lacked any natural aptitude or skill to make that happen. That's where I came in. Harry thought he knew everything about picking stocks when he actually didn't know a thing. Ten years ago, when the market was about to crash, he decided he was the smartest guy in the room. That's the day our partnership ended. Our five years of success crested like a giant wave that day. After that, Harry still tried to ride it, but it kept losing momentum until the last bit washed up on the shore and sank into the sand. See, there was no one around after I left to tell Harry what stocks to buy or when to sell. But as always, his ego and arrogance wouldn't let him admit it."

I saw he'd stopped moving, so I continued. "But Swenson, I'd have to say Harry did have one great talent that he never lost; his ability to convince rich people like you to invest with him. I'm guessing he not only claimed he could deliver the highest possible return on your investment, but he guaranteed he'd pay that outlandish return. It was a sales pitch that proved too hard to resist, am I right?" Swenson nodded slightly, reluctant to admit I was right, then resumed moving towards me. It seemed I had his attention but not the answer to how to stop him, so I kept on talking. "I'll bet when Harry first spoke to you about investing in his fund, he wanted to know just how much money you were talking about. I'm sure you proudly told him you were thinking about starting with a couple hundred thousand of your million-and-a-half-dollar estate. It must have shocked the hell out of you when that amount turned Harry off...and fast! See, he couldn't waste his time on your measly couple hundred thousand when he needed to feed his fund with enough money to keep everyone happy. Am I getting any of this wrong?"

"No," he replied quietly, sounding surprised. He had stopped moving forward.

"Well, that was the first step of his con. After you balked at investing all of your money, he dropped you from his active list of possibilities but kept you on the back burner as a so-called social friend. I suspect that whenever the two of you met, he told you how he was minting money for all his investors, which I imagine at some point started to really bother the hell out of you. But that was by design. Harry knew it was only a matter of time before he wore you down...and you'd bite. I'm sure he saw the greed in your eyes. You know, Swenson, I'll bet you tried to resist risking your entire estate on Harry's siren call, but you couldn't, could you? You wanted financial security, so you wrote a check for a million and a half dollars."

"How do you know all that?"

"It's standard procedure for a con artist like Harry."

"You're right," he said slowly and sadly. "I did tell him I'd invest two hundred and fifty thousand as my first investment. I wanted to be a little cautious and see if he could really deliver. But then he told me he'd think about it. I was shocked that my two hundred and fifty thousand wasn't good enough for his fund. Still, we continued to spend a lot of time together, drinking at local bars, having fun dinners, and chasing a lot of women. All that time, he was telling me how every one of his investors was making such a great return and loved getting paid month after month. So yes...I finally couldn't resist. I heard the stock market was going up, and I thought my million and a half would grow like hell. I'd be richer than I ever thought possible, and step into a great retirement. When I handed him my check, you know what he said to me? 'Tim, this is the best investment you'll ever make!'"

Swenson's face had lost some of its intense anger, and his fists had opened up. I breathed a silent sigh of relief. "I'm sure you felt it was the best investment for a while," I said, hoping to keep him calm. "It had to be gratifying to have those checks rolling in every month until, unfortunately, he ran out of new investor money. I bet you and all his other investors were caught completely off guard when that first letter came, telling you he was cutting the monthly payment in half, then soon after, in half again. But then Harry promised to quickly restore full payments...and the back payments too, didn't he?"

"Yeah, he did," he replied quietly, obviously humiliated at being so easily suckered.

"I understand, Swenson. No one likes to be made a fool of," I replied sympathetically.

Well...the word *fool* set him off again. I wanted to kick myself for being so stupid. "Do you, Lowe? Do you really understand what that money meant to me? It was all the money I had in this world. It took me years to earn it and save it. I spent a hell of a lot of years in tank towns across the country wrestling, getting bounced and beaten up every night, whether I was the bad guy or the good guy. The money was peanuts! It took me ten years to crack the big time. That's when the bucks started rolling in. I was on top of the world when I broke my back getting thrown to the mat one night. It took me months to heal and get back in shape. I was real careful after that. I knew I had to watch my money and not blow it stupidly. But I admit I somehow did with Harry. Now I'm fifty-eight and too old to wrestle. So, what do I do now? How do I live? I've got no money…no future…no life!"

As he took a couple of steps forward, I panicked, sure this was going to be the end of me. I felt the stitches in my back pull tight as I slowly retreated. Suddenly, without any warning, the living room lit up as bright as day from multiple flashes of lightning, followed by deafening claps of thunder that shook the house. Swenson looked nervously at me, and I glanced anxiously at Maude, wondering if she'd ever experienced a storm like this before. Her calm expression signaled she had, but I stood frozen in place, alarmed over what this violent storm was capable of doing, and desperately trying to figure out how to stop Swenson. As lightning continued to ricochet across the sky and cracks of thunder reverberated overhead, Maude somehow had the presence of mind to say to Swenson, "Why don't you sit down. This storm should blow over in a little while. Have a drink with us."

"Lady, I already told you this isn't a social visit…I'm here to collect my money! And you know what, Lowe? I don't give a damn whether I was greedy or not. All I want is my money back. And now!"

"Look, Swenson, I'll tell you again; you're not getting a dime from me!"

Surprised at first, he quickly turned furious and started taking the last few steps towards me. That's when Maude decided to be a hero and tried to step between us to protect me, thinking he'd back off from a woman. But Swenson was too angry and too determined. He pushed her out of the way and kept moving closer. She screamed at him, "This is my house, and you're trespassing on private property. Leave now, or I'll call the police!"

"You're not calling the police, lady! Lowe and I are going to settle this now. Right, Lowe?"

Fearing the prospect of this powerfully built, bull-necked man slapping her around, Maude got out of the way. That left me standing face to face with a furious and desperate man, firmly convinced I was going to end up in the hospital for quite a while. I knew I had to do something, even if it was a long shot, and probably a dumb one at that. "Look, Swenson, you don't expect me to write you a check tonight for that amount of money, do you? Why don't we meet tomorrow to talk about it?"

"Not on your life, Lowe! I don't buy that one. Pay up now or else!"

"Do you really think I've got a million and a half dollars sitting in my checking account? Are you crazy? I work at a bank in New York...on a salary which couldn't pay you that amount of money in a lifetime!"

"Okay, then. Write me a check for a down payment...say, two hundred thousand, and I'll be back tomorrow for the rest."

"You're not listening, Swenson. I'm just an employee! I don't have that kind of money. And even if I did, I still wouldn't pay you a dime. I owe you nothing! Now get the hell out of here!"

"Well...maybe this will help you change your mind, Lowe!"

With that, he cocked his arm back, ready to take a life-changing swing at me. I cringed, anticipating the blow, only to see him hesitate, maybe waiting to see if his threatening size, and giant fist, were enough to scare the hell out of me into giving him the money. And they were...until I remembered I only had a couple thousand in my bank account. "No, it doesn't," I answered.

"Okay, pal, you asked for it!"

"Wait!" Maude shouted.

"Wait for what?" he snarled at her.

"I'll write you a check for the two hundred thousand now, but only if you leave my house and never come back. Agreed?"

He stared at Maude for a long moment before saying, "Lady, if you can write a check for two hundred thousand now, that means you've got plenty of money. So, if you want to protect your loverboy here, you better have a check for the rest tomorrow. Then I swear I'll be out of your lives forever."

"Maude, I don't want you to pay him a dime...now or ever!"

"That's it, Lowe!" Swenson reached back again, ready to prove beyond a doubt he meant business. I waited until his swing started forward, then quickly stepped aside, ignoring the sharp pain in my back. Just as he missed me, I threw the hardest punch I could. It hit him on the side of his jaw, sending him reeling backward, but not down. I stood there rubbing my throbbing hand, certain it was broken, while Swenson shook his head a couple of times to get rid of the cobwebs. Glaring at me, he charged again, expecting to tackle and beat the hell out of me. I waited nervously to almost the last second and then stepped aside again, which caused him to miss and land face-down on the floor. I jumped on his back to hold him down and shouted to Maude, "Get something I can hit him with...now!"

She ran off into the bedroom as I struggled to hold him down, but he was too damn strong. He got to his knees with me riding on his back, then began to stand up. I tried grabbing him around the chin and twisting his head as far to the right as I could, hoping that would stop him long enough for Maude to bring something...anything to hit him with. But that bull neck of his wouldn't budge. He flicked me off his back, then turned to face me. His face was now bright red, either from anger or embarrassment at not being able to finish me off.

I stepped back again and found myself pressed against the window, which surprised me. With no room to maneuver, all I could do was watch him raise his arms into a fighter's stance, his large hands clenched tightly into large fists. He took a step towards me just to see how I would react. I couldn't help but show my concern...no my unmitigated fear! He gave a sly smile and began to shake his head from side to side as if to say, *You're going to be glad to give me the million and a half before I'm done with you!*

Just then, Maude came back into the living room, screaming, "Don't you dare move a muscle, Swenson!"

He slowly turned to her with a disparaging grin on his face, only to see a Colt .22 pistol pointing straight at him. It surprised the hell out of him, and frankly, me too! It took a couple of seconds before he grinned again, obviously dismissing the idea she would shoot him if he took one step closer to me. But then…he must have noticed the steely look in her doe-shaped blue eyes, the same look she had before shooting Harry, the same one when I visited her in prison…the one I knew meant business. Swenson just stood there, trying to decide if she'd actually shoot him if he laid a hand on me. He stared at her pistol, pointing straight at him, then up at those steely blue eyes. It took him only a moment more before he made a very wise decision. Slowly raising his hands chest high, he turned his palms up to show he wasn't going to challenge her. Shaking his head in disbelief that he was actually backing away from this woman and her pistol, he walked to the front door. As he reached for the knob, he turned back and gave first Maude, then me, a threatening look that clearly said, *Neither of you will like it when I come back.*

"Before you get the hell out, Swenson," I shouted across the living room, "tell me, were you at Harry's dinner last Saturday night?"

"Yeah, I was there," he replied in a disinterested tone.

"Did you meet him down at the beach later that night?"

"No. But if I had, I wouldn't have shot him, I can tell you that much."

I had one last question. "Swenson, were you the one who shot at me yesterday afternoon?"

A nasty little smile appeared on his face. "I'd never do that to you, Lowe. If I killed you, how would I get my money back?" He opened the door. "I'll be back tomorrow, you can count on it. And Lowe, you better have my money ready!" With that, he stepped out into the pouring rain and swirling wind, slamming the door behind him.

Chapter Twenty-Two

I dropped down on the sofa, trying to control my loud sighs of relief. My back was hurting, but my hand was killing me. The worst part was that this wasn't the end of my dealing with him. God, he was one tough son-of-a-bitch, which I could attest to, as evidenced by the pain and rapid swelling of my hand. I tried to flex it, but it hurt like hell. Still, I concluded, the pain in my hand and back was a far cry from what Swenson could have done to me. What a bull of a man, I thought, with a steel jaw to boot. I reached for what was left of my drink with my good hand and quickly swallowed what remained, but it didn't seem to help. I looked over at Maude; she was frozen in place, her pistol still pointing toward the front door, seemingly contemplating what she had just done.

I turned away and stared at my hand to see how much more it had swelled, all the while trying to rationalize the ugly fact of her lying to me once again. The gratitude I had felt for her saving my life was starting to curdle into contempt. I was convinced I wanted nothing more to do with her, yet even as I thought this, I couldn't help but appreciate how she'd saved me from a deadly beating. I glanced over at her again. She was still standing in the same spot, pistol in hand, looking at me, waiting for me to say something, anything that would excuse her for lying about the gun. But what could I say? All of her lies were making it easier for Brantley to build a case to charge us both with murder.

That thought made the pain in my hand feel worse. Minutes passed before I looked back at Maude. She was still standing in the same spot but was now shaking her head from side to side, obviously angry that I still hadn't thanked her for saving me. Finally, realizing that wasn't going to happen, she abruptly walked into the bedroom, slamming the door behind her.

I kept sitting there, trying to decide which was worse: Her lies or the beating I had narrowly escaped. Finding no answer, I headed to the kitchen for some ice. As I passed Maude's bedroom, she suddenly opened the door and stood there with a pleading expression on her face. "Don't you realize, Davis, I had to save your life? Swenson would have killed you. My choices were to let him beat you to death…or risk your hating me for lying to you and the police. Well, guess what? I chose to save you, believing your life was more valuable than what you'd think of me afterward. Was I wrong?"

"No," I replied softly. "I can't thank you enough as I probably would have been dead by the time he was finished with me. And Maude, I've got to say that I admire your guts for standing there ready to shoot him."

"You fool! I did it for you…I did it for you!" She burst into tears and covered her face with both hands.

"I know you did, Maude." I put my arms around her. "And I really do appreciate it. But right now, we find ourselves trapped between a rock and a hard place, and I'm feeling overwhelmed just thinking about it. Never in my wildest dreams did I think something like this would ever happen to me…and I'm sure neither did you!"

Maude looked up at me, clearly frightened. "We've got to run, Davis! We've got to run now! This minute! It's the only way out of this mess. I've got plenty of money. We can escape to some small Caribbean island and live out our lives there."

I shook my head slowly. "Maude, you know that wouldn't work. The police will eventually catch us. Or our friend, Swenson, will spend a lifetime searching for us. No. We've got to stay. And as futile as it sounds, we've got to find Harry's killer!"

She looked at me like I was a fool, but then slowly nodded in agreement, adding one proviso: "I'm telling you right now, Davis,

I'm keeping my pistol. It's the only security I've got if Swenson attacks me. Or wants money from me. Without it, I'll be totally defenseless, and I won't be defenseless ever again!"

"I understand. But the police won't. Keeping your gun could add years to a prison sentence. But if you want to keep it, then you better make sure you hide it well, as I'm sure your house will be searched again."

Hearing this, Maude did a double-take, realizing I had just forgiven her. But if I was sure of anything in this world, it was that this decision was going to come back to bite me...and badly! *I guess I'll just have to accept it, as I know all her lies are going to be our downfall sooner or later.* Suddenly it dawned on me that *sooner* could be tomorrow...when Brantley comes knocking at the door with a warrant for our arrest. Maybe it'll be the same time that Swenson shows up. That would be interesting. My God, what am I thinking? Hoping the police arrest me to protect me from that muscle-bound gorilla has to be the height of desperation!

"Oh, Davis, thank you! Thank you! I did it for both of us. I need you so much in my life." Maude threw her arms around my neck and kissed me a half dozen times, which I must admit I enjoyed, even with all the pain.

Chapter Twenty-Three

"Come on, Davis," Maude cried out enthusiastically, "let's celebrate our short-lived freedom from the police and our bull-necked friend!"

I reluctantly nodded my agreement, thinking that our freedom was indeed going to be short-lived as we were trapped from every direction...no question about it. In fact, I was more inclined to ditch the whole idea of a celebration and sink further into abject fear and frustration. As I debated which course to follow, the sky literally lit up the ocean with multiple lightning flashes. They danced everywhere, creating a monstrous light show that we watched with fascination, waiting for the inevitable thunderclaps to boom overhead any second. And they did with ear-shattering fury, rolling over the house, again and again, accompanied by large raindrops pelting the windows. The experienced storm watcher held me tightly, no giggles or laughter this time. It was an awesome display of Mother Nature's power.

It took a few more minutes before the lightning flashes disappeared out to sea, and the thunder and rain stopped. Still, neither of us moved a muscle. We just stood there anxiously listening for any sign of the storm doubling back. But it was gone, and we smiled at each other in relief. Shaking her head in awe, Maude said, "That was a biggie, Davis! But the house is still standing and without any damage. Isn't it amazing how a well-built house can withstand a storm like that?"

"Are you sure it did, Maude?"

She gave me a quick, puzzled look as if I knew something that she didn't, then proudly replied, "Definitely! Now let's open the champagne and celebrate our survival."

"Okay," I answered hesitantly, still not convinced there was anything to celebrate. We walked into the kitchen together, where she took a bottle of champagne from the refrigerator, and I reached into the freezer for some ice.

"Davis, your hand is definitely in no condition to open this bottle, so let me." It took a little time, but she popped the cork, filled our glasses, and then raised hers, toasting, "To us, Davis! Somehow we're going to get out of this mess."

"I'll drink to that," I replied, adding solemnly, "and God willing, we'll find out who murdered Harry before Swenson tries to beat the hell out of me again!" Maude's nod of approval appeared less than enthusiastic, but she recovered quickly with a warm smile. I couldn't help but wonder what that meant as we sipped our champagne.

We took our drinks and the bottle into the living room and walked over to the floor-to-ceiling windows to see what the ocean looked like after the storm. It was definitely calmer, no white caps spraying white foam, but the sky remained dark and threatening, indicating the possibility of another one brewing. But that didn't matter to Maude as she raised her glass to propose another toast. "To us, Davis," she said excitedly. "To our long future together after this mess is cleared up!"

I took a step back, stunned. Maude pretended to ignore my reaction and patiently held her glass high, waiting for me to clink on her toast. But I was too shocked to nod my agreement, wondering, *What made her think I was ready to spend the rest of my life with her?* Finally, I raised my glass and said, "To our freedom! May it last a lifetime."

Maude shrugged her shoulders in obvious disappointment but drank up anyway. Champagne has always hit me with a sudden mellowness, which was a godsend at this moment. She quickly poured us two more, which we downed without any thought of proposing another toast. She then hooked her arm around mine and walked us back to the sofa. As we sat down, she turned and stared at me with a loving look in those beautiful doe-shaped, blue eyes. I knew what she wanted…a commitment to our relationship no matter what we were about to face and my willingness to forget our age differences. I don't know why, but I suddenly thought of Harry facing the same situation. He balked…and look what happened to him! Sure, we'd had incredible sex two days ago with no strings attached. But now, I sensed that having sex would imply something more serious, a long-term commitment should we ever make it out of all of this unscathed.

Maude quickly guessed my dilemma and slid closer to me. Before I knew it, she had her arms around me, kissing me with a passion that matched her desire two days ago. How the hell could I not be aroused…even with a swollen hand and a back with twelve stitches? Before I knew it, we were taking off each other's clothes while kissing passionately. After that, it all became a blur, and we didn't stop until we were exhausted.

****

We had fallen asleep in each other's arms on the sofa and woke to the early morning sunlight shining through the windows. I kissed her several times, and she responded with that wanting look again, which swiftly led to another wonderful time. Afterward, we fell back asleep in each other's arms again.

The pain from my hand woke me, and I slowly pulled myself away, hoping not to wake her up. I walked into the kitchen looking for more ice and some painkillers. I found both and sat down at the kitchen table to wait for them to take effect. This gave me a chance to think, which led to a very disheartening question, *What in the world have I gotten myself into?* Between Maude's possessiveness, the police wanting a scapegoat, and Swenson seeking revenge, I couldn't see any way out of my predicament.

Feeling agitated at getting so involved, and frustrated at not knowing how to extricate myself, I decided to take a break and head into town to find out about my car. I showered and shaved, and then woke up Maude to get her car keys. She immediately put up a fuss, warning me that the police would spot her car and arrest me. I responded that they could easily come out here and arrest both of us, but Maude kept putting up obstacles to stop me from leaving. At first, I hesitated, as I could understand her being scared at being in the house alone, but then it dawned on me that wasn't what her objections were about; she was afraid of my not coming back. Damn, Harry had definitely done a number on her. Finally, after swearing numerous times that I wasn't going to leave her to face Brantley or Swenson alone, she reluctantly handed me the keys. I kissed her goodbye and drove off.

****

The auto body shop was located on the main road a mile or so outside of town. The news was what I had expected...the car was totaled, and they were waiting for the insurance company to confirm it. *I can now add that to my list of problems.* Feeling overwhelmed, I decided a cup of coffee would help calm me down. I remembered seeing a coffee shop next to the ice cream stand when I was here two weeks ago. Since it was a little further out of town, I'd probably be safe. As I opened my car door, my focus was squarely on how good coffee would taste right now, so I didn't notice the car until it screeched to a halt alongside mine. "Oh no," I gasped. Was that Brantley in an unmarked cruiser? I stood there frozen for several seconds until the car window rolled down, and Ellen Hauser leaned out the window and called my name. I gave her my best smile while breathing a huge sigh of relief.

She appeared agitated and frightened. "Oh, Mr. Lowe, am I thankful I ran into you. I'm in real trouble. Can we talk for a few minutes?" she asked, all the while glancing up at her rearview mirror.

"Sure, of course. But if you don't mind, I'd like to get a cup of coffee first. Would you like one?"

"No!" she replied sharply, with an expression indicating she did mind…and very much.

But hell, it was my bad day, so whatever she wanted to tell me was going to have to wait. She followed close behind my car all the way to the coffee shop. I parked and walked over to her car to ask again if she'd like some coffee. She rolled down the window, still looking scared.

"What's the matter? What's wrong?"

"Someone has been following me, Mr. Lowe."

"I don't see anyone," I replied, looking in both directions.

"He was right behind me…so close that he actually bumped my car. I didn't know what to do. I tried to speed up to get away, but he just stayed close behind me. He must have driven off when I stopped to see you."

"Okay, I'll be out in a minute, then we'll talk," I said, hoping to calm her down. I watched her quickly roll the window back up, then entered the coffee shop, wondering what was going on with her. The line was short, and as I walked out with coffee and donuts, it suddenly dawned on me that what she had just described was exactly what had happened to me. Only in my case, bumping had led to shooting. I walked quickly over to her car. She rolled down the window again, and I asked, "Where can we go that's private?"

"Well…there's a small beach nearby that's pretty private. We can go there. I don't think we'll be seen."

"Okay," I replied. I got back in my car and scanned the road in both directions for any suspicious-looking cars before following her to the other end of Beach Drive, where we turned onto a long, narrow road that ended in a small parking lot. We walked down a narrow path lined with dunes and tall grass to a small, empty beach facing a cove full of moored sailboats. A half dozen sun-bleached benches arched around the back of the beach. We sat down on the nearest one and took a moment to collectively survey the beach, the sailboats, the ocean, and the dark, threatening skies.

"Mr. Lowe…"

"Please, call me Davis. May I call you Ellen?"

"Yes, of course! Davis…I'm so glad I ran into you. I have a confession to make, and I'm hoping you can help me. You see, I witnessed a murder, and I fear it's coming back to haunt me!"

Surprised, to say the least, I nodded okay, wondering, *Why not tell the police?* "A murder? Whose murder?"

"It was Harry Miller!"

"You saw who murdered Harry?"

"Yes! Well…not exactly."

"What does 'not exactly' mean?"

"Please, Davis, let me start from the beginning."

"Please do."

"Well, last Saturday night, I went to Harry's dinner. I know I shouldn't have gone, but I did. I purposely sat at the table next to his, frankly hoping he'd notice me. I'm sure this sounds ridiculous to you, but I wanted to talk to him. I'll admit…I was hoping there was still an outside chance we could renew our relationship. Oh, I can see by your expression you're surprised. To tell you the truth, I wasn't very optimistic, but I still wanted to try. I'm sure you're thinking, why do that when Harry was engaged and about to marry Lucy Grimes? I was quite aware of that, but knowing Harry…and what he did to me, their engagement didn't necessarily mean marriage."

It was tough to hold back my grin at her cynicism. But trying to fathom Harry Miller's magic was something else. There were now three women that I knew of who gave him a hell of a lot of money to buy his affection. And yet, this arrogant son-of-a-bitch gladly took their money and ditched all three of them. I couldn't figure out what kind of spell he held over them, but someday I was going to spend some time trying.

Seeing my reaction, Ellen hesitated for a moment before continuing. "I must say that Harry appeared in a jovial mood that night, basking in the town's adulation for his contributions. We started to talk, but in short order, it became all about him and his generosity in making the town a better place. That's when Maude Williamson stopped by his table. She ignored me and congratulated him eagerly. At first, Harry looked at her suspiciously, as though he expected some nasty crack or threat to follow. But he relaxed after she smiled warmly and kissed him."

"Are you sure, Ellen?"

"Yes, I was sitting right there and saw everything. That's what happened!"

"Well...was that all?"

"No, she then proceeded to ask him to meet her down at the beach that night around 11:30 for old times' sake. I saw Harry's eyes open wide as he nodded a very doubtful *yes,* and then I watched as he slowly smiled, realizing exactly what she meant. Maude returned to her table, as the ceremony was about to start. Harry graced me with a quick smile and a hurried 'thanks for coming tonight,' and that was it. Then he turned his attention to the introduction of the town selectmen as everyone else turned theirs to him. By then, I had realized that any hope of rekindling our relationship was clearly gone. But there had been a second part to my madness. I wanted to press him on getting my money back. I had given him a lot, which frankly has left me in a shaky financial position."

Ellen waited for my reaction. But to tell the truth, I was still thinking about Harry and the three women. Getting no response from me, she decided to go on anyway. "What I did afterward, I must confess in hindsight, was most embarrassing and quite stupid. It has put me in this awful spot. I don't know what came over me, whether it was jealousy at Maude's apparent relationship with Harry, or my anger at his jilting me, or stealing my money. Anyway, after the dinner ended, I got into my car and drove to the big beach up the road where I guessed Harry was rendezvousing with Maude. I parked at the very far end of the lot, hoping no one would see my car. Clouds had dimmed the moonlight, so I turned on my flashlight, and walked the long way around to the beach. I found a place to hide behind some tall, thick grass along one side of the dune, near where the path ends, and the beach begins. My plan was to wait for Harry there."

"When did he arrive?" I asked.

"He was already there! In fact, he was standing not far from the water, looking out at the incoming waves. I had just started to walk towards him when a woman came running up the path with her flashlight bobbing up and down, shouting excitedly, 'Harry...Harry, I love you!' I dashed back behind the tall grass. She ran past me, shouting, 'I love you so much, Harry!' until she reached him. At first, I thought it was Maude. That is until I heard Harry yell at her, 'What the hell are you doing here, Lucy? I told you to meet me here in an hour!'"

"Lucy Grimes? But she told me she was meeting Harry at the beach around 12:30. What time was it when she got there?"

"Maybe 11:15, possibly 11:30."

"That's interesting...what happened next?"

"Well, I stepped from my hiding place to get a little closer to hear what they were saying. Just as I did, another woman called out Harry's name as she walked up the path. I ran back to my hiding place. Harry recognized the voice immediately, which I guess startled him as I don't think he really expected Maude to show up. I heard him order Lucy in a threatening voice to run across the beach and wait there until he got rid of Maude."

"How did that go over with Lucy?"

"As you can imagine, she was quite upset. She hissed, 'No, I won't go!' Then I heard a loud slap, and she started to cry. I saw her turn and run."

"My God, this doesn't jibe with anything I was told!"

Ellen looked very surprised, thinking I didn't believe her. But then she shrugged her shoulders and continued. "Then I saw Maude walk up to Harry, and heard her say she still loved and needed him. He started laughing at her with that arrogant laugh of his, but I couldn't see much from where I was hiding. I thought he pushed her away, saying, 'I've got your money, so why would I need you anymore?' I heard her plead with him, but he kept on laughing at her until finally, she turned and ran back down the path in tears."

"My God, this is quite the saga! What did he do about Lucy?"

"Well, he stood there alone looking out at the ocean for what seemed like minutes, watching the waves pick up as the wind increased. I assumed he was waiting for someone else to show up. I guess he forgot about Lucy until she was standing next to him. He yelled at her to get back across the beach again, but she refused. In tears, she screamed at him to go to hell, and then ran right past me down the path to the parking lot, with Harry shouting after her, 'Don't come back! The wedding's off! And you're not getting your money back either!'"

Ellen hesitated, obviously trying to control her emotions, then said, "I couldn't believe what had just happened. That's when I made up my mind not to speak to him after the way he treated those women. I knew I had to get out of there. I waited a few more minutes to be sure no one was in the parking lot. But as I started towards my car, I heard another voice call out to him. That surprised and frightened me. I couldn't tell whether the person was coming up the path, or going the roundabout way like I had, so I had no choice but to run back to my hiding place."

"Was it a man or a woman's voice?"

"Definitely a man's voice!"

"What happened next?"

"It was hard at first to make out what they were saying, but it was clear they were arguing…and very loudly. The man demanded money from Harry to close some sort of deal they had made. Things grew more heated, and I tried moving closer to see who Harry was arguing with, but all I could make out was he was a short, older-looking man…I couldn't get a good look at his face. He was mad, though, and right up in Harry's face, demanding he go along with the deal as he'd made a commitment and couldn't back out now. That's when Harry shouted, in no uncertain terms, that he was terminating his end of the deal. He didn't care, he yelled, he wasn't going through with it. The man cursed him out. Said he couldn't do that as he'd made a down payment, and the deal was ready to be signed, sealed, and delivered. Harry just laughed, telling him, 'To hell with the deal and your down payment. I don't need your money anymore…I've got enough right here to last me for quite a while,' patting his stomach several times. But the man wouldn't give up. He kept arguing that Harry made a deal, and a deal is a deal. Harry started to walk away as if to end the conversation, but after a few steps, he stopped, turned, and shouted back that he was leaving town on Monday for good. That's when the man screamed at Harry, 'This is the second time you've screwed me over, but this time you're not going to get away with it!' Harry pointed at the parking lot path, bellowing, 'Get the hell out of here before I beat you to a pulp!' The man vowed that he'd be back and then took off."

"My God, Ellen, this is beyond belief!"

"I know, but it's the truth, Davis! By then, I'd definitely seen and heard enough to know I had to get out of there…and the faster, the better! I waited about five minutes after the man walked back down the path toward the parking lot before running to my car. I was just about to go when I suddenly realized that he'd see me driving away if he was still there. That's when I panicked! The only place I thought I'd be safe was in my hiding place, so I ran back there to wait for Harry to leave."

"What was Harry doing?"

"Well, when I finally felt safe enough to stand up to see what he was doing, I couldn't believe it! He was down at the water's edge, watching the waves come in. The wind was blowing harder, and the water was choppy with white caps. But none of this seemed to bother Harry. He sat down, took off his shoes and socks, and rolled up his pants as if he was going to enjoy a Sunday afternoon at the beach. He walked into the water, I guess to feel the waves break over his feet, and then turned around to watch them race up on the beach before dying out.

"After a few minutes of watching this, I heard someone come

running up the path, really fast. I quickly slipped back into the tall grass and hid. They ran by me and onto the beach before stopping. Stepping out of my hiding place, I watched as they spotted Harry walking in the water and started running towards him. Harry didn't seem at all surprised. From my angle, I couldn't tell whether it was a man or a woman. Harry walked out of the water slowly and up on to the beach, and when the two got close enough, I could hear Harry shout, 'So, you're back again. I knew you would be! You just can't stay away from me, can you?' The other person didn't say a word. 'Can't you understand, we're through, and I'm leaving for good!' Suddenly, the arrogant tone of his voice changed as he cried out, 'What are you doing? No, don't do that! Let's talk. Please! Don't shoot! Please…I beg of you!' Then I heard a gunshot and saw Harry fall backward. He wasn't moving. I watched as the shooter flashed a light on Harry's face, I think, to make sure he was dead."

"Was it a man or a woman?"

"I don't know…it happened so fast. Whoever it was, never spoke a word. And the flashlight was only on for a couple of seconds. Next thing I knew, they were running back towards the path and me. I ducked down as fast as I could, praying they wouldn't see me."

"What happened then?"

"I don't know. I had my head down, and my eyes closed, trying my best to hide. After they ran by me, I sat up, not knowing what to do. I'd just witnessed a murder! I'd never seen anyone killed before…it was horrible! All I could think about was getting away from there as fast as I could. I tried to get up to run, but my legs were shaking so. And I couldn't catch my breath. It took me a while before I was able to force myself to get up and walk. But just as I did, I stopped, thinking the murderer might still be in the parking lot. And the last thing I wanted to find was the murderer sitting there in their car. I can't tell you how afraid I was of also ending up dead!"

Ellen stopped and looked at me, I guess wondering if I believed her story, but I didn't react. She shook her head, obviously disappointed. "Davis, I was so frightened that I stayed hidden in the dunes for what seemed like hours. Just as I got up enough courage to run to my car, I heard loud footsteps coming up the path towards me. I could hear heavy breathing, I guess from running all the way from the parking lot. I quickly got down again as low as I could, and being so scared, didn't even try to look up to see who it was. I just crouched there, praying the dune grass was tall and thick enough to hide me. If it wasn't, I could end up lying dead on the beach just like Harry!"

I waited for her to calm down, before asking, "What did you do next?"

"I struggled to control my shaking body as I couldn't get over seeing someone shoot Harry just like that! I still can't believe it. And then to see him lying there...dead. It took a while before I was able to breathe normally. I knew I had to get out of there before I was spotted, but I was too afraid to move."

"Wait a minute! You said the murderer left after shooting Harry. What did this person do?"

"After he...it was definitely a man this time...passed by me, he ran onto the beach. I quickly got up and saw him flashing a light all around the sand. When he spotted Harry, he ran over to him. He stood there looking down at him for a minute or so, before angrily shouting, 'Serves you right, you son-of-a-bitch!' I watched as he then kneeled down and searched Harry's jacket pockets and opened his wallet, obviously looking for something. He sat back on his heels for a moment, then unbuttoned Harry's blood-stained shirt, unfastened some sort of belt, and pulled it off him. I didn't understand what he was doing until he opened each pocket in the belt and took out what looked like pieces of paper, which he stuffed into his own jacket. After making sure all the pockets were empty, he re-buckled the belt around Harry. He stood up, looked down at Harry's lifeless body, and without any hesitation, kicked him hard twice, shouting, 'Goodbye you son-of-a-bitch, you had it coming. May you rot in hell!'"

Ellen stopped and gave me a long look, as if asking, *Now do you believe me?* I nodded, *Yes*, and she continued. "He stood there for another minute or two, then bent down, grabbed one of Harry's bare ankles, dragged him down to the water, and pushed him out. But the high waves brought him back to shore. He tried a couple more times without any luck, then just left him there drifting back and forth on every incoming and outgoing wave."

"What did you do then?"

"What could I do? I was scared to death. I stayed in that tall grass, praying he wouldn't see me. When he finally walked past me, I could see him organizing, or maybe counting, the paper he had stuffed into his pockets. My heart was beating so loud, I was sure he could hear it. I waited five…maybe ten minutes, hoping he'd left the parking lot, then got up, and even though my legs felt so wobbly, somehow managed to walk the long way around just to be sure I wouldn't be seen. When I finally got to my car, I felt so relieved that I did the stupidest thing. I forgot that when I opened the door, the light would go on. I quickly looked around the dark parking lot, hoping no one was there to see me. But then, nearby, I saw the light on in a car. I immediately knew it was his car. I guess he was counting those pieces of paper again when he saw my light."

"How did you get out of there?"

"My heart was in my throat as I jumped into my car, got it started, and shifted into drive as fast as I could. I jammed my foot down on the gas pedal so hard the wheels spun, and I could hear pebbles flying in all directions. The car skidded around, but somehow, I managed to control it and raced over to the long road out of there. I heard him start his car, but he had to turn around, which gave me a few seconds head start to get to the main road. My heart was pounding…I was so scared, and I knew I was traveling too fast as I could hardly steer the car down the narrow lane. Somehow, I don't know how, I got to the main road, turned towards town, and sped off, almost losing control going around that first bend. I slowed down to look back but didn't see any lights following me. As I pulled into my driveway, I realized that bend in the road had saved my life, as there was no telling which way I'd gone."

For the next few minutes, we sat in silence on the bench while she tried to get her nerves under control, and I tried to figure out whether the murderer was a man or a woman. *Too many suspects*, I thought, gazing out at the darkening ocean where the wind was now whipping up the waves. The air suddenly felt colder.

I turned to tell her we should think about leaving, as it looked like it could start raining at any moment, only to find that her frightened expression had disappeared, replaced with a very appreciative smile. She reached over and squeezed my hand. Figuring she was sufficiently composed to discuss what to do next, I asked, "Ellen, don't you think you should tell the police what you just told me?"

"No! Absolutely not, Davis!" She pulled her hand away from mine. "I can't be involved in any of this. Don't you understand that I'd be risking my life? What if the murderer finds out I witnessed Harry's murder? He'd try to kill me too. No way, Davis, I'm not going to the police."

"But you should, Ellen. They need to hear your story. And they'll protect you!"

Ellen shook her head and stared icily at me. *She's definitely making a mistake,* I thought, but I didn't know how to persuade her otherwise. We sat in silence, watching the dark rain clouds come rolling towards us. "Ellen, we've got to leave, it's about to rain." As she nodded okay, the rain began, and we ran to the parking lot where I opened her car door, expecting her to jump in. Instead, she stood there and smiled warmly at me. I smiled back, frankly surprised after her sharp rebuke, and gestured at her to get in. But she kept smiling as the rain poured down, drenching both of us. Hers was a beautiful smile on a beautiful face, and we stood there staring at each other for another minute or two, soaked to the skin, before I put my finger on it: she was going to reward me for listening and believing her story! But why? I guessed she wanted someone to back her when the police came calling. That led me to quickly conjure up a scenario in which she murdered Harry in a fit of anger and then realized what she'd done and panicked. But still, she didn't impress me as the type who could lie so vividly about the goings-on of all those people running up and down the beach path. Ah…I guess my cynicism was getting the better of me. But why shouldn't it? Everyone else involved in Harry's murder has lied. So why not add her name to the list?

As we stood together in the pouring rain, I tried one last time to convince her to go to the police. "Look, Ellen, I know you're scared, but believe me, the police will protect you. They'll assign someone to guard you around the clock. You'll be safe."

"I can't, Davis. Don't you understand? I'm too afraid."

Feeling disappointed and a little angry, I replied, "You're making a big mistake, Ellen. I wish I could convince you to listen to me."

"Davis, I'm not making a mistake!"

"Well then…I guess there's nothing else to say." We stared at each other for a moment before I asked, somewhat dejectedly, "Do you want me to follow you home?"

"Yes, I would appreciate that very much."

I stood there, holding the car door open, waiting for her to step in. Instead, she stepped around the open door, threw her arms around my neck, and kissed me. At first, I thought, *What a nice reward for being a good listener.* But the kisses that followed were longer and a hell of a lot more passionate, leaving me to wonder if she had something more in mind. *God, why didn't I think of moving to this town years ago?* As I gazed into her beautiful green eyes, I realized that as fate would have it, I was in too much trouble to get involved. As the rain dripped down our faces, I tried to smile as warmly as possible to thank her for those ardent kisses, while wondering if I wasn't making the same mistake I'd made fifteen years ago with Maude.

I motioned to her again to get in the car and said, "I'll follow you." I could see the disappointment in those green eyes as she slammed the door and drove out of the parking lot towards home. There, I waved goodbye as she unlocked her front door. She gave a half-hearted wave back and stepped inside.

Chapter Twenty-Four

The sky had darkened, and the rain came down hard as I started back to Maude's house. *Why not wait out the storm in town, I thought, and where better than the coffee shop?* The place was empty, so I took my coffee and sat down next to one of the giant windows in the front. The coffee proved to be the right catalyst to reflect on Ellen's account of everyone's comings and goings at the beach the night Harry was murdered. It seemed they each had an incentive to kill him. What a bastard he was... destroying their lives and their dreams...just as he destroyed mine! The more I thought about it, the angrier I got. I took another sip of coffee and tried to cool down.

As I sat there watching the rain stream down the window, I found myself drifting back to Ellen's account of how Harry was shot at close range. He had to have known the person well enough to let them get that close to him. But that didn't help to narrow the list of possible killers at all. Frustrated at not getting closer to finding an answer or anything that even resembled one, I slammed my empty cup down on the table with an accompanying *damn*! I looked back out at the rain pouring down and suddenly thought about Maude, and how anxious she had been at my leaving so abruptly this morning. Feeling guilty that I had left her alone most of the day, I decided to call her and try to make amends. Luckily, the coffee shop had a pay phone, so I didn't have to go out into the storm. I started apologizing as soon as Maude answered, and was about to tell her that I'd be back as soon as the rain stopped when she interrupted me to say in an unsettled voice, "Davis, I have company. Fred Simmons and Lucy Grimes, and my nemesis, Charlie Reynolds, are here. They stopped by to talk."

"What about?" I asked nervously.

There was a moment of silence before she responded, "About you."

"What about me?"

"They believe that you murdered Harry!"

"And what do they want from you, Maude?" I asked slowly.

"To join them in making the case to Brantley."

"So that's their game! Maude, I'm leaving now, and should be there in twenty minutes."

"Davis…they had me call Brantley to come out here tonight. Oh, how I want to get this whole thing over with as quickly as possible!"

"Don't do or say anything, Maude. I'll be there soon!"

****

The rain pounded against the car as I started back to Maude's house, not only limiting my visibility but creating an eerie darkness that made Beach Drive's winding turns even more treacherous. And as if that weren't enough, as I rounded the first sharp bend in the road, a series of lightning flashes lit up the sky, closely followed by loud, rolling claps of thunder. Needing no more convincing to wait out the squall, I looked for a spot to pull over, but the next bend came up too fast. As I slowly rounded the turn onto the straightaway, I saw only thick brush on both sides of the road, so I kept on going. I don't know what possessed me to check my rearview mirror to see if anyone was closing fast behind me, but the road was empty. All I could do was shake my head in embarrassment at my lingering anxiety.

The rain suddenly became torrential, cutting my visibility to practically zero and giving me no choice but to pull over and wait for a lull in the storm before driving on. Just as I put my flashers on, two police cars raced past me with their red and blue lights flashing wildly. *There could be only one place they were going,* I thought, which made me nervous as hell. Now I had no choice but to continue on…and fast. That turned out to be a major mistake because as I navigated around the next sharp bend, my car slid off the road with the right-side wheels sinking into roadside sand. "Damn it!" I shouted in frustration. "I've got to get back on the road. If those wheels sink in further, I'll be stuck here all night!" Holding my breath, I slowly pressed down on the accelerator and prayed the wheels wouldn't spin. Somehow, it worked. I sighed with relief, thinking, *Finally, a little luck!*

Taking the experience to heart, I drove slowly around the next bend, which opened up onto another straightaway, taking me past Harry's imposing wrought iron gates and those large initials of his. The sight irritated me so much that I drove the last two miles faster.

When I pulled into Maude's driveway, I saw the two police cars parked near the front entrance, their colored lights still flashing in every direction and reflecting on everything that glistened. I parked off to one side and was turning off the windshield wipers and headlights just as Sergeant Brock ran over with one hand resting on his revolver.

I rolled down my window and shouted through the rain, "It's me, Sergeant. Davis Lowe. Is it okay to park here? I'm going into the house."

"Of course, Mr. Lowe. Detective Brantley is expecting you. Let's get inside before we both get soaked."

****

As we entered the living room, Detective Brantley called out, "Ah…Welcome, Mr. Lowe. I've been waiting for your arrival."

"What's going on here, Detective?" I asked as calmly as possible, sensing a trap. I looked around the room. There was Maude, sitting up against one arm of the sofa, feet tucked under her, obviously upset, her expression seeming to suggest she had just committed some kind of mortal sin…hopefully not against me! Charlie Reynolds sat slouched down in a nearby armchair, his hands simultaneously moving slowly back and forth along the arms as he observed the room. There was no gloating smile this time. His eyes darted back and forth from Brantley to Maude, then over at me, as though he was trying to figure out how to pin Harry's murder on the two of us while absolving himself. On the other side of the sofa sat Lucy Grimes and her new...er...old lover, Fred Simmons. She was staring contemptuously at me, obviously convinced that I'd murdered *her* Harry. And now, *her* Fred was holding her hand tightly, giving me a look that I'd come to know so well...one that just oozes hatred for me.

I looked back over at Brantley, standing in front of the floor-to-ceiling windows that were now laced with thick white foam from the turbulent ocean below. His arms were folded across his chest, and he sported a 'gotcha' smile on his face. "Sit down, Mr. Lowe. Please...over there on that armchair. The one I've reserved just for you." As I sat down, he slowly and carefully surveyed the room. Apparently satisfied that all the key suspects were there, he cleared his throat and began to speak. "The last time we met, except for Miss Grimes, of course, Sergeant Brock and I were in the early stages of gathering critical evidence in the investigation of the murder of Harry Miller. I must say we've made great progress since then. The case is moving right along. Yes, right along." He gave a proud nod.

Radiating confidence, Brantley continued. "There has been a new twist in the case however, which may be connected to Harry Miller's murder. We were notified yesterday afternoon that there was an attempt on Mr. Lowe's life. It involved someone taking four shots at him from a speeding car. Sergeant Brock and I have been working to determine who fired those four shots. Our first clue came after examining the damage to Mr. Lowe's car. Although totaled after hitting a tree, we still found plenty of evidence on both the car's sides and undercarriage. Our impression was that Mr. Lowe's car must have been forced off the road multiple times by the perpetrator. To verify our theory, we went out to Beach Drive to look around and found tire tracks and large amounts of sand, rocks, and debris spewed more than two miles along the road. We concluded that Mr. Lowe's adept driving must have frustrated the perpetrator, preventing him from making it look like a fatal accident. Instead, he was forced to use a pistol and fired four shots, one of which grazed Mr. Lowe's lower back just before he crashed into the tree. When Mrs. Williamson arrived at the scene, Mr. Lowe was sitting dazed and bleeding on a rock. Isn't that right, Mrs. Williamson?"

Maude responded with a rather uninterested *yes,* obviously still wrapped up in her own problems. Brantley nodded, and after glancing quickly around the room again, said, "We assumed that whoever was involved in the wild chase with Mr. Lowe likely also sustained significant damage to their car. We then spent time talking to junkyard owners in the area and examining a number of recently junked cars." Just as Brantley pointed his finger at Fred Simmons, a huge roar suddenly echoed throughout the living room as a wave smashed against the rocks below, startling all of us. We heard the sound of rushing water quickly follow, then smack hard against the pillars supporting the house, causing it to sway slightly from the force. We all gasped...surprised and frightened.

I looked at Brantley, who was staring wide-eyed at Maude, anxious for reassurance that the house was in no danger of collapsing on the rocks below. She looked up at his worried face, smiled, then said, rather nonchalantly, "Oh, don't worry, we're quite safe here."

Brantley shook his head in disbelief. Taking a deep breath, he turned back to the now wary Simmons. "As I started to say, we looked at several junked cars, and concluded that the car we were searching for belonged to you!" Simmons started to respond, but Brantley waved his hand to stop the anticipated denial. "Oh, please, Mr. Simmons, don't try to plead innocent. We know it was your car. The junkyard owner immediately recognized your picture. It seems you had quite an argument with him over the price. After making a deal, you removed the license plates, but unfortunately for you, not before he wrote the numbers down and called us. When we got there, we not only found multiple dents and scratches on your car, but the undercarriage was badly battered too. We thought it was quite remarkable that you were able to drive it to the junkyard in the first place."

Simmons started to speak, hesitated, then said defensively, "I don't deny it was my car, Detective. But I wasn't driving it that day. Maybe you weren't aware that I reported it stolen?"

"Oh, come now, Mr. Simmons. You expect us to believe that? Seems awfully convenient, doesn't it?"

"I'm telling you...someone stole my car! How would I know what they'd do with it?"

"Not true, Mr. Simmons. Not true at all! We found four shell casings that must have rolled under the seat after shots were fired at Mr. Lowe. They were .22 caliber casings...just like your pistol's casings."

"That doesn't prove they were mine!" Simmons quickly retorted.

"Not yet anyway, Mr. Simmons...not yet! We've checked the used casings for marks left by the firing pin, and all four were perfectly matched. We want to recheck your pistol to see if it has been fired since we last tested it, and if so, whether the casing marks match those from your gun. Where is your pistol now, Mr. Simmons?"

"It's at home."

"Sergeant Brock will stop by to pick it up tonight. And if it was your pistol, that's all the evidence we need to verify that you fired those four shots. In the meantime, I strongly advise you not to leave town."

Brantley turned and gazed at the foam sliding down the picture window for a few moments. Swinging around, he pointed his finger again at a now nervous-looking Simmons and said, "I'm wondering, Mr. Simmons, is it possible you murdered Harry Miller at Miss Grimes' urging?"

Sounding shaken, Simmons replied, "No! That's not true, not at all! I resent you even asking me that, Detective! Lucy...ah...Miss Grimes would never ask me to do anything like that."

Brantley stared hard at him, then asked, "Did you go down to the beach the night of the murder to confront Harry Miller on Miss Grimes' behalf?"

"I certainly did not, Detective!" he shouted defensively.

"Were you down at the beach that night, Mr. Simmons?"

"No, I wasn't there, Detective!"

"Are you sure you weren't there, Mr. Simmons? Perjury can bring you jail time."

Simmons hesitated, obviously debating how to answer, then weakly offered, "Well…yes, okay, I did go. But Miller was already dead, Detective!"

Brantley quickly turned to Lucy Grimes. "Do you own a Colt .22 pistol, Miss Grimes?"

"I do, Detective. Fred bought it for me years ago to go target practicing with him. We haven't done that in quite a while, now have we, Fred?"

"Where is your pistol now, Miss Grimes?"

"At home on the top shelf of my closet."

"Are you sure, Miss Grimes?" Brantley demanded with a questioning stare.

"Why…ah…yes, Detective."

"Could Mr. Simmons have used your pistol to shoot at Mr. Lowe, not wanting to use his own after the police tested it?"

"No! I told you, it's in my closet."

Brantley paused, then turned to gaze at the foam-covered window again, deciding where to go with his questioning. When he looked back, his eyes were wide open as if he had just discovered a new angle to the case, and was anxious to spring it. "Miss Grimes, did you murder Harry Miller?"

"I did not!" she shouted indignantly.

"Did you give your pistol to Mr. Simmons the night Harry Miller was murdered?"

"No! I had nothing to do with Harry Miller's murder!"

"I'll ask you again, Miss Grimes…did you murder Harry Miller? You had every reason to, didn't you? He called off your pending marriage and then refused to give back your five million dollars. Isn't that when you returned to the beach and shot him?"

"No! That's not true! I didn't shoot Harry Miller. I'm telling you, Detective, my pistol is on the top shelf of my closet," she whimpered.

"We'll see about that when Sergeant Brock comes by tonight to pick it up for testing, Miss Grimes."

The living room fell silent. Lucy's face tensed, and her eyes opened wide as she turned to Fred for help, but he just smiled confidently at her and patted her hand. Suddenly, another wave hit the rocks below with a resounding roar. From the sound, this one was bigger and seemed more powerful than the last. Instinctively, everyone turned to the floor-to-ceiling windows and watched as a sheet of ocean spray slammed against them, applying a thick coat of foam. The water surged up against the pillars with a tremendous force, smacking them so hard that the house seemed to sway backward a little before slowly righting itself.

We all held our breath, positive the worst was about to happen. Brantley turned anxiously to Maude and asked, "Is your house about to collapse, Mrs. Williamson?"

Maude answered, "Oh...there's really nothing to worry about, Detective. We've had much worse storms than this before, and I assure you that nothing has ever happened to this house," but she sounded a little less confident than before.

The worried expression on Brantley's face clearly indicated he wasn't convinced. After taking a deep breath, he returned to questioning Lucy. "Did you know that Harry Miller deposited your bank check for five million dollars last Wednesday, Miss Grimes?"

"Yes, I did. Well...not actually on Wednesday. My banker called me late that afternoon to verify that I had written the check. It wasn't deposited until Thursday." Sounding a little surer of herself, Lucy continued. "After I gave Harry the check, he promised he wouldn't put it into his investment fund until after he bought the insurance policy. He swore to me he'd buy the policy on Friday. I told him that was fine as long as he bought it then. I had no reason not to trust him,

Detective; after all, he was going to be my husband."

"Ms. Grimes, were you down at the beach that night?"

"Yes, Harry asked me to meet him there around 12:30."

"Was he alive at the time?"

"Why yes! We spoke before being interrupted by Maude."

"Did she stay long?"

"No, she left in quite a hurry."

Her answer seemed to surprise Brantley. He stared at her for a moment, then turned to Maude, demanding, "Mrs. Williamson, what were you doing down at the beach that night?"

"Harry asked me to meet him there."

"What time was that?"

"Around 11:30."

"Did you see Ms. Grimes?"

"No, I did not."

"Ms. Grimes, how did you know Mrs. Williamson was there then?"

"Um, I must have the time wrong. I was very anxious to see Harry and talk to him about our wedding plans and our honeymoon."

Brantley's long, suspicious glare said it all. "Tell me the truth, Ms. Grimes, just when were you there?"

"Oh...I really don't know, Detective. I was so excited about getting married!"

Brantley looked up at the ceiling in disbelief at her answer, then nodded to Brock as if to say, *We definitely have to come back to this.* Turning to Maude, he asked, "Mrs. Williamson, what were you doing down at the beach?"

"As I said, Detective, Harry asked me to meet him there."

"Why would he ask you?"

"To say goodbye."

Apparently caught off guard by her answer, Brantley started to ask a follow-up question, hesitated, and instead changed the subject. "Mrs. Williamson, why did you lie to me? We now know that you gave Harry Miller the four hundred-thousand-dollar check he deposited that Wednesday."

"I'm terribly sorry I lied to you, Detective. Frankly, I didn't want to be involved in any of this. But Harry forced me. He was a desperate man and would have done anything to get the money. I was afraid he'd hurt me!"

A quick shake of Brantley's head indicated he wasn't buying her story. Just as he began to ask Maude another question, a heavy deluge of rain pelted the windows, followed by a series of waves that slammed hard against the rocks below with a deafening roar. Brantley abruptly stopped his questioning. We all froze, petrified, waiting to hear the rush of water crash against the pillars, which it did, with a frightening force. The house swayed further back than before from the impact, then started to slowly right itself. But the next wave came quickly, smacking the pillars harder, tilting the house back again. The lights flickered, then went out. Seconds later, they came back on, but dimly, then went out again. No one moved. No one could move! We were all scared to death...even Maude! As the house creaked back into place, the lights flashed on and off several times more, then stayed on. We all held our breath waiting for the next big wave, but this time it hit the rocks below without the telltale-deafening roar. The same with the next...and the next...and the next. We looked around at each other, not believing the worst was over. But it was! Everyone relaxed, and there was a collective sigh of relief.

I glanced over at Brantley. He was standing with his back to the room, appearing to look out the window, but more likely trying to regain his composure. It took a minute or so before he turned back to us. I was right! His face was pale, but he seemed determined to get back to business. Wiping his forehead with his handkerchief, he fired his first question at Charlie Reynolds. "Mr. Reynolds," he asked with a nervous tremor in his voice, "tell me exactly, how much money was Mr. Miller going to invest in your business project?"

"Why...ah, he agreed to put in five hundred thousand at the contract signing."

"Did he come up with the money?"'

"No, he never did!"

"Mr. Reynolds, did you believe Mr. Miller had the money to invest in...?" Brantley suddenly stopped mid-sentence, distracted by a series of lightning flashes that lit up the sky, turning the living room as bright as day. Again, we all sat holding our breath, fearing the storm's possible return. But the lightning moved away, just as a barrage of booming thunder reverberated directly overhead, rattling the house. Sitting there, looking as though we were frozen in time, we listened...waiting and wondering what would happen next. But thankfully, the thunder moved off into the distance, too, followed by another round of grateful sighs.

Brantley turned his attention slowly back to Reynolds. "I'll ask you again, Mr. Reynolds, did you believe Mr. Miller had the money to invest in this project?"

A little smile crept across Reynolds' face. He stared at Maude for a moment before replying, "Yes, at first I did. When I approached Harry, I understood his investment fund was still doing okay, although a few rumors were circulating as to just how well. I kept asking him if he was sure he could get the money. His reply was always the same...*That he could get it anytime he wanted it from a dear friend.*"

"The dear friend was Mrs. Williamson, was it not, Mr. Reynolds?"

"That's correct, Detective."

Brantley turned to Maude to ask a question, thought better of it, and returned to Reynolds. "What exactly was your deal? And just how much did you and Mr. Miller expect to make from it?"

Reynolds appeared taken aback by the question, and hesitated, probably thinking it was too personal. But when he saw Brantley standing there with a stern look on his face, he knew the detective wasn't backing down. With a shrug of his shoulders, he acquiesced, and replied, "Well...it was a real estate deal, Detective, one that I had been searching for a very long time. It started with a chance meeting in town with a good friend of mine, George Addison. He told me that he was going to sell his home and land overlooking the ocean...ah, the property was further up Beach Drive…and move into a senior residence closer to town. I knew he had about forty acres, which had been in his family, I guess, since the eighteen or nineteen hundreds, and frankly, the place looked it! George was now in his mid-eighties, and not in particularly good health. He had disowned his two adult children years ago, so he asked me if I could help him sell it. I said I'd do better than that…I'd buy it from him. We agreed on the spot that I'd give him two hundred thousand dollars in good faith, and five hundred thousand more on signing a contract with him. And he'd get thirty percent of the selling price when the deal closed. George agreed. But he wanted the deal to close quickly. That's when I asked Harry to partner with me as I was sure he'd be able to come up with the five hundred thousand fast…from his dear friend!"

Reynolds stopped, hesitant to say anything more in front of us, but Brantley pressed him. "What did you think you could sell the property for, Mr. Reynolds?"

Reynolds' face turned a shade of red, but Brantley's persistent stare and willingness to wait gave him no choice but to answer. "Well, I showed Harry the property, and he got excited as hell! We agreed it could easily be subdivided into twenty, maybe thirty lots…maybe more. We were sure that on seeing the fabulous ocean view, any developer would jump at the chance to pay fifteen million, at least. Harry was already counting his share in his head, as he needed this money to help solve his financial woes, which I had heard were starting to mount up. As for me, I'd be set for life!

"As we were leaving the property, Harry slapped me on the back, and in his usual arrogant way, told me not to worry about a thing, that the five hundred thousand would be ours with the snap of his fingers. Detective, I'd been searching for this kind of a deal for nearly ten years. It was one sweet deal!"

"So what happened, Mr. Reynolds?"

"Well…" he replied in a defeated voice, "Harry hemmed and hawed about delivering the five hundred thousand. Rumors were flying that his fund was in trouble…deep trouble! George kept asking when I'd have the money, and I kept telling him to be patient, I'd have it within a week. I kept asking Harry again and again when he'd have the money, but he wouldn't give me an answer. He finally called last Friday and said to meet him down at the beach after the dinner Saturday night. I asked him if he was going to have the money by then and he said he'd tell me when we met. I told him I wasn't going to come unless he gave me a check for the five hundred thousand. The next thing I know, Harry's dead. The deal's off. And I'm out two hundred thousand dollars!"

"Weren't there any other investors willing to write a check, Mr. Reynolds?"

"Not any I knew, especially after what Harry did to them."

"Then you didn't meet him down at the beach that night, Mr. Reynolds?"

"No, I didn't!"

"Are you sure, Mr. Reynolds? Didn't you want to make one last try before Mr. Miller left on his honeymoon?"

"Absolutely not, Detective!"

"Why not, Mr. Reynolds?"

"I was positive Harry didn't have the money. It would have been a waste of my time."

I had watched Brantley shake his head as Reynolds told his story, especially when he denied going down to the beach that night, so I figured he was going to pressure Reynolds with more questions about not meeting up with Harry that night. Instead, he turned to me with a 'gotcha' smile on his face that made it glow. Whatever surprise he had been saving up for me, he was about to spring it.

"Ah...Mr. Lowe. You're the banker here, or you were, so you must know all the ins and outs of banking. Please tell me in detail just how you'd go about converting the five million dollars in Harry Miller's bank account into a dozen or so pieces of easily transportable negotiable certificates of deposit in just a few days."

"I'd have to think about that, Detective."

"Come, come, Mr. Lowe! Why do you need to think about it?

Didn't you do just that for Mr. Miller?"

"Did what for Miller, Detective?"

"Please don't be evasive, Mr. Lowe. I know you did it. And I'm sure there was a fee involved for you…and a very stiff one at that!"

I sat there stunned, not knowing what to say. But before I could come up with a response, Charlie Reynolds jumped out of his armchair, shouting and jabbing his finger at me. "I knew it! I knew it! I spotted him as a thief the first time I laid on eyes on him. I just knew it! He told me that he came up for Harry's funeral 'just out of curiosity.' Curiosity, my ass! He came to murder Harry for the money. And I was right! I could always spot a guy like that!"

This elicited a strong Brantley headshake. "Now, now, Mr. Reynolds, I didn't say anything about murder. My question to Mr. Lowe was, 'How do you take five million dollars and convert it into a dozen or so pieces of negotiable paper in just a few days?'"

That burst Charlie's bubble. He slowly sat back down in his armchair and stared in disbelief at Brantley's out-of-hand dismissal of my murdering Harry.

Brantley turned back to me, his gotcha grin still firmly in place, impatient for my answer. But I was in shock as to how he even knew about the transaction. I had to come up with something quick, but what? My thoughts raced as I searched for an answer that would get me off the hook without admitting a thing. I came up blank. All I could focus on was, *How in the world had he learned about the transaction?* Could he be bluffing? Did he call my bank and ask them? Or did Maude tell him about my confession to her? She could have made a deal with Brantley not to prosecute her after Brock found those bullets, and believed she still owned a gun. What about Swenson? Maybe he went to the police and told them about her gun? No, that doesn't make sense…he wants his money. No, it had to be Maude! She needed to get Brantley off her back, so told him about the certificates as if I had confessed my part to her in helping Harry. Ah…so that explained her mortal sin look.

But still, what the hell do I tell Brantley? I can't lie as it sounds like he already knows my bank handled the transaction. But if I tell him the truth, he's going to leap to the conclusion that I murdered Harry for those certificates. Damn it, I've got to come up with something he'll believe.

"Mr. Lowe, I'm waiting for your answer. And I want the truth, Mr. Lowe. Only the truth!" he commanded, loving every bit of my squirming.

I looked over at Maude, who was busy watching the thick layer of foam slide slowly down one of the floor-to-ceiling windows. *And here I helped her,* I thought. Well, that's gratitude for you!

"I'm waiting, Mr. Lowe. Now!"

"All right, Detective...I'll explain." I started slowly, still searching for a way out. "A little over two weeks ago, I was sitting at my desk at the bank when I got a phone call from Harry. I couldn't believe it! Ten years...and never a word from him. But now out of the blue, he calls, asking me for a favor. Ten years...and now a favor! 'The hell with him,' I thought and hung up. A minute later, he called back, shouting, 'Davey wait! Don't hang up again. I have a proposition that will make you a hell of a lot of money...and fast!'"

"So, that's how you quickly overcame your animosity, Mr. Lowe?" Brantley needled.

"Well...I guess you could say that, Detective."

"So tell me, Mr. Lowe, exactly what was his proposition? And again, tell the truth, please! I'm sure you understand the consequences if you don't."

I stared long and hard at Brantley, then glanced at Maude, who was still staring at the foam on the window. I sensed this was fast becoming a trap with no escape. All I could think was, *Would I go to prison...and for how long?*

"Please, Mr. Lowe. We don't have all night!"

"All right, Detective. Two weeks before Harry's dinner, he asked me to come up to Connecticut to meet with him. I told him *no* a half a dozen times, but if you knew Harry, Detective, he never took no for an answer, especially when he wanted something. That was Harry's unique talent, Detective. He could make the most convincing offer that you just couldn't turn down."

"Get on with it, Mr. Lowe."

"His offer? Well…Harry went right to my weak spot. Money! He swore to me he'd make it worth my while. It was like old times with him holding a pot of gold in his hand to tantalize me. And before I knew it, he hit my other weak spot, telling me I'd be able to quit my bank job tomorrow and get back into the real action of buying and selling stocks. Having been stuck in a dead-end job for eight years, I couldn't resist. So, I drove up here, and we met at a little place outside of town near that ice cream shop for lunch. He laid out what he wanted me to do, which was to have my bank convert the five million he was getting from Lucy into negotiable certificates of deposit that he could take with him when he left on his honeymoon. I laughed at him! I told him I was in no position to do that. Higher-ups in the bank did that. Harry was shocked, to say the least. At first, I thought that would scuttle his plan. But Harry wasn't one to give up easily. It wasn't in his DNA. So over a sandwich, he devised another plan."

"And what was that, Mr. Lowe?"

"He asked who had to approve the transaction. I told him a senior vice president, reminding him that we're a small bank. Then he asked, what if he overpaid the bank a fee for converting the money into certificates in say…two days? I told him that I didn't think the bank would do that. They would follow their normal procedures to avoid the usual concerns about money laundering. But I told him that I'd try to find out."

"And what did he offer you as a reward for making it happen, Mr. Lowe?"

"Well…he pulled out his checkbook and said he'd write me a check for half of the two hundred and fifty thousand dollars he was going to pay me. And that I'd get the balance when he got the certificates."

"A lot of money for finding out something as simple as that? Did you take it, Mr. Lowe?"

"Yes, of course, I took it!"

"And what did you do with the money, Mr. Lowe?"

"The first thing I did was buy an ice cream cone!"

"So you lied to me, Mr. Lowe, when you told me you were not in town two weeks before the dinner."

Charlie Reynolds sneered, "Anyone could see that he didn't make the trip up here just for ice cream!"

"That's enough out of you, Mr. Reynolds."

Ignoring them both, I continued. "The senior vice president told me the bank would do it and would be very happy to accept an additional fee for the rapid processing. I called Harry about it, and he agreed to send me a check for the balance, which he did."

"So that's why he bullied me into giving him the four hundred thousand dollars," Maude hissed. "And you knew all along where the money came from, didn't you, Davis?"

Brantley cut my response off, demanding, "So when did you bring the certificates up here, Mr. Lowe?"

"The bank approved my being the courier last Thursday, and I brought them up and gave them to Harry on Friday."

"Do you know what he did with them?"

"No."

"Did you get a signed receipt for the certificates, Mr. Lowe?"

"Yes."

"Did you stay in town that Saturday for the dinner, Mr. Lowe?"

"No, I didn't."

"Don't lie to me, Mr. Lowe."

Before I could deny it again, Lucy Grimes jumped up, shouting, "So you're the one who murdered *my* Harry! I always believed it was you, you bastard! You killed him for the money!"

"I didn't kill him! I wasn't even here last Saturday night."

"You did too! I just know it!"

"Maybe you and *your* Fred did it," I shot back.

"How dare you say that to me!" Her face was crimson with rage as she headed straight towards me with Fred close behind.

"Sit down, Ms. Grimes! You too, Mr. Simmons!" Brantley shouted, motioning to Brock to block their path. They stopped but continued to glare threateningly at me while Brock guided them back to their seats. Brantley glared at me, too, accompanied by an angry headshake.

I don't give a damn what Brantley thinks. I'm not going to let her get away with accusing me of murder without a fight. "Lucy," I shouted at her, "You said you were meeting Harry to talk about your wedding and honeymoon. But I know that Harry slapped your face when you didn't want to obey his order to run across the beach just before Maude showed up. That doesn't sound like the actions of a loving couple...now does it? Then, after she left, you came back and screamed at him, telling him to go to hell! That got him really angry, and he told you the wedding was off. And on top of that, he was keeping your five million! That's a combination that gives you one hell of a motive to come back and murder him! And maybe...you told *your* Fred here what you did before going to the police. He then hustled down to the beach to make sure Harry was dead. Where just by chance, he found the certificates before dragging Harry into the water."

"Not true! Not true! You did it for the money. It's so obvious!" Lucy shouted back, her body shaking with anger.

Simmons put his arm around her, trying to calm her down. Pointing his finger at me, he said, "Lowe, I'm going to get you this time...you can count on it!"

"It hasn't worked so far, now has it, Simmons?"

"Stop this!" Brantley bellowed. "Stop this at once! I'm the one asking the questions here. Does everyone understand that?" Turning to me, he asked suspiciously, "How do you know all this, Mr. Lowe?"

"There was a witness at the beach that night who saw it all happen."

"A witness? Who?" Brantley's face lit up with anticipation.

"The witness has refused to come forward for fear of being killed, Detective."

Brantley's anticipation quickly turned to anger. "I don't believe you, Mr. Lowe!"

"It's true, Detective!"

"Mr. Lowe, you are up to your ears in this murder. So let's start from the beginning. Tell me where those certificates are now."

"I have no idea!"

"Stop lying to me, Mr. Lowe. You were the only one who knew Mr. Miller had those certificates."

"That's not true, Detective."

"What do you mean it's not true, Mr. Lowe?"

"Let me explain. The witness saw five people come down to the beach that night. Lucy and Maude already admitted they were there. But there were three others, starting with Charlie over there."

Reynolds jumped up. "That's a lie, Lowe! You can't use me to cover up your murdering Harry for the five million!"

Ignoring him, Brantley said with an exasperated sigh, "Mr. Lowe, I don't believe any of this!"

"Detective, just let me tell you what else the witness saw."

"You're wasting my time, Mr. Lowe."

I stared at him, wondering how the hell he got off being so arrogant. Ah…the hell with it. "Let me start with Reynolds over there. You had a heated argument with Harry, didn't you, about him calling off your deal. You kept pressing him to pay up the five hundred thousand as promised. But Harry told you *no* every time you asked. The last straw had to be when Harry bragged to you that he was leaving on Monday with all the money he ever needed…and patted his stomach as if he had the certificates with him. The witness said you cursed Harry out for killing the deal, and before you left, threatened him with, 'This is the last time you'll do this to me!'"

"Lies…all lies!" Reynolds sneered. "He's trying to make me the fall guy, Detective!"

"Mr. Lowe, this phantom witness of yours isn't going to save you."

"Then, Detective, I have nothing to lose by telling you the rest of what the witness told me, now do I?" Brantley looked surprised but said nothing. I started to speak again when suddenly I realized that I knew too much about Harry's murder. A cold chill ran down my back at my stupidity. But what choice did I have? Brantley needed to hear about what Ellen had seen, yet the thought of being the sacrificial lamb who brought out the murderer scared the hell out of me. Taking a deep breath, I continued. "According to the witness, about ten minutes after Reynolds left, someone else arrived. Harry had taken off his shoes and socks and was walking in the water, but came out to tell the person, 'I knew you'd be back.' The person didn't answer, but instead approached Harry, stopping only a few feet away before pulling out a gun. Harry appeared shocked, then frightened, clearly not expecting this. He pleaded not to shoot. But the pleas obviously fell on deaf ears as the person shot him once in cold blood."

"Was it a man or a woman, Mr. Lowe?" Brantley demanded.

"It was dark, and the witness couldn't tell from their angle of sight, Detective."

"Then what good is your witness?" Brantley grumbled.

"I'd say damn good, Detective!"

"Fine. Let's hear the rest of it, Mr. Lowe."

"The witness said that after shooting Harry, the murderer ran off down the path. About fifteen minutes later, a man, yes, a man came running up the path out of breath. He stopped and turned on his flashlight, searched over the beach until he spotted Harry, and then ran over to make sure he was dead."

"What are you driving at Mr. Lowe?"

"Well, Detective, the man seemed to know that Harry was already dead. Suppose for argument's sake, this man was told that before he came down to the beach. And suppose he got there ahead of the police, just to make sure it was true. He could have known about Harry's money belt, searched him, and found the certificates. Realizing what they were, he probably thought he had just received manna from heaven. Now he had everything he ever wanted: a lifetime's worth of untraceable money, and the love of his life back in his life. Who, by the way, would be obligated to do whatever he wanted under the threat of his telling the police about Harry's murderer. It couldn't have happened more perfectly if he'd planned it himself!"

Simmons flew out of his seat. "I should have beaten the crap out of you that day in the bar, Lowe! How dare you accuse Lucy of murdering Harry after all she's been through! And now...now you're trying to blame me for stealing those certificates?"

"Simmons, you forget that I started out by saying 'suppose.' The two of you have perfect motives. But did you actually kill Harry? That's Detective Brantley's job to determine."

"What do you think you're doing here, Mr. Lowe...playing detective?"

"I'm just trying to show you that there are motives to go around."

"But so far everything you have said hinges on your phantom witness. Until I can question that person, all your speculation means nothing. Is that clear to you, Mr. Lowe?"

"Well, then, Detective, I might as well tell you my last theory based on what the witness told me. At Harry's dinner, Maude went over, congratulated him, then asked him to meet her down at the beach that night. He agreed, and she kissed him before leaving. She's already admitted meeting Harry down at the beach. But according to the witness, what she left out was how horribly Harry treated her after she made a desperate attempt to convince him to love her again. She left the beach in tears. But whether she was the one who came back to shoot him, the witness couldn't say."

"How could you do this to me, Davis?" Maude howled, jumping up with her hands outstretched as if her last friend in the world had deceived her. She fell back down, and with head bowed and shaking, asked, "How could you even think that after all I've been through, I could kill him?"

"Maude, you still loved him! That's what you told me when you saw that yellow tape on the beach."

"You know I didn't murder Harry! I've already paid my debt!" she cried, tears flowing down her cheeks.

From the look on Brantley's face, it appeared I'd confused him even more. There were too many motives, and he didn't know which way to turn. "Mr. Lowe, I want to know the name of your witness now! If you don't tell me, I'll arrest you for suppressing evidence and obstructing justice."

"Detective, I'm not going to break the witness's confidence."

"Well, Mr. Lowe, a night in jail might help convince you otherwise."

"At least I'll have a place to stay tonight!"

"Don't be so flippant, Mr. Lowe. I assure you that you won't like it."

Our attention suddenly turned to Lucy. "How can you not arrest him for murdering *my* Harry?" she screamed. "It's so clear he did it. He already told you his motive: money and the chance for a life he's always wanted. Can't you see that, Detective?"

Brantley could hardly control his anger as he walked over to where she was sitting, and looking down at her with a piercing stare said threateningly, "Ms. Grimes, there's enough evidence to hold you too for Harry Miller's murder!"

Lucy burst into tears as Fred put his arms around her. "As you can see Detective, she's distraught, and didn't know what she was saying."

Brantley's eyes widened in disbelief, followed by a quick headshake at Simmons' flimsy defense of her. He walked to the window and looked out through the remnants of foam at the ocean, obviously buying time to think about what to do next.

"Davis, I'm trying to figure out who your phantom witness is," Maude hissed through her tears. "From what I remember, I only saw two people besides myself stop by Harry's table to congratulate him. Everyone else was too furious at the closing of his investment fund to even talk to him."

I tensed, knowing that if Maude came up with Ellen's name, she'd be in real trouble…and I had put her there. Everyone in the room turned to look at Maude. She shook her head several times and then smiled deviously. Looking up at Brantley, she practically shouted, "I know who it was!"

"Well, who?" demanded Brantley, turning around quickly.

"It has to be Ellen Houser!"

"Why?" Brantley asked.

"Because she sat at the table next to Harry's and was talking with him when I stopped by. I remember as I was leaving, she gave me a dirty look. I'm positive that my interrupting had stopped whatever she was trying to tell him." Maude thought about it some more and added, "I'd swear she overheard my earlier conversation with Harry. By the way, Detective, did you know that Ellen had been informally engaged to Harry? That was before you, Lucy. Who knows, maybe she gave Harry money too."

I grimaced at the thought of having put Ellen in harm's way, but I didn't say a word. I saw Brantley out of the corner of my eye, looking at me for confirmation, but I just focused on Maude. Finally, a frustrated Brantley demanded, "Well, Mr. Lowe, is that your phantom witness?"

"I'm not answering your question, Detective!"

Brantley was furious at my refusal. He started to stutter an angry reply but thought better of it. I could see in his eyes that he'd love nothing more than to slap the cuffs on me and cart me off to jail right now. Turning his back to the room, he stood looking out the window, most likely deciding what to do with me, and I assume the others too. We all just sat there on tenterhooks waiting for his next move. It took a minute or two before he faced us again, looking angry and confused. "We'll meet at police headquarters tomorrow at 11:00 am sharp, and Ellen Houser will be there too!" He then turned and walked out, followed by Sergeant Brock. At the front door, he stopped to take a long look back at us all before stepping out into the rainswept night.

Chapter Twenty-Five

Nobody moved! We all sat there, practically in a daze, trying to figure out who among us was the murderer. As we eyed each other suspiciously, I could feel the penetrating stares of Lucy and Simmons as if they were pondering whether to punch me out...or murder me right then and there! Simmons finally shook his head in disgust and putting his arm around a still distraught Lucy, led her out the front door.

Reynolds got up to leave. When he reached the front door, he turned back to look at me, and the abject hatred I saw in his eyes made me cringe. He gave a nod that said, *I'm going to get you...trust me!* Then he walked out, slamming the door behind him.

I looked over at Maude. She was sitting on the sofa in her usual pose with legs tucked under her, staring at me with that steely, intimidating stare of hers. I was sure she'd first curse me out, then throw me out, but she remained silent. I didn't know what to say, so I just sat there and waited, but as I did, I could see a bit of doubt about what to do with me creep across her face, so I decided my best bet was to keep sitting there, waiting.

She finally took a deep breath, shook her head reluctantly, and got up, saying, "Davis, I can't believe what you just did to me. You've put me at the top of Brantley's list, and I'm sure he's going to go all out to put me behind bars again. I trusted you, and this is how you treat me. I can't believe it...I just can't!" She then began to cry...the desperate cry of no escape. I felt guilty as hell, but I also knew that what I had said would have come out sooner or later. And if she was the killer, I certainly didn't want to be in the position of trying to shield her, as Brantley would surely nail me as her accessory. "I think you ought to leave, Davis!" she cried out through her tears as she walked into her bedroom and slammed the door.

I stood there, knowing she was right about leaving. "I'm sorry it has to end this way, Maude," I shouted at the closed bedroom door. *But I have to protect myself,* I thought. I went into the kitchen, picked up the phone, and dialed Ellen's number. When she answered, I told her I had to see her. Could she pick me up at Maude's house on Beach Drive?

"Be there in twenty minutes," she replied, sounding quite curious.

Chapter Twenty-Six

As I stood in the driveway waiting for Ellen to arrive, I looked up at the imposing, and still standing, steel and glass house perched high on a dune, wondering if I'd made the right decision about Maude. Out of the corner of my eye, I caught sight of her standing at the bedroom window watching me, but she moved away quickly. Did she feel torn about kicking me out after all we'd been through together? Maybe, but I knew she thought I'd broken our bond of *we're in this together*. And now, she had to face Brantley without me. I felt awful about that, but I had to protect Ellen since I had brought her front and center into this murder case.

I watched as Ellen drove slowly into the driveway, stopping when she saw me standing there. When I opened the car door, she appeared quite anxious, obviously wondering why she was picking me up here at this hour of the night. I hesitated to tell her until we got back to her house, thinking it would be easier there.

"Ellen, I need to rent a car and was hoping that one of the car rental places might still be open. Could you drive over to the strip where they're located?" She nodded yes, but when we got there, they were all closed. "One last request, could you drive over to the motel just off the highway so I can book a room for the night?"

"Stay with me tonight, Davis. I have plenty of extra room. You can pick up a car in the morning."

"That would be wonderful! Thanks so much."

"Now, tell me what's going on and why you're not staying with Maude?"

"I'll tell you when we get to your house."

****

Ten minutes later, Ellen started to turn into her driveway when we saw the police car and two officers standing next to it, talking. I shouted to her, "Keep driving! We've got to get out of here!" The officers turned to watch us drive away but thankfully didn't follow us.

Ellen sped to the outskirts of town, stopping at the entrance to an old dirt road. Shutting off the motor, she took a deep breath, then turned to me with a distrusting eye and loudly demanded, "Tell me what's going on, Davis! Why are the police sitting in my driveway? What did you tell them? You promised to keep me out of this! Wait, you did...didn't you?"

"Let me explain, Ellen, please!"

"Oh, my God! The police know that I witnessed Harry's murder! How could you, Davis? How could you do that to me!"

"Please, Ellen! Let's get some coffee, and then I'll explain."

"Why, Davis, why? I told you how I felt at being involved, yet you still involved me!" She was screaming now.

"Ellen, please, calm down, and I'll tell you what happened."

We pulled into the coffee shop parking lot five minutes later. Ellen turned off the lights and motor, and sat there staring furiously at me, impatient for my explanation.

"Would you like some coffee?"

"No!" she growled through gritted teeth.

When I got back into the car, I took one look at her and saw she was ready to explode. "Ellen, please let me explain. I told Brantley, the detective on the case, there was a witness to Harry's murder, but I refused to divulge your name. He threatened to arrest me, but I still refused to tell him. It was then that Maude Williamson remembered you were sitting at the table next to Harry's at his dinner and guessed the rest, which Brantley was happy to believe.

I said absolutely nothing about you!"

Her furious stare remained frozen on me, as she tried to decide whether to believe me or not. Finally, she shook her head, seeming to accept that she had no choice, and nervously asked, "Well Davis, now that you put me in the middle of all this, tell me, what should I do?"

"We're both in the middle of this!" I exclaimed. "The murderer must be worried as hell, thinking you saw who shot and killed Harry. And by telling me, it makes us both targets. We're in this together, Ellen."

"Okay then, what do *we* do now, Davis?" a now frightened Ellen asked.

"We can't go back to your place, that's for sure. Let's find somewhere to stay tonight. That will give me a chance to come up with something."

"My mother's house is at the far end of Beach Drive. We can stay there."

"I don't want to get your mother involved in this."

"Don't worry, she's in Paris for the month."

"Okay, then let's go there."

****

Ellen stopped the car in front of a massive black wrought iron gate. She took a door opener out of the glove compartment, clicked it on, and the huge gate slowly squeaked open. She carefully drove up a long, steep winding driveway to the top of a hill overlooking Beach Drive and the ocean beyond. There stood a large, stately white nineteenth-century colonial house with long, black shutters on every window, and a widow's walk built into the roof.

We pulled up to a stone path lined with a multitude of colorful flowers on both sides, leading up to the front of the house. Unlocking a large, black door, we stepped inside, where Ellen fumbled for the light switch. When she finally turned it on, I saw that we were standing in a shiplap paneled foyer with wide-planked wood floors. I followed her into the living room, where I was taken aback not only by its size but its spectacular ocean view through floor-to-ceiling windows stretching the length of a large, expensively furnished room with paintings of earlier generations of Housers.

Ellen led me to a side door that opened onto a large deck. Hoping to calm things down, I said, "Ah...isn't this a beautiful night, Ellen? And just look at that ocean with the moon shining across it." We stood transfixed for several minutes watching the moonlight shimmering across the vast becalmed ocean, and enjoying the warm sea air. Finally, I turned sheepishly to her and asked, "By any chance, does your mother have a bar? I'm desperate for a drink!"

Smiling knowingly, she led me back through the living room to a large nook with a well-stocked bar. "What will you have, Davis?"

"Scotch, straight up, please!"

"I'm going to have some wine...to steady my nerves."

We clinked our glasses in a silent toast and drank.

"Ah, that's better! Thank you, Ellen."

Her weak smile was brief as she quickly asked, "So what happens now that the police know I'm the witness to Harry's murder?"

"Unfortunately, we have to be at police headquarters tomorrow morning at 11 for more questioning," I replied hesitantly, hoping she wouldn't become hysterical again.

Ellen's eyes and mouth opened wide in disbelief at the trouble she found herself in. She appeared quite shaken and quickly reached for the wine bottle to pour another glass. After a long, slow swallow, she declared angrily, "You can't believe how sorry I am that I told you what I saw. You've put me right in the middle of all this, Davis! And that's exactly where I didn't want to be, damn it!"

I walked over and put my arms around her, trying to comfort her. "We're in this together, Ellen. And we're going to get out of this...together." She looked up at me with the same angry expression, then pushed me away. I can't say I was surprised by her reaction, but there was nothing I could do about it right now. "Let's go out on the deck again," I suggested. "The ocean is such a beautiful sight after a storm."

She followed me out, and we stood silently for a few minutes. Then, Ellen turned to me and asked curiously, "So how did you know Harry?"

"Oh...I thought I told you. I worked for him as a stock analyst for five years. How did you meet him?"

She took another long swallow of wine. Smiling to herself, she said, "I met him at a charity costume ball held annually in the town. He was dressed as a southern gambler, and I was Scarlet O'Hara. When we saw each other, we just laughed and spent the rest of the evening talking. That led to our whirlwind romance and introducing him to my mother right here on this deck."

"Knowing Harry, he must have been very impressed with all of this," I said with a wave of my arm.

"Yes, he certainly was! He said he loved the house and the view. But Harry being Harry, he immediately began to brag about how fabulous *his* house and view were. Then, he boasted how devoted he was to the town, and how proud he was to make so many contributions, which he proceeded to list one at a time, obviously trying to impress my mother. Clearly, he thought he'd found another potential investor, and quickly steered the conversation to how successful his investment fund was, and why so many people in town had invested in it. My mother listened intently. I could see she had taken a liking to him. I wasn't sure why, nor would she tell me. Maybe because he had given so much back to the town? Or, maybe she just liked young, ambitious, handsome men. Who knows? Anyway, she soon gave me that mother-daughter nod that Harry was the right guy. At first, I couldn't have agreed with her more! But as I got to know him better, I realized just how arrogant and self-centered he was. Davis, why I didn't act then, I don't know, but damn it, I should have! I guess I was leaning on my mother's judgment. And how well Harry understood my mother. It was as if he knew exactly what she liked to hear and fed it to her. It took me a while to find out what a real knack he had for doing that. At every chance he got, he never failed to mention how proud he was to be supporting the town's longstanding heritage, something dear to my mother's heart."

"Ellen, Harry was a master at that. He promoted himself all the time."

"I guess you're right, Davis. But truthfully, it wasn't too hard to learn just how much the town meant to my mother and me. You see, our family settled here in the early nineteenth century, and have been devoted residents ever since. My mother is tenth generation, and I'm eleventh! We're descendants of a sea captain whose wealth came mostly from trading rum and spices in the Caribbean. His was a Horatio Alger story. As a young man, he started out sailing up and down the Connecticut River in a small schooner, trading all kinds of foods and wares with the local towns along the river. Then, he became a large sailing ship captain, first trading in the Caribbean, then Europe. And before long, he captained one of the first steamships crossing the Atlantic. He loved living here in town, so he built this house...widow's walk and all. And our family has lived here ever since."

"I'm curious, Ellen. Did Harry really appreciate your family's heritage?"

"Well...I guess up to a point. But it was our money that impressed him even more. All he cared about was how to get his hands on it."

"That sounds like Harry!"

"I know! But still, we did have some wonderful romantic moments together. Of course, he never passed up an opportunity to ask Mother to join us on day trips to Long Island or Block Island or for dinner, often to my chagrin. Looking back now, it's easy to see what inspired our relationship. Mother eventually saw it too, and then egged him on unmercifully by bragging how rich she was. Funny, as hard as Harry tried, and let me tell you he tried awfully hard, my mother never invested a penny with him!"

"Ellen, I'm sorry all this happened to you. Harry was a real con artist. Everything he did was directed towards attaining his one goal in life...to become a rich Wall Street tycoon."

She started to reply, but then suddenly looked startled and turned away. "Davis, do you hear something rattling? It sounds like someone's down at the gate trying to get in. Do you think someone's after me?"

"I doubt it. But at this hour of the night, let's be on the safe side. Is there another way out?"

"Yes! There's a back driveway behind the garage. We never use it, but it's still there."

"Then let's get out of here!"

"I don't understand…how would anyone know to come out here, Davis?"

"I don't know, but let's not wait to find out!"

We ran out the front door to her car. She started it up, swung around, and sped over to the partially hidden, narrow dirt road behind the garage. I could hardly tell it was there with all the small, dead branches and weeds covering it. But that didn't stop Ellen from barreling down its steep, curvy descent. "Slow down, Ellen. Please! This looks treacherous!"

She either didn't hear me or ignored me because she kept on maneuvering around one sharp curve after another way too fast. As we neared the bottom, she overshot a curve and ended up in some tall dune grass, but then managed to steer her way back onto the road again. The ride down took no more than a minute or two, yet it felt like a lifetime!

Once on Beach Drive, Ellen stepped on the gas and raced towards town. "Ellen, you've got to slow down, we'll get there!"

We whizzed by the front gate, where I saw a smallish man wearing a baseball cap, pulling on the gate, trying to get it open. It looked like Charlie Reynolds. When he saw our car race by, he waved his fist and shouted something at us. I looked back to see him running to his car to follow us.

Ellen sped down Beach Drive with me shouting, "Damn it, slow down!" As we passed Maude's house, I thought I saw two cars parked in her driveway, where there should have been only one.

"Stop, Ellen, stop!" I shouted.

"Why?" she shouted back.

"Please, just stop! I'll tell you later!"

She did about fifty yards down the road. I jumped out and ran back. When I reached the driveway, I just stood there with my hands on my knees, gasping for breath. As I stared at the second car, trying to figure out who it belonged to, I had this sudden sense that something was definitely wrong. I ran up to the house where I heard Maude screaming 'get out' through the partially open front door. I pushed the door open to find Maude sitting on the living floor with blood trickling from the side of her mouth as Tim Swenson stood over her, shouting, "This time you're not going to point a gun at me, lady. I want my money...now!"

"I don't have that kind of money in my checking account," Maude cried out, trying to back away from him.

"Remember, lady, you volunteered to give me the money when Lowe couldn't. So write that check now for the two hundred grand, and you won't get hurt."

Still inching away from him, she yelled bravely, "You better get out of here, or I'm going to call the police!"

"Pay up, lady, or you're going to regret it!"

"Get out now, Swenson!" I shouted, running to Maude.

"Well, well...look who's here! The hero on a white horse returns to save the lady in distress!"

"Swenson, you're the one who blew the million and a half. You have no one to blame but yourself for investing in Harry's scam. So get the hell out of here!"

"I'll go right after your lady friend here writes me a check. Although on second thought, maybe I'll stick around and deal with you once and for all, Lowe."

"She's not writing you one, so deal with me!" I shouted at him, surprised at myself for saying that, but then quickly realizing I was in too deep now to talk my way out of it. I looked around for a spot where I could get away from him if he charged me. The best place seemed to be near the door to the deck, as he'd have to cross the living room to come after me, and I'd be able to get outside fast, getting him away from Maude.

Giving me an *I'm going to get you* smile, he said, "I'm not falling for your little trick, Lowe. She's going to write that check right now...aren't you lady?" He turned to Maude and cocked his arm back, ready to hit her, thinking it would force me to come closer to him.

He was right...it did. But as I moved closer, I spotted the poker next to the fireplace. I ran over and grabbed it, then raised it shoulder high and started towards him. He took one look at me and began to laugh as if I had a little toy in my hand that wouldn't hurt him. I glanced over at Maude, whose expression clearly said, *Are you out of your mind?* Maybe I was! But I couldn't back down now.

I stopped about six feet away from him and prepared to stand my ground. But this thick-necked, broad-shouldered gorilla with a sinister smile on his face kept beckoning me to come closer...poker and all. Which I did, surprising the hell out of him! His smile faded, replaced by anger at my willingness to challenge him. He shook his head slowly from side to side to signal that I had just made a really stupid mistake. As I looked at his size, and the mad, determined look on his face, I couldn't have agreed more. I stopped and began to backpedal, realizing I needed more room to swing the poker. Just as I did, he charged past Maude like an angry bull, straight at me. Somehow, I managed to sidestep him at the last second, then swung the poker as hard as I could, hitting him on the side of his head. He fell to the floor.

I felt pretty confident that would change his mind, but to my amazement, he absorbed the blow with a loud grunt. Getting up slowly, he shook his head to clear the cobwebs, then reached up to touch the side of his head and felt a trickle of blood. When he looked at his hand, his expression changed to one of angry embarrassment that someone like me had been willing to stand up and hit him with a poker. He became enraged and ready to teach me a lesson…maybe my last!

We began to circle each other cautiously. I held the poker shoulder high, searching for the right moment to hit him again. He kept eyeing me for an opening to charge, grab the poker, and beat the hell out of me. As we maneuvered around each other, I couldn't help but be reminded of a lion stalking his prey until he was ready to strike. He slowly and deliberately moved in for the kill, forcing me to backpedal towards the door to the deck. He must have seen the rampant fear on my face because he nodded to himself as if to say, *That's what I've been waiting for*!

When I was only a step or two away from the door, he rushed towards me with fists clenched tight and ready to throw that one punch to put me away. My response was to quickly open the deck door and run out. Unfortunately, Swenson wasted no time in following me. And for a fifty-eight-year-old, he came running out damn fast, his right arm cocked, ready, and eager to knock me out. All I could do was to keep on backing away, but he matched me step for step. I shifted the poker from one hand to the other, hoping that might confuse him as to which way I'd swing it at him, but he kept moving forward, maybe a little slower, and a bit more cautiously, but determined as ever. Suddenly, to my shock and dismay, I found myself pressed against the deck railing without any more running room. I was trapped!

I needed to come up with a way to escape…and fast! But I was overwhelmed with fear and fell back to the only thing I could do: hold the poker high and ready to swing as hard as possible when he charged. He stopped and stepped back, then gave me a sly smile as though he had just planned his next move to finish me off. I felt as if I was one of his opponents in the ring. I took a couple of quick, deep breaths, trying to steady my nerves, but I knew it was only a matter of seconds before he would charge. I gripped the poker as tight as possible out of fear. *Not much of a defense when your opponent was a wrestling champion who wanted to kill you*, I thought. I decided my only chance to break out of this trap was to feint a move to my left, and hope he'd fall for it. That would give me room on my right to run to the center of the deck to face him again. But he wasn't buying it. Not only did he block my move, but he used it to lock me tighter into the corner. I was desperate now.

"Your girlfriend isn't going to like what she sees after I get finished with you, Lowe!" he growled, his sly little smile becoming a full-fledged one at the prospect of beating the hell out of me.

"You're all talk, Swenson," I shouted nervously. "She's not going to give you a dime, nor am I! So get the hell out of here before you do something you'll regret. Prison's going to be a tough place to spend the rest of your life."

"That money was my life, Lowe. And I want it now!"

"You're not getting a dime!" Maude shouted, standing in the doorway with her pistol pointed at Swenson.

He turned to her, glanced at the pistol, and with a dismissive smile, said, "Go ahead and shoot, lady! But you could hit your loverboy too!"

When I saw Maude hesitate, I yelled at him, "It's gone, Swenson! Your money is gone! Guys like Harry knew how to spend it without giving a damn about guys like you. Lots of Harry's clients ended up the same way you did: angry, bitter, and broke. But forcing Maude or me to pay for your mistake is worse than what happened to you. You'll pay for it. The police will be after you for the rest of your life!"

"I don't care!"

"Then you're a fool, Swenson!"

"No, you're the fool, Lowe! For working with a guy like Miller to bilk people like me out of their life savings, and then think you can get away with it. That isn't going to happen! You or your girlfriend here are going to pay me back...right now! I'm too old to wrestle. Too old to find a job. Too old to learn anything new. Without that money, my life is over. Do you understand that, Lowe? You and Miller have destroyed everything I worked and lived for. I have nothing left. Absolutely nothing! So I have nothing to lose if I get a little revenge by beating the hell out of you."

It was clear there was no use in arguing with him. And Maude appeared afraid to shoot. All I could do was pray I'd survive. Suddenly, I realized how close he was to me, his eyes dead set on me, searching for that one opening to charge and throw a punch, all before I could swing the poker at him. Even Maude's frightened, "I'll shoot if you touch him, I swear!" didn't break his concentration. Then he charged! His right arm cocked back, ready to swing. He moved so fast, I couldn't defend myself. I felt his punch graze off the side of my head with such force that it slammed me back against the railing. But he missed grabbing the poker. My head began to spin wildly, my eyes were in and out of focus, and all I could think of, and try to do, was somehow protect myself with one last swing.

As dizzy and wobbly as I felt, I knew survival meant standing and moving, ready to hit him. *If I can do that, I just might have a chance*, I thought encouragingly. But my wooziness grew worse to where I could barely see his smile as he forced me tight up against the corner. I grabbed onto the railing for support, but it felt loose. All that shaking during the storm must have damaged it. Damn it! I needed something steady to help me stay on my feet. I raised the poker with all the strength I had left, shouting, "Don't come any closer, Swenson!"

Every good wrestler has the innate sense to know when his opponent was on the ropes. And he knew I was on the ropes. He feinted to his left, then right, and back to his left, hunting for an opening. I shuffled from side to side as best I could, hoping it would make me a tougher target. But the dizziness had taken its toll. Most of my strength was gone, and it was an effort to hold the poker shoulder high. Suddenly, he charged. My head was spinning faster, and I felt faint, so I knew this was it. I swung at him as hard as I possibly could…and missed when he ducked. He lunged at me, just as my momentum was about to drape me over the side of the railing, and grabbed the poker out of my hand, but his punch was wild, and done from an awkward position, throwing him off balance. His forward momentum was too great to stop. He crashed headfirst into the loosened railing, his body weight shattering it, and plunged to the rocks below with a loud, surprised shout, a mournful grunt, then dead silence.

****

It took a minute or two to pull myself up as my head wouldn't stop spinning. I reached over and grabbed the nearest unbroken part of the railing as tight as I could, thinking that if I fainted, it would keep me from falling to the rocks below. But the spinning wouldn't stop, to where I felt on the verge of passing out. I sat down, or maybe I fell down; at this point, I wasn't sure. The worst problem was my eyes, which kept going in and out of focus. I'd never felt so helpless and unprotected...until two arms wrapped tightly around my neck, followed by a flood of kisses, and saved me!

"Oh, thank God you're okay!" Maude exclaimed. "I was sure he was going to kill you and then kill me!"

"Is he moving down there?" I slurred, turning my head slowly in that direction.

"It's hard to see. I'll go inside and get a flashlight."

I sat there wondering how long it would take before this infernal spinning stopped when a voice dripping sarcasm shouted from the direction of the house, "Well, well now. I knew you were up to no good the minute I laid eyes on you, Lowe. But now you've gone and done it. You've murdered a guy! Who was he? Someone else you've screwed along the way?"

"Oh...shut up, Charlie!" Maude hissed as she ran past him towards me. "Can't you see he's hurt?"

"*He's* hurt? What about the guy lying down on the rocks? He's got to be dead! Your friend here, Maude, just killed him!"

"He didn't kill him. Swenson was attacking Davis and fell when he grabbed the poker Davis was defending himself with," she shouted back while shining her light down on the rocks.

"Well, is he moving?" Reynolds asked, sounding as if he was

- 244 -

hoping for the worst.

"Ah…no, he's lying there very still."

"So, he is dead. And your dear friend Lowe here just murdered him!"

"It was self-defense, Charlie!"

"Brantley is not going to believe you, Maude, take it from me."

I could make out Maude shaking her head in disgust at Reynolds, as she kept shining the light on Swenson, hoping he might move. As I waited for her report, my dizziness slowed, enough so that I thought I'd try to stand. But when I got up on my knees, the spinning started again, forcing me to sit back down, disappointed, to say the least, as my urge to punch Reynolds would have to wait.

As I struggled with my renewed dizziness, I saw a blurred figure step out on the deck behind Reynolds. I correctly guessed it was Ellen. She ran across the deck to where Maude was standing, looked down at Swenson's limp body, and, shaking her head sadly, shouted, "I'll call the police." She ran off to find the phone before a surprised Maude could tell her where it was located.

Maude knelt down beside me again to see how I was doing. I tried to smile, as I wondered just how *we…or maybe just me…*were going to get out of this one. It quickly became *we* when Charlie casually asked, "Oh, Maude, I believe you dropped your pistol over here. You know, the one you shot Harry with?"

Well…if anything could start my adrenaline flowing, that was it! Reynolds pressed the subject some more. "Oh, by the way, Maude, do I remember correctly that you told Brantley you haven't owned a gun since you went to prison? Obviously, that's not true, is it?" I could only imagine how steely-eyed her stare was as she slowly walked over to pick up the gun and put it in her pocket. "That's not going to change anything, Maude. I'll testify that you have a pistol in your possession. And you know as well as I do that Lowe here will be forced to verify my testimony…unless of course, he wants to lie for you again."

"What do you want, Charlie?" Maude asked slowly and

suspiciously.

"I'm glad you asked me that question, Maude. For my not seeing your pistol lying here on the deck and supporting Lowe's testimony that he used that poker in self-defense, I want those certificates of deposit…all five million dollars of them!"

"Are you crazy? What makes you think that I have them?"

"Well, maybe you don't. But your friend sitting by the railing probably does. Or don't you remember that he told Brantley he gave them to Harry the Friday before the dinner? Except nobody knows if that's really true, now do they? Maybe he had a change of heart and didn't give them to Harry on Friday as he claimed, but decided to keep them for himself. After all, five million could get him out of a dead-end job and into the lifestyle he's always wanted. Maybe with that kind of incentive, he decided that night on the beach to finally take his revenge after all these years. So, he shot Harry, and dragged his body down into the water, hoping it would drift out to sea and be gone forever!"

Reynolds paused to let his accusation sink in before adding, "You must admit Maude, how five million dollars, plus a lifetime of wanting revenge, can be a wonderful inspiration for murder!"

That did it for me! Adrenaline soared through my body, almost stopping the spinning. I tried standing again, but my legs still wouldn't cooperate. I collapsed back down, overcome by desperation, wondering how in the world I was going to defend myself. Why would anyone believe I gave Harry the certificates after I lied about not being here two weeks before the murder? I was trapped!

My heart was racing as I asked myself, *Who could have taken those certificates?* Reynolds said he didn't, but even if he did, why bother trying to blackmail Maude and me now? Maybe Simmons? But he swore up and down to Brantley that he didn't have them. And yet, Ellen was so sure a man took the certificates from Harry's body, which could have been Simmons or someone who looked like me. Paranoia started to take over as I struggled to figure out some way to defend myself.

"Well, Charlie, I'll tell you again," Maude said as she walked back towards me. "I don't have them. And Davis wasn't at the beach that night. Are you sure you don't have them? Accusing Davis or me would take the spotlight off of you, now wouldn't it?"

"That's not a very clever tactic, Maude."

"Well…maybe Fred Simmons took them, Reynolds," I offered, hoping he'd bite at that possibility.

"It was definitely a man!" Ellen chimed in as she stepped out on the deck again. "He came down about fifteen minutes later and found the certificates on Harry's body. He took them. I'll swear to that! And by the way, the police said they'll be here shortly."

The four of us fell into a tense silence. I could feel the suspicion mounting as everyone eyed each other, wondering who murdered Harry and took the certificates. Maude kept shaking her head that it wasn't her. I turned in time to see Ellen and Reynolds nod to each other as if convinced the evidence pointed to only one person…me!

I was frankly surprised by their kangaroo court judgment, but not feeling quite ready to defend myself. Instead, I asked Maude, "Could you take another look to see if Swenson is moving?"

She flashed her light down at him and held it there for a minute or so, then announced quite solemnly, "No, he's not moving…not at all."

Another moment of silence followed, tinged with a feeling of sadness from everyone but me. Then Reynolds gave me a look of being ready and eager to drag a confession out of me. I tried to delay the inevitable by taking a long, slow look down at Swenson's body. When I looked back up, Reynolds was standing in the middle of the deck, ready to pounce. My surprised expression must have convinced him I was cornered because he folded his arms across his chest and shook his head for emphasis, as if to say, *I've finally got you checkmated, Lowe.* I shouted out my only defense again, "Reynolds, I wasn't here last Saturday night!" But that didn't seem to make a difference. Trying to distract him, I said, "Why don't you call

Simmons and ask him what he's done with all those certificates?"

Injecting a little doubt did the trick. His smile disappeared, and he looked a bit angry as he walked quickly into the living room to make the call. I nodded slightly to myself and thought, *Maybe that will help remove the onus from me.* But deep down, I knew Reynolds was determined to get me.

As the three of us waited for Reynolds to return, Ellen walked over to the broken railing to take another look down at Swenson. After a few seconds, she sadly shook her head, then turned to me and said, "Davis, perhaps you're right that Fred Simmons took the certificates from Harry after all. Do you think it's possible Lucy Grimes told him that Harry was dead before she went to the police? In her grief, maybe she said it in a way that Fred thought she'd murdered him? Trying to protect her, he then raced down to the beach to dispose of the body, and that's when he found the certificates?"

She stood there staring at me as Maude and I thought about what she was suggesting. I guess our long silence surprised her as she seemed to change her mind. "Well, maybe it wasn't Lucy who murdered Harry after all." Then, in the next breath, she said, "But Davis, I'm still certain it was a man who took those certificates from Harry's body. If it wasn't Fred, it was a man...say just about your height and build. Oh, how I wish I had seen his face!"

What? Me? I was stunned! How could she even make such an accusation? But before I could recover and defend myself, Maude jumped in, demanding, "Ellen, tell me...was it Lucy and Fred, or Davis, who you think murdered Harry and stole the certificates?"

Backtracking again, she responded, "Well, ah...I'm not really sure! It was too dark for me to see who killed him. But I'm positive it was a man who stole the certificates."

Maude questioned her again. "Ellen, do you think Lucy could have murdered Harry?"

"Didn't she have every reason to, Maude? Being jilted like that...and then to lose all that money!"

"Maybe you're right," Maude replied thoughtfully. "But if Lucy didn't do it, do you still believe Fred took those certificates?"

"Well...I just don't know!"

"Do you think that Davis murdered Harry, left, then came back fifteen minutes later looking for the certificates?"

Looking flustered and a little foolish, Ellen cried out defensively, "As I said before, I don't know who murdered Harry because I couldn't see the person. But I'm positive it was a man who took the certificates. If it wasn't Fred, well then..." her voice drifted away as she turned towards me, her stare piercing.

"Why are you accusing me of taking them, Ellen?" I said indignantly, struggling to stand again.

"I could be mistaken, Davis, as it was dark and I was scared to death, but it could have been you. Yes, it could have been you!"

"Well, well, Lowe! It sounds like she's identified you," Reynolds said with glee, stepping out onto the deck. "And I'll bet you never gave Harry those certificates when you met him down at the beach that night. I'd also bet you shot him too!"

"Wait a minute!" I shouted, finally managing to stand, but wobbly enough to need to grab hold of the railing. "Reynolds, you're in this damn deep too! Ellen told me that she saw and heard you arguing with Harry at the beach that night. He finally got disgusted with your demands for the five hundred thousand and told you off. And she saw you watch Harry pat his stomach and tell you he wasn't going to pay you, as he didn't need the money anymore. Sounds to me like you knew Harry had the five million with him in a money belt. And come to think of it, why couldn't you have stayed at the beach after Harry told you to get the hell out of there? You know, Reynolds, it would have been so easy for you to wait for the right time to come back and kill him, and then take those certificates. And your blackmail attempt just now could be a ruse to deflect attention since you already have the certificates."

"You're not going to get out of this one, Lowe. I don't have them because you do!" Reynolds bellowed back.

I turned to Ellen and said, "Couldn't it have been Reynolds you heard running up the path fifteen minutes later?"

"Well…it was a man breathing heavily, but other than that, I can't say for sure. She was becoming distraught. "Please, stop this. I'm not going to point the finger at anyone without being totally sure."

"Wait a minute now! You had no problem pointing your finger at me just now. And Simmons, too! But you're not going to point your finger at Reynolds?"

"I told you, and I'll tell you again…I just don't know!" she replied angrily.

"Lowe, you're just trying to confuse her and shift the blame to Simmons or me so you can to get off scot-free!"

"All I'm trying to do Reynolds is prove that when she says it was a man, that doesn't mean it was me."

"But Lowe, she's absolutely convinced it was someone who looked exactly like you."

With that, the four of us waited in silence for the police to arrive. I stood against the railing, squeezing it hard, still furious at Ellen's accusation. I had no doubt Reynolds would keep coming after me to divert attention from himself. He'd probably start making his case the moment Brantley arrived, but the truth was that I didn't have any real defense to stop him, so any denial by me would be meaningless. Besides, I knew Brantley was just looking for a reason to pin it all on me, and Reynolds would be more than happy to give him one.

****

Maude finally broke the silence. "Let's all take a seat since the police seem to be taking their time," she said and proceeded to sit down on the nearest chair, while Ellen and Reynolds sat nearby. I tried to make myself comfortable leaning against the railing. Everyone appeared on edge, as we were all no doubt anticipating Brantley's questions, and trying to prepare our responses. I looked over at Reynolds and saw his eyes darting from me to the broken railing, obviously scheming how to link me to Swenson's death,

Harry's murder, and the missing five million. Maude appeared terrified as she gazed out at the dark ocean, most likely struggling to come up with a story of why she lied about her pistol. And there was Ellen, looking distraught at being the key witness, and unsure of everything she was once so positive about.

As the minutes passed, our anxiety only grew. Suddenly, Ellen jumped up and dashed across the deck to the open living room door.

"Where do you think you're going, Ellen?" I shouted after her.

"I've had enough of this. I'm leaving! I'm not subjecting myself to any more questions and challenges as to what I saw!"

"That's not a smart idea right now," I said as soothingly as possible. "The police should be here any minute. Your leaving like this will put you under more suspicion."

"Ellen, please don't go," Maude begged. "Davis is right. Detective Brantley will want to question you."

While Ellen stood hesitating at the doorway, Lucy and Simmons pushed their way past her onto the deck. As the others turned to look at them, I watched as she gave a determined nod, and then stepped into the living room. "Ellen," I yelled after her, "Please, don't go! You'll end up being Brantley's prime suspect if you do!"

I stood there, not believing how foolish she was acting. Thinking that I couldn't let her leave this way, I pushed myself away from the railing to go after her. But before I got to the middle of the deck, she looked out from the doorway and cried, "I'll say it one more time: I don't know who shot Harry, and I didn't recognize the person who took the certificates." With that, she turned back into the living room.

"Ellen! Please don't leave…you'll regret it!" I shouted again, dismayed she didn't understand the situation she was putting herself in.

My final plea must have made an impression, as a few seconds later, she walked slowly out the door onto the deck again. She stopped and glared hatefully at me before hurrying past me to her chair. There she sat down in a huff, her arms folded across her chest. I was shocked! *What in the world is going on with her,* I wondered, as I headed unsteadily back to the railing.

Lucy and Simmons were still standing by the door, watching us. When Simmons saw me stop at the broken railing and look down at the rocks below, he began walking towards me. "What happened, Lowe?" he asked. "Have you murdered someone else and plan to accuse me like you did with Harry?"

I turned to him and said sarcastically, "As a matter of fact, no, Simmons, I'm not! Are you surprised? Well...I'm not like you. I don't just jump to conclusions."

Stopping a few feet away, he stared at me with contempt. Then, in his typical plodding fashion, he froze, apparently trying to make up his mind about what to do next. I couldn't help but think he was debating whether or not to take this opportunity to push me through the broken railing to the rocks below. It must have been an appealing idea, as a slow, menacing smile crossed his face, signaling his decision, which I assumed was going to be a fitting end to me.

As he moved closer, Lucy asked, "Who's down there? Is someone dead down there?"

We all turned to her, as Maude replied, "Yes! A wrestler by the name of Tim Swenson. He tried to kill Davis, but broke through the railing and fell to his death. We're waiting for the police to arrive."

"Too bad he missed you, Lowe!" Simmons hissed, now only a couple of steps away.

"Simmons, you always have the nicest things to say to me."

Simmons's face turned beet red as he took another step, then cocked his right arm back, ready to punch me.

"What in the world are you doing?" Maude yelled at him. "Stop it this minute, or you'll be sorry!" She started to reach into her pocket.

"Fred! Stop it right now!" Lucy demanded.

"Lowe and I have a score to settle," he yelled over his shoulder, still eager to take a swing at me.

"Fred, stop right there and now! Do you hear me?" Lucy commanded.

The tone of her voice stopped him in his tracks. He stood there, deciding whether to accede to her demand or not. After a few seconds, he stepped back and gave me an evil, *I'm still going to get even with you,* look, then headed back across the deck to an empty chair, angry as hell.

Lucy pulled up a chair next to him and reached over to hold his hand as we waited for the police to arrive. The tension finally exploded when Maude turned to Simmons and said accusingly, "Fred, you took those certificates from Harry's dead body...didn't you?"

"No, damn it! I didn't!" he shouted, jumping out of his chair and heading toward Maude.

Maude stood up, and jabbing an accusing finger at him as he neared, declared, "It's true! You were seen searching Harry's body before dragging him into the water."

"Who said that?" Lucy demanded.

"Ellen saw everything that happened," Maude responded forcefully. "She believes the person who took the certificates looked exactly like you, Fred!"

We all turned to stare at Ellen, who stood up and moved quickly behind her chair as if it would provide some sort of protective barrier. "That's not true!" she cried out. "Not true at all! I never said it was Fred who took them. All I said was, it looked like him, that's all! But I'll tell you right now...I won't swear to it! It could've been somebody else here." She glared at me.

"Fred, how could you even think of doing that?" Lucy yelled in his face. "After what I've been through with Harry and his stealing my money. And...and you weren't even thinking about giving the money back to me, were you?"

Fred's face turned crimson. He scowled at me, then at a frightened Ellen, before turning to Lucy. "What do you mean, sweetheart?" he asked. His tone was soothing, but it was clear he was still seething. "Remember when you screamed about being so glad *your* Harry was dead? What else could I think but that you had shot him?

All I was trying to do was help you! Don't you understand that I love you and I'd do anything to help you? But when I got down to the beach, Harry's body was floating out in the water. I never went in to get him…and I never took any certificates from his body."

"Don't lie, Simmons!" Reynolds yelled. "It had to be you. Who else was strong enough to drag him into the water and push him out to sea?"

"How about Lowe over there?" Simmons lashed out, pointing his finger at me.

"I wasn't even there that night, Simmons!" I shouted back, pushing myself away from the railing and toward him.

"You've lied too many times, Lowe," Reynolds said, jumping up from his chair. "And there's no reason why you're not lying now!"

Somehow, and I didn't quite understand how, I'd become the rallying point for the two of them as they'd quickly buried the hatchet for the sake of coming after me. Together, they headed towards me with one obvious intent in mind…to beat me into a confession. And here I was in no position to stop them.

"Stop all of this now!" Maude shouted, reaching into her pocket. "Don't you dare touch him!"

They stopped, shocked at seeing her point a pistol straight at them. It surprised me too! It didn't take long before they reluctantly backed away from me and returned to their chairs.

This brought a momentary silence, which I thought might help calm all of us down. But Lucy apparently wasn't done with Fred. Shaking her head furiously at him, she shouted, "How could you have taken those certificates, Fred? They're mine! It was my money that Harry stole under the pretense of marrying me. I want them back this minute! Do you hear me, Fred?"

Simmons' face couldn't have gotten any redder. He gritted his teeth before replying, "I didn't steal those certificates! And I didn't murder Harry! But now, Lucy, you had every reason to shoot him. After all, first, he slapped you, then later, called off your wedding after arguing with you on the beach. You could have gone home, gotten your gun, come back to the beach, and shot him before running to tell me he was dead."

"That's not true! Not one bit of it! How could you even think I'd do that, Fred?" she cried, tears rolling down her cheeks.

The deck fell deathly silent as everyone absorbed and sorted out all the different accusations. Yet, I couldn't take my eyes off of Simmons. His expression ranged from despair at losing Lucy to hot anger at her alleging he stole her money. Not knowing how to appease her, he decided to lash out at Reynolds, instead of me for a change. "Maybe you shot Harry when he refused to come up with the five hundred thousand for your land deal. It's no secret how much you've hated him since he destroyed you and your brokerage firm, or don't you remember that?"

"Don't try to pin Harry's murder on me, Simmons!"

After a protracted standoff, they both turned an accusing eye at Maude, likely rationalizing that her bitterness at spending five long years in prison was reason enough for revenge. Maude appeared surprised at first, but then waved her pistol at them, stating in no uncertain terms, "Don't look at me! I left Harry standing near the water, and besides, I didn't even know he had the money on him. And how could I have dragged him into the water? He was too damn big and heavy!"

Well, by process of elimination, that left just me. But before the two of them could even begin to accuse me, I let out a loud, defensive, *no!* Which didn't mean much, since, in their eyes, I was the guilty one, no question about it. Why even bother arguing with them? It was clear they were just looking for an excuse to give me what they thought I deserved. Thankfully, Maude realized what they were up to and rushed to my side, pointing her pistol at them as she shouted, "You don't seem to understand that I mean business!" Deciding not to test Maude's resolve, they quickly backed away and sat back down. I guess Maude's pistol and her known record for shooting Harry in a fit of anger, were the convincing factors.

I smiled my thanks to her. She nodded back, then slipped the pistol into her pocket and returned to her chair. An anxious silence resumed as we all waited for Brantley's imminent arrival. I glanced over at Ellen and saw that she was still standing behind her chair, glaring at me. *What was going on with her?* I wondered. It was only this afternoon when I'd sat beside her at the beach, and listened as she told me what she'd seen and heard that night. How thankful she'd been that I believed her. And I had believed her, every word! I remember thinking...another pretty, sweet, and trusting woman Harry had destroyed.

She caught me staring at her and cried out, "I'm leaving!"

I pushed myself away from the railing and hobbled as fast as I could across the deck, practically begging, "Ellen, you're not under suspicion, so don't be a fool and leave now!"

She stopped short and turned slowly around to face me, seething with anger. "I'm not a fool, Davis! Even if my mother thinks I am after how Harry treated me."

"I certainly don't think you're a fool, Ellen," I replied softly. "You've been caught up in this awful mess Harry created just like the rest of us. He took us all in with his lies and cons, not caring at all about how it hurt us...or how he ruined our lives. He was an evil son-of-a-bitch who deserves to be dead. But I certainly don't believe you're responsible for what happened to him!"

"Nor do I!" Maude agreed.

"Oh, yes, you do! You've both doubted what I saw that night from the very beginning. And you Davis...you're the one who told the police everything I told you in strict confidence. Now I'm right in the middle of this mess, exactly where I never wanted to be."

"But don't you understand, you have to be in the middle," I said. "You're the key witness who saw everyone and everything that happened that night."

"No! That's where you're wrong. As I told you a hundred times, Davis, I can't identify who murdered Harry, and I'm not sure who stole the certificates. So, I'm *not* in the middle! Stop saying that I am!"

- 256 -

I stood there, frankly shocked at the animosity in her voice when she said, *Stop saying that I am!* It was how she said it...with such anger and nastiness. And to me, a friend. It made no sense.

I started to walk haltingly toward her again, trying to understand her changed attitude. She stood waiting at the doorway, angry as hell...and ready to do battle.

"Ellen, I'm puzzled. Why the sudden angry denials? You were the only one who saw what happened at the beach that night. Without your testimony, the police haven't a clue as to who murdered Harry. And knowing how Brantley thinks, he'll end up picking one of us as Harry's murderer based solely on circumstantial evidence."

She didn't need to reply, as her scornful expression of, *I really don't give a damn,* said it all. It was clear that no words of mine were going to change her mind. But why? She'd been more than friendly when confiding in me at the beach. Yet, looking at her now, there's no doubt she'd point straight at me and tell Brantley that I took the certificates from Harry's body. She'd make me Brantley's prime suspect... and her, the innocent bystander!

"Ellen, before you leave, tell me again...why was it so difficult for you to see who shot Harry from your hiding place when you were able to clearly describe how Maude and Lucy and Reynolds confronted Harry?"

"How many times do I have to tell you?" she answered impatiently.

"Well...I know you said it was dark, and the murderer stood at an odd angle, which prevented you from seeing whether it was a man or a woman. But weren't you standing the same distance away, and in the same darkness, when you identified the three of them? How could you not see Harry's murderer? It's just not making sense."

"That's what I saw! That's it! End of story!" She sounded agitated and defensive.

But her answer, and that tone of hers, made me wonder just how true her story was. So, I repeated my question. "What I don't understand is how you saw Harry slap Lucy's face...and Maude run away in tears…and Reynolds argue heatedly with Harry over money. And until a little while ago, you were sure that Simmons took the certificates from Harry's money belt. And yet, after seeing and hearing all that, the only people you couldn't recognize were the ones who shot Harry and stole the certificates!"

"This is the last time I'm going to tell you," she responded, eyes flashing furiously. "It was dark, and I could only make out it was a person standing there. When I heard the shot, I saw Harry fall backward on the sand, and watched the person run away. Don't you understand? It all happened so fast, and I'd never seen anyone murdered before…I was in shock!"

"Davis, stop it! You're browbeating her into a confession," Maude shouted angrily. She walked over to Ellen and put her arm around her shoulder to comfort her.

"As always, Lowe, you're way off-base," Reynolds chimed in.

"Maybe I am. But after what she's told us, it's getting harder to believe her."

"Lowe, you're not going to wriggle out of a murder charge," Simmons said with a sneer.

"That's right, Fred, he won't!" Lucy joined in. "He's lied too many times!"

Who the hell are they to point the finger at me? I thought. Every one of them has just as strong a motive to murder Harry as I did. Still, it doesn't answer the question as to why Ellen saw everyone but Harry's murderer and whoever stole the certificates.

I stood there, asking myself over and over again, *What am I missing?* I went back over Ellen's description of what she'd seen that night after Harry was shot. A man running down the beach path, breathing heavily. He stopped to look around, then spotted Harry's body near the water. He ran over to him, and made sure he was dead, then searched his body as if he knew Harry was hiding something valuable. And then, after finding what he was looking for, dragged Harry out into the water. I was sure I didn't forget anything, yet, something didn't make sense. Damn it, what am I missing? I just couldn't put my finger on it.

Then it hit me. *Why search him?* Seeing a dead person lying on the beach, the first reaction by most people would be to run and call the police. But if you knew Harry had a large sum of money on him...yes, that's it! Only two people had heard Harry brag about having all the money he needed while patting his stomach...Reynolds and Ellen. I'll bet Reynolds was too angry after Harry backed out of their deal to have paid attention to what he was saying. But Ellen...she could have thought Harry was carrying around her three million dollars, and this was her chance to get it back. That makes sense!

But how to be sure it's her? I hobbled up to Ellen and Maude, and said, "You know Ellen, you can't cash those certificates without creating a great deal of suspicion."

"What are you talking about? I don't have them!" she shot back, her eyes wide open in shock.

"I think you do!"

"Lies! Not true...not true at all!" she screamed at me, furiously shaking her head, looking to Maude for support.

"Well, Ellen, let me tell you what I think happened that night. You realized what Harry meant when he patted his stomach, and so after Reynolds left in a huff, you decided to come out of your hiding place and confront him. He must have been surprised to see you, of all people. My guess is that typical arrogant Harry was waiting for Lucy to come back and beg him not to break up with her. And I'll bet he wasn't the least bit interested in seeing you as you'd been out of his life for weeks after taking your money."

"Again, lies! All lies!" she cried out. She pushed Maude away, and with her head down and in tears, started to walk toward the living room to leave.

"No, they're not lies!" I shouted after her. "Knowing Harry, he probably told you to get lost after you confronted him. And I'll bet in your own sweet way, you asked him for an apology for breaking up with you. He must have said some very derogatory things to you, designed to hurt you even more. I know how it feels, and so does everyone else here."

She stood still in the doorway, looking quite frightened at my description of what had happened. I paused a moment to think through the rest of it. Then, I said as sympathetically as possible, "My guess, Ellen? All those nasty things he said to you brought all your latent hatred for him to a head. Suddenly, you had an uncontrollable urge to see him dead for treating you like dirt. You wanted to see him suffer for all those despicable lies he had told you along the way. Lies about loving you; lies about dreaming of your wonderful future together; and lies about the money he'd make for you by investing in his fund. You gave him the three million...your inheritance...to prove your love and loyalty, only to have him betray you with someone else.

"You became obsessed with the idea of ridding the world of this evil man. And on the beach that night, every element of your hatred came together into one burning desire...to take your revenge! You probably made him beg before you shot him at close range. I can imagine the pleasure you derived from watching him fall dead onto the sand, payback for all the dastardly things he said and did to you. You then opened his shirt, found the certificates in his money belt, and took them, thinking it was the money he had stolen from you. And even though it must have been difficult, you dragged him down to the water, hoping the tide would pull him out to sea where nobody would ever find him."

Her frightened expression changed into a cold, angry one. "Why are you making up this story, Davis? Do you want to hurt me too?"

"Unfortunately, I'm not making it up. It all fits! And believe me, I certainly don't want to hurt you. But it had to be you, Ellen. You had him right where you wanted him...all alone where you could make him squirm and beg for his life as retribution for all the heartache he caused you. Then, and only then, could you pull the trigger. That would complete your revenge. How shocked he must have been to see such a sweet and trusting woman at the end of a pistol pointing at him!"

"Lies! Lies! Lies! You're making it all up to blame me for Harry's murder!"

"No, I'm not, Ellen," I replied. "I'm looking for the truth." I paused a moment before saying, "You know, Ellen, the more I think about it, the more it all comes back to me. I remember you telling me that you and Harry were unofficially engaged, and to celebrate, he took you to Barcelona for two weeks. But after returning, you didn't see or hear from him for a week. You were so upset and worried that he hadn't called that you thought something had happened to him. So, you went to his house and found him having sex with Lucy on the couch. Why? Because she was his next target for her five million dollars!"

"You're lying!" Lucy shouted at me, turning to Fred with pleading eyes. He angrily shook his head and stepped away from her.

"How devastated you must have been at Harry for doing such a despicable thing to you. Your first impulse had to be revenge. But look around, Ellen: we've all had the same impulse after succumbing to his humiliations, deceitfulness, and the biggest betrayal of them all...stealing our money!"

"Stop it, Davis! Stop it right now!" Maude shouted. "Can't you see what you're doing to her?" She went over to Ellen and put her arms around her. The two of them turned back to me, outraged at my accusations.

But I wasn't finished. "One more thing, Ellen, that convinces me that you shot Harry as an act of revenge. It had to be utter humiliation for you to tell your mother the engagement was not only off, but that you had foolishly invested your inheritance in Harry's fund, even after hearing rumors that he was close to shutting it down. Revenge had to be your answer to all the shame he caused you."

Letting go of Maude, Ellen yelled, "I'm not listening to any more of this!" and disappeared into the living room.

Maude started after her, but I grabbed her arm and whispered, "Don't go in there; you don't know what she's capable of doing in her state of mind. Let me go."

I hobbled past Maude into the dimly lit living room where I spotted Ellen sobbing in the corner next to the liquor cabinet. Her face, as best I could see, was taut with fear. When she saw me, her sobbing slowed to a whimper, then stopped. She glared hatefully at me.

I suppressed my first instinct to leave before something ugly happened. As I stood there waiting for her to say something, the hate on her face seemed to intensify. Hoping to calm her down, I said quietly, "Ellen, I know what the need for revenge feels like. We all do! Each of us hated Harry with as much passion as you did. And we all fervently hoped and prayed that he'd sooner than later get his just reward. But I believe what he did to you with his deceit and humiliation was far greater than what he did to any of us. He was a rotten bastard! He took advantage of your sensitivity, your sweetness, and your love, and it distorted your mind and your emotions to where you lost control. I'm truly sorry for what he did to you."

"Nice of you to say that now, Davis, but it's too late to help me."

"No, it's not! I'll help you. Maude will help you with money and lawyers. Just calm down and let us help!"

"No one can help me…least of all, you! You're the one I trusted the most, yet you've made me the prime suspect with your stupid theories and lies! I hate you for it!"

"Please, Ellen, I know we can help. Don't shut us out! We'll be there for you with whatever you need!"

"You're a damn liar…just like Harry was!" She suddenly was in front of me with a pistol pointing at my face.

"Ellen, shooting me isn't going to help you," I stammered nervously. "The police will be here any minute; you won't escape!"

"Yes, I will! But I'm not going until I get rid of the other person who destroyed my life…you! I had a perfect alibi until you ripped it apart. Now I'm going to make you pay." Smiling crazily, she shouted, "This is for you…you bastard!"

I heard the first shot and instantly felt the pain. Then the sound of a second shot and the pain became so great that I could hardly breathe. I found myself too weak to stand and crumpled to the floor. As I drifted in and out of consciousness, I suddenly heard a burst of noise and Brantley shouting, 'Put the gun down, now!' Then I passed out.

****

I was jarred awake to find myself lying on a stretcher in a speeding ambulance with the siren blaring, the EMT holding the IV up high, and Maude gripping my hand tightly. From the fear on her face and the excruciating pain in my right side and shoulder, I was sure I was dying.

****

I awoke in a semi-dark room to find a nurse smiling down at me, nodding that I was going to be okay. The agonizing pain made me doubt her immediately. She bent over and whispered near my ear, "There's someone who's been here all night worrying about you. I'll let her stay for a minute or two to be sure that you're all right."

A moment later, Maude came in. She walked over to my bed and nervously took my hand, very happy to see me awake. With a cautious smile, she leaned over and kissed me, then said in a whisper, "Davis, I'm looking forward to having a drink with you out on the beach…and damn soon!"

"Maude," I whispered back, feeling better already, "I'll go anywhere with you…but never to the beach."

Acknowledgment

I can't thank my daughter, Jaime, enough for spending untold hours helping to bring this mystery to publication. Her effective editing work included many cogent suggestions that kept the plot moving and gave the characters greater dimension, which added significant suspense and intrigue to the book.

Books by this Author

Peter Bernard is also the author of *The St. Michel Legacy,* a mystery in which past events haunt the present, and the fate of a multibillion-dollar media empire is at stake.

Following the shocking murder of the CEO, his four adult children battle over who will be chosen to lead their company. But they soon receive another shock, when during the reading of their father's last will and testament, events from the past are brought to light, revealing the century-old secret that nearly destroyed the company four generations ago.

Now history could be repeating as bitterness intensifies against the favorite son, who finds himself the prime suspect in the murder of his father. Wanted by the police, pursued by his embittered siblings, and hunted by progeny from the past, he realizes the only way to stay alive and clear his name is to find his father's killer.

The St. Michel Legacy is available on Amazon.com.

Made in the USA
Coppell, TX
23 December 2020